## Praise for *The End of Longing*

*The End of Longing* is a cleverly written piece of historical fiction…a complex story of mystery and intrigue…I was completely absorbed from the first page until the final scene.
BOOKSELLER + PUBLISHER MAGAZINE

Compelling…intense…poetic…it stayed with me and has been hard to shake off.
THE SYDNEY MORNING HERALD

Filled with allusions to nineteenth-century literature, history and mores, *The End of Longing* is distinguished by its sense of place, which is ironic really, as one of the themes in this richly layered book is that of travel and the peripatetic lives of the married couple at the centre of the story. But wherever his characters go, be it Japan, Canada or Honolulu, Ian Reid places us vividly there.
THE AGE

Reid scores a considerable success in recreating the hard-scrabble frontier towns of an age that is increasingly alien to our own…The reader encounters a pageant of nineteenth-century lives here…a realistic portrait of a bleak world.
AUSTRALIAN BOOK REVIEW

Ian Reid's fine and unusual historical novel…concerns a man who is a fugitive not only from the law and his past misdeeds but perhaps more essentially from his repressed better nature…Maybe – as Reid subtly suggests – it is the desire for revenge against the angels of his own nature that Hammond self-destructively seeks.
THE AUSTRALIAN

A tale rich in historical detail, creating two memorable and affecting main characters.
THE WEST AUSTRALIAN

Frances is a 30-year-old spinster living in Dunedin, New Zealand, restless and dissatisfied with the parameters of her life…Typical of colonial heroines, Frances is destined to satisfy a terrible curiosity – what is it like out there? Her husband, and perhaps her nemesis, is the Rev. William Hammond…Reid's exploration of William's background is suspensefully threaded through the book…very seductive.
THE WARRNAMBOOL STANDARD

An imaginative story of two people struggling to understand themselves and their relationship to the world around them.
WRITING WA

Skilfully realised…How well does any person know the 'truth' of another?…This question underpins much of the novel and keeps the reader turning the pages…The gradual revelation of clues… allows the reader to become the detective in pursuit of truth.
TRANSNATIONAL LITERATURE

Beautifully told.
THE LAUNCESTON EXAMINER

What Reid has done is to subvert the usual [family history] genre by telling the tale of an ancestor not at all respectable, and not at all predictable…Reid is also a poet, and he writes beautifully.
ANZ LITLOVERS LITBLOG

Loved it! Great mix of history, travel and psychological study… Clever and engrossing.
GOODREADS

## Praise for *That Untravelled World*

Reid has deftly woven some fascinating WA history into the
narrative, giving a very vivid and familiar sense of Perth in days
gone by. This history provides a fitting backdrop to a story that is
compelling and satisfyingly unpredictable.

WRITING WA

Celebrated author Ian Reid's latest tale is the incredible journey
of a young man through the Great War, the Depression, and the
years after.

WORLD LITERATURE TODAY

This fine novel presents a story faithful to its period... *That
Untravelled World* covers the gamut of human emotion, from
passion to apathy, ecstasy to dysphoria, sacrifice to indulgence, and
love to racism.

BONZER

Perth comes alive in Reid's hands, and throughout the book
Western Australia's regional towns are deftly depicted...We are
persuaded to ask to what extent we can let unfair disadvantage
dictate how we live the remainder of our lives.

THE AUSTRALIAN

*That Untravelled World* draws the reader into a walk through time...
The descriptions of Western Australia ground the novel in an
almost tangible sense of place...Dreams and disillusion, difficult
and concealed family relationships, racism, the Depression, regional
disenfranchisement, the tyranny of distance, as well as the pros and
cons of technological advancement...They are themes that speak
to our present society.

TRUST NEWS AUSTRALIA

This has everything – snippets of Perth's history, lots of philosophy, a little geography and marvellous descriptions…Ian Reid cleverly steers the reader into false assumptions…[as he] acquaints us with our own journey into the untravelled world of our aspirations, and the life experiences that are encountered as we struggle with broken dreams and upheavals on our way to becoming older and wiser. Buy this book – you won't be disappointed.
HAVE-A-GO

The perennial outsider, Harry drifts between places and jobs following Nellie's disappearance, never really finding his niche. His tale of early confidence followed by recurrent disappointment is evocative of the period in which it is set…With its rapid technological change and economic ups and downs, it's a period which resonates with our own.
THE WEST AUSTRALIAN

It's essentially a gentle tale of one man's life. It was not the life he had envisaged but, really, how many of us have the life we dreamed of when we were young and hopeful? There is a synchronicity about events, though, which leads to a satisfying conclusion for him – it doesn't feel contrived and reminded me, once again, of the often small degree of separation between us all.
GOODREADS

# The Mind's
# Own Place

Ian Reid is the author of a dozen books – fiction, non-fiction and poetry – whose work has been widely anthologised, awarded prizes, and translated into several languages. His previous historical novels are *The End of Longing* and *That Untravelled World*, both published by UWA Publishing. He lives in Perth, where he is an adjunct professor at the University of Western Australia and an emeritus professor at Curtin University. He blogs at ianreid-author.com.

# The Mind's Own Place

*A novel*

## IAN REID

UWA PUBLISHING

First published in 2015 by
UWA Publishing
Crawley, Western Australia 6009
www.uwap.uwa.edu.au

UWAP is an imprint of UWA Publishing,
a division of The University of Western Australia.

THE UNIVERSITY OF
WESTERN AUSTRALIA

National Library of Australia
Cataloguing-in-Publication entry:

Reid, Ian, 1943– author.
The mind's own place / Ian Reid.
ISBN: 9781742587479 (paperback)
Pioneers—Western Australia—Fiction.
Convicts—Western Australia—Fiction.
Swan River Settlement (W.A.)—History—Fiction.
Great Britain—History—19th century.
A823.4

Cover image by Thomas Browne (arrived Australia 1863)
Rose Hotel, Bunbury 1863
watercolour and black pencil  23.8 × 43 cm
National Gallery of Australia, Canberra
The Wordsworth Collection, purchased 2010

Inside photograph of the Old Mill, South Perth, 1890. Sourced from the collection of the State Library of Western Australia and reproduced with the permission of the Library Board of Western Australia.

Typeset in 11pt Bembo by Lasertype
Printed by Lightning Source

This project has been assisted by the Australian Government through the Australia Council, its arts funding and advisory body.

Australian Government

*To Gale*
*my ideal reader*

The mind is its own place, and in itself
Can make a Heaven of Hell, a Hell of Heaven.
What matter where, if I be still the same...
                    So *Satan* spake...
                            John Milton, *Paradise Lost*

The people of Fremantle were used to convicts. A generation
was nearly grown up who had always seen the grey-clad
gangs at work on jetties and bridges, roads and government
buildings; who knew that the curfew tolled at ten o'clock each
night, and after that the policeman on rounds challenged late
wanderers with the words, 'Bond or free?'
                            Alexandra Hasluck, *Unwilling
                            Emigrants: A Study of the Convict
                            Period in Western Australia*

There is neither Jew nor Greek, there is neither bond nor free,
there is neither male nor female: for ye are all one...
                            St Paul, *Epistle to the Galatians*

OLD MILL SOUTH PERTH W.A.

# Prologue

# Mill Point, January 1882

She was loosening soil in the vegetable patch with a heavy-pronged fork when a large frog hopped out lopsidedly from behind the bean row, one leg entangled in a piece of string. She caught the hobbled wriggling thing in her hands. Its emerald skin felt moist but waxy as she carefully unwound the string to set it free. Bounding away, it disappeared somewhere among the plants in search of another hiding place. She returned to her rhythm of digging, and then decided after a few minutes that the sand needed more humus mixed into it. Going over to a corner of the garden where leaves had been heaped and rotted, she swung her big fork vigorously into the pile. There was a high-pitched noise, a long reedy wail. Aghast, she saw that she had impaled the frog. It was squeaking in anguish as it squirmed on one of the tines, which had entered its gullet to skewer its body and the full length of one leg. She forced herself to grasp the clammy creature a second time, pull it off the fork and throw it quickly back into the rubbish mound, out of sight. Nausea made her tremble.

Later that same day there was a stranger on her doorstep, bringing dire news from the prison.

Her husband had been short in stature, and this man who now stood before her was almost a head shorter – not much more than five foot, she guessed. But his manner was quietly authoritative, with a solid presence despite the lack of height. He looked as thickset and weathered as a quayside bollard. A bollard with a fat moustache. She was aware that his eyes, pale blue, unblinking, had closely watched her reaction to the grim tidings he had just imparted.

'I know you were estranged from him, ma'am,' he was saying as she led him into a small drab room, sparsely furnished. 'But setting aside the rights and wrongs of all that, it seemed only proper to let you know what's happened before gossip arrives at your door or you read about this matter in the newspaper. *The West Australian* may well report it in a lurid way.'

'I thank you, sir. It's considerate of you to come here and tell me. I wasn't on the friendliest terms with him of late, I won't deny that, but to hear what he's done now is shocking. Truly shocking.'

She lowered her eyes and put a hand to her mouth. He observed a tremor in her cheek. *So she's not unfeeling after all,* he thought. *Unless it's just the drink.* Satan's letter was in his mind.

'Telling my little boy will be hard,' she said. 'He's in the bedroom now, playing jackstraws, the poor mite.' After a pause, she added quietly, 'And people will talk. No doubt much of the blame will fall on me.'

There was a knock at the cottage door and she went to answer it, returning in the company of a sprucely dressed gentleman.

She began to introduce them: 'This is my uncle...'

'We're acquainted, Polly,' said the new arrival with a nod of greeting and a brisk handshake. 'How are you, Sergeant Rowe?'

'Well enough, Mr Letch, well enough, but it's a sorry business that has brought me here. You've heard?'

'I have.' Sighing, Letch glanced down as if the scrubbed floorboards might suggest some consoling thought. 'And so I came directly to break the news. It seems you've told Polly already.'

The woman gestured to the threadbare armchairs. 'Do sit down, please, both of you. I'll put the kettle on the hob and fetch you some tea.'

She left the room and the men sat in silence for a few moments.

'He had exceptional qualities,' said Rowe. 'That's the pity of it. But his spirit was badly bruised. He deserved better fortune. And the colony is much the poorer for his loss.'

Nodding, Letch frowned. 'He felt bitter towards some of us at the last. Perhaps justifiably. I've often thought about the similarities, in bygone years, between his situation and mine,' he said. 'About the reverses we both suffered as younger men, through our own folly, the mistakes that brought us to this place always lingering in our minds. But then such different eventual outcomes. I've been lucky and he was luckless.'

'You've toiled for your success, Mr Letch. Everyone acknowledges that.'

'He could hardly be accused of working less hard than I did. And he had talents beyond mine. His character may have been flawed, but God knows that's just as true of me. Yet I've prospered beyond my deserts, while he's ended in disgrace.'

'Our endings are sometimes shaped by our beginnings, are they not? The child may continue to inhabit the man. If we knew more about his early years, that could help to explain his later tribulations.'

'Perhaps so. He wouldn't be the only person who never quite finished growing up.' Alfred Letch clasped his hands and inspected the nails pensively before continuing. 'But in the final count, I believe, each of us embodies something enigmatic – a riddle that no story of failed adulthood can fully decipher.'

# Thomas

# 1

# London to Lancashire, August 1833

Teeth clenched, neck bent sideways, he inched himself into the crevice above the ledge. Fear clutched at him, sweat stung his eyes, but Eddie's scoffing words made him try to continue.

'What's the matter, Tomtit? Fraid, art tha?'

'It's much tighter,' he gasped, his voice muffled and distorted, 'than I thought it would be. I can hardly squeeze in here.'

'Nonsense. Th'art small and skinny enough to fit easily. Go on.'

'I reckon this is far enough now.'

'No, th'art only halfway. The dare was th'd get right in under the rails. Th'art not going to funk it now?'

The cavity was dark and dirty, with an oily smell. He fervently wished he hadn't been goaded into this.

Eddie had put the challenge to him: 'Bet th'd be too scared to climb up in there, between that rampart and the railway track.'

'Would not!'

'Do it then. Go on, do it.'

So Thomas had to show he wasn't a coward. But now he was seized by the alarming sensation that he could neither move further in nor wriggle out again. He seemed to be jammed. Wedged tight. There was a painful crick in his neck, and his arms and legs felt frozen. He began to tremble. The trembling was not only within his body but also in the beam on which he lay, and in the track close above him. Then the trembling became a shuddering vibration, and with it a rumble that grew louder and louder into a terrible approaching clamour. He squirmed, sobbed, but there was no escaping the throb and quake of it. Although he knew he was crying out, screaming now, he could not hear his puny voice above the great snorting roar of the steam engine as the train hurtled past, just a few fearful inches overhead, carriage after racketing carriage, on its boisterous headlong charge from the embankment out across the viaduct.

As the monstrous noise receded he was conscious of his own feeble whimpering and of the shameful wetness spreading around his crotch.

'Eddie!' he wailed desperately. 'Help me, Eddie!'

'What? Can't get out by thaself?'

'I'm stuck fast.'

There was a tentative tugging at his arm, but it seemed impossible to budge him.

'I'd best get someone.'

'Don't leave me here! Eddie! Eddie?'

There was no answer. He was alone, convulsed with self-pity. Time stretched out wretchedly.

∽

But the previous ten days had been like a blissful dream. First there was the long journey with his father, all the way from Islington up here to Newton in Makerfield, twenty hours without a pause except for changing the horses. Never before had he left the familiar little district of his upbringing, and it felt momentous – almost adult – to be waving farewell to his mother and sisters as dawn broke. He walked proudly beside his father along their foggy streets to the coaching inn, Grice staggering behind them with their bags. As a starting point for this expedition, their villa could hardly have been more conveniently located: a short stroll took them along Richmond Avenue to the corner of Liverpool Road, and on down to the Angel, the first staging post on the journey from London to the north.

Every little thing was imbued with excitement, even the smells of horses and harness, of sweaty ostlers, of pungent pipe smoke. Hubbub filled the inn yard, as the men around him raised their deep phlegm-thickened voices to make themselves heard above all the whinnying and barking and shouting. Early sunlight brightened the colours of coaches and uniforms. The yellow of the post-chaise carriages, three of them in a row, stood out in vivid contrast to the livery of their own mail coach with its maroon doors and lower panels, black upper panels, scarlet wheels, and the royal coat of arms on the doors. Grice, sweating and huffing, hefted their bags up into the foreboot, inclined his head deferentially towards Mr Browne, muttered, 'I wish you safe travelling, sir,' and took his leave, looking as glum as ever.

'If Grice has smiled even once in all his years as our servant, I've not seen it,' remarked his father. It occurred to Thomas that nobody ever exhibited a cheerful demeanour in his father's presence.

One of the post-chaises was being readied for departure. A smart-looking postilion stood nearby, booted and spurred, hand firmly on his horse's bridle, awaiting the moment to move the animal into a lead position. Thomas admired the flamboyance of the man's uniform: he was resplendent in short blue jacket, top-boots, shiny white hat, white cord breeches, white neckcloth and a yellow waistcoat with glinting pearl buttons. But his manner seemed vainglorious, and Thomas was not the only one who saw this. His father nudged him, saying, 'A bit too pleased with himself, that peacock, eh, Thomas?' At this moment something startled the horse and it reared up suddenly, jerking the postboy so that he toppled into a pool of mud, soiling his white hat and breeches. There was much coarse laughter around the inn yard at the sight of his bedraggled finery. Thomas felt a twinge of sympathy but his father hissed a familiar scriptural proverb in his ear: 'Pride goeth before destruction, and an haughty spirit before a fall.'

Though uncertain about their expedition's precise purpose, Thomas was solemnly conscious of the privilege of accompanying his father. He half understood that it involved a business scheme – and also, in some vague way, his own employment prospects.

'Your schooling days are behind you now, Thomas,' his father had said the evening before their departure, stern as ever, puffing on his little clay pipe. 'It's the working life for you from this point onwards. Time to learn how to make your way shrewdly in the world, m'boy, and earn a living. Diligence! Application!' He wagged an admonitory finger, as if to forestall any waywardly indolent impulse his son might be tempted to indulge.

'But this place you're taking me to...'

'Newton. Up north.'

'But why travel so far away, Papa? What is it we're going to do there?'

Henry Browne inhaled deeply, frowning to dramatise the gravity of their purpose and the authority of his pronouncement. 'We're to spend time in this part of Lancashire because it's where new ways of designing and manufacturing are at their boldest. At their most advanced. In particular' – coughing, he paused to wave away the acrid pipe smoke curling around his head – 'in particular, there's no better place in all of England to understand the commercial opportunities being quickened by the development of railways. That's where the future lies, mark my words.'

When his father deepened his voice in that orotund way, one hand slowly rubbing his belly with satisfaction as he spoke, he reminded Thomas of Mr Wiggins addressing the school assembly – but Henry Browne's command of long instructive sentences was even more impressive than the headmaster's.

'It's fortunate,' he continued in the same teacherly tone, 'that my brother Ralph, canny fellow, is right there in the thick of it. By staying with him and observing the work he does as a foreman at the big new foundry that's just been constructed in Newton, we can find out what openings are likely to come up when the railway moves south. You can be sure London will become the centre of a railway system before long. Oh yes. A grand system! Locomotive transport will transform this nation, I know it.'

'But if —'

Impatient with buts or ifs, his father waved away the interruption. 'Engineering,' he went on, haloed in smoke, 'is going to be the most vigorous and prosperous profession in the years ahead. Civil engineers, mechanical engineers. There'll be a whole new world of innovation and investment, Thomas. Those of us who've thought ahead and studied the prospects can take advantage of that transformation before others have woken up to the magnitude of it all.'

'Why is Newton such a good place to see these —?'

'Because of its location! In the past, Ralph's letters tell me, Newton has just been a little market town, but it's situated halfway between Warrington and Wigan on the great northern road, and halfway between Liverpool and Manchester, too – the new railway line goes through it east to west. Great achievement by that Stephenson fellow – the first railway in the world to carry passengers along with many kinds of freight! So business is coming to Newton from all corners of the country.'

Thomas quivered with awe at his father's self-assurance, his knowledge of the commercial world, his ability to explain how things worked. To be the offspring of a well-educated successful businessman who could speak with such profundity, that was enough to make any son proud – though anxious, too: anxious about what such a father expected of him. Not to succeed would apparently be unforgivable.

But now they were climbing into the coach and setting forth. Their fellow passengers presented a comical contrast: an extremely thin, tight-lipped old lady with a doleful-looking dog at her feet sat opposite Thomas, and beside her, taking up most of the space on that side of the coach, a florid corpulent man with splayed legs making frequent recourse to a liquor bottle as he read aloud various sections of his newspaper and voiced tangential rambling thoughts on a miscellany of loosely associated topics.

The road north from London began to take them through landscapes Thomas had previously been only able to imagine. He wished he could look at more of the countryside along the way, but the shape of the coach window restricted his line of vision. Intermittently there were brief glimpses of farms and fields, ragged hedgerows and dark copses. He caught sight now and then of wind-swayed wheat on hillsides, ready for the harvest, and of little twisting lanes, stone bridges, tollgates, quiet hamlets, lively-looking market towns. At times he dozed. The hours slipped by until afternoon faded into dusk. As they left the solid macadam surface behind and their carriage lurched along a rough stretch of rutted roadway with sombre trees on either side, he asked his father anxiously about highwaymen.

'No, no,' replied Mr Browne with a dismissive shrug. 'We won't encounter any of those rascals. They belong to the past. The country's much more law-abiding these days, what with the Peelers in London and the severe punishments our courts now mete out for wrongdoing.'

A mile up the highway, in the day's last dim light, they saw and smelt a gibbet at a crossroads. As they passed close by, Thomas stared open-mouthed at the barred iron cage swinging in the breeze and the shackled, half-decayed body he could barely discern inside. He could think of no fate more terrible than to be hung in chains, rotting away as a public spectacle.

His father nodded at the grim exhibit and sniffed noisily – perhaps with righteous satisfaction, perhaps with sheer disgust; Thomas couldn't be sure.

# 2

# Newton in Makerfield, August 1833

'Watch and learn, m'boy – just watch and learn!'

His father's gravelly voice repeated this stern injunction each morning as they walked with Uncle Ralph through the entrance to the foundry. High above them, set into the imposing structure that encased the huge iron gates, was a slab of stone inscribed with the previous year's date: 'T. & S. – 1832'. 'Tayleur and Stephenson,' his father explained. 'That's Robert Stephenson, son of the great engineer. Impressive in his own right, the young one. A partner in this enterprise.' Surmounting the stone, framed by bolts of lightning, the fearsome visage of Vulcan glared down at them.

Watch and learn? What exactly was he supposed to learn? By no means clear. But in every corner of the Vulcan Foundry there were always plenty of things to watch. Agog, he stared at all the bustle in the boiler shop, where men sweated, spat, shouted, as they moved around the benches, operating massive rollers to shape the iron plates into curves, wielding shears to cut them precisely to size, punching holes for the rivets, handling the mechanical drills like toys. In other buildings they were making all sorts of things — big things like girders for bridges, little things like switching devices and miscellaneous replacement parts for the locomotives.

What excited him more than anything else was the casting process in the centre of the foundry. He didn't dare approach closely — the way Mr Tayleur the manager glared at him from under a shaggy eyebrow was enough to keep Thomas out of harm's way — but he stood tiptoe on a box against the wall and peered at the large pit into which men were placing the moulds. Then the fiery molten iron was transferred from the cupola furnaces to an enormous receptacle beside the pit, and poured into the moulds. Blazing. Frightening. Diabolical. Magical.

Watching was only part of it. There was the unforgettable smell of hot metal, too, and the incessant noise — the clanking, scraping and ringing, the sonorous ding and dong, the utter cacophony of it all.

His father observed all these foundry processes closely, asking questions, taking notes in a pocketbook. And a couple of times he took Thomas beyond the western end of the township to see where a wagon works was being built with cottages for its labourers.

And so the mornings went, informally inducting Thomas into the adult world, regulating his pulse in accord with industry's throb.

But the afternoons were different. In later life he would remember them as the final strands of boyhood — his own boyhood, and also his cousin's. Tall big-shouldered Edmund was to begin his apprenticeship with Spragg the butcher before the month was out. For both boys, this fortnight of afternoons seemed like a large bowl to fill with playfulness, with impulsive little excursions and half-baked schemes.

'Let's go up to Castle Hill!' exclaimed Edmund. Or, 'Want to see the Roman road, Tomtit?' Or, 'Know how Gallows Croft got its name, dost tha?'

So they walked to Castle Hill, half a mile north of the town, where a tinkling brook flowed into the River Dean. 'That big mound up on the bank there,' Edmund pointed, 'folk say it's an ancient barrow. Burial place. Of a king, could be. Or some sort of hero.'

They reckoned the barrow's height at eight or nine yards, and its width as three times that. Wandering in the shade of the oaks that grew thick on its summit and sides, they threw sticks at squirrels and rooks, rolled a sleepy hedgehog down the slope, wrestled with each other like puppies, imagined that a decaying hut was a robbers' lair.

There was a creaking of feathers close overhead as a pair of ravens flew towards the trees. 'Black as coal!' Edmund exclaimed. 'Just like thy locks. Th'art a tomtit with a raven's plumage.' His cackling laugh made Thomas wince.

Another day they went out to Red Bank. 'Folk tell of a gory battle here,' said Edmund as they came over the stone bridge and along a green lane towards the steep bank. 'Time o the Civil War. They say Cromwell's force captured some o the King's men who'd come from north of the border, highlanders. And that Cromwell, he were a bloody hard man, he hanged the prisoners in that field across the way – over there, look. That's why it's still called the Gallows Croft.'

The township itself was like a fairground of diverting entertainments. Outside the churchyard, just along from the marketplace, they ran their hands over the stone uprights of the old stocks, imagining the humiliation of miscreants held fast there, taunted, exposed to the weather, pelted with mud and food scraps and pig shit. Beside the large willow-fringed lake they sent flat stones skipping across the water. In the doorway of the smithy they watched Big Ned bashing the tips of red-hot bars into flattened ends for some obscure purpose.

But the place they kept going back to was the Sankey Valley, with its little brook running beside the large canal, and above them George Stephenson's mighty viaduct stretching across the whole wide valley – a thing of wonder. The boys would spend hours looking at this marvellous edifice from all angles. More than sixty feet high, it gave ample clearance to the Mersey flats that plied the canal. Thomas took his sketchbook down to Newton Common, where he had a clear view of the nine great rounded arches spanning the valley, and painstakingly drew each component of the structure. The process of drawing could absorb his attention for long periods. In the schoolroom he had shown a talent for fine graphite pencil work and porte-crayon sketching. Nothing gave him more pleasure than representing on a sheet of paper the shapes and textures of buildings and street scenes. Sitting now below the viaduct while aimless Edmund watched the barges and rambled around idly nearby, Thomas applied himself to rendering with patient exactitude the design that combined so proportionately the ginger and yellow sandstone slabs with a patterning of red brick. The way the afternoon shadow fell on stepped plinths and banded jambs – he wanted to capture the detail of that, and show precisely how the corbelled square pilaster on each pier carried the moulded cornices, and the cornices in turn supported the square-capped stone parapets.

The sun's warmth leaked away and damp air from the canal began to drift over the common. Edmund, tired of random pottering, slouched up to look at his cousin's sketchbook.

'Not bad, Tomtit,' he conceded grudgingly. 'But next time we come down here, tha can leave thy sketchbook at home. Tedious for me just filling in time while tha sits here and toys with thy pencil. We should be doing things together.'

So the following afternoon, at Edmund's bidding, they walked along the railway line from the village station until they were approaching the point where the edge of the viaduct rested on the shoulders of the high clay embankment. Swivelling his head this way and that, wishing he could see in all directions at once, Thomas felt giddy with a surfeit of prospects. Southward the vista led his eye towards a spire rising in the distance, and he pointed to it questioningly.

'That'd be Winwick,' Edmund told him. 'Near Warrington. Th'd have come that way in the coach. Spire of St Oswald's. Father tells how they dug up three giant skeletons under the church there, just four or five year back. That Cromwell, he took his troops to St Oswald's after the battle at Red Bank. Smashed up the statues. He were a bloody hard man, that one.'

To the north, at intervals in the landscape where the canal was no longer visible, they could see masts and sails of the flats. East and west ran the railway, its pair of solid iron rails nearly five feet apart, forming a shiny track that extended into the far distance.

Beneath their feet were those sturdy rails, and beneath the rails were the dark recesses where the edge of the viaduct rested on the embankment. They peered into the narrow shelf-like aperture. Then Eddie had issued his challenge, and soon after that it all went frighteningly wrong.

∞

After an eternity of waiting he heard his father's gruff voice and felt big firm hands pulling at him. His shoulder was being squeezed hard, his forehead was pressing against a rough surface, and his hip seemed to be jammed tight. He let out an anxious yelp but Mr Browne hushed him impatiently, and then with a sudden wrench Thomas was set free. He crumpled at his father's feet, snivelling. Blood trickled into his eye from the graze on his brow.

Mr Browne reached down, seizing and twisting his son's ear, and yanked him upright. 'Now listen to me, you foolish boy!' he shouted. 'I don't want to know why you got yourself into this predicament. The answer is all too obvious: stupidity! Sheer stupidity! What I do want to know is this: has it taught you a lesson?'

'Yes, sir.' A whimpering whisper.

'Then what *is* the lesson?' yelled his father, shaking him by the shoulders. 'What have you learnt from this sorry episode? Eh? Eh? Louder!'

This catechism made Thomas shed more tears, and curl his fingertips so tightly into his palms that the nails stung his flesh. What was the right answer? 'Not to be led astray?' he ventured. 'Not to be talked into doing stupid things?'

'Ah, so you're telling me someone else is to blame. Someone made you do something against your will. Am I to believe that? Then you accept no personal responsibility for your puerile behaviour?'

Thomas wailed. It wasn't his fault. He would never have done such a thing if Eddie hadn't dared him to.

'Oh, enough of that! Fifteen years old but you sound like a fretful baby. And you've wet your breeches. Stop the bawling and come with me.'

His father strode ahead, with Thomas stumbling behind him.

# 3

# Newton,
# September to December 1833

Although the memory of disgrace flickered through him
nightly as he lay down to sleep, there was so much else to fill
his daylight hours and evenings that Thomas soon ceased to
be utterly abject. In the course of each day he felt a kind of
hunger growing in him – a hunger beyond anything physical.
Midday dinners of soups and stews were substantial enough,
and for every supper the food was plentiful, though plain, but
as afternoon drew towards twilight it was to the abundance
of table talk that he always looked forward with the keenest
appetite, eager to consume all the facts and ideas the men
would be discussing. Their vigorous conversation was usually
prompted by his father's many questions about the operations
of the foundry, about other businesses in the district such as
the chemical works down at Bradley Lock, and about the
likely further developments of the railway system. His uncle,
never short of opinions, enjoyed holding forth.

On this particular evening, Ralph Browne was waxing
vehement on the theme of the lack of useful vocational

education. 'Even in a town such as ours,' he declared, grasping his tankard of porter in one big hand and clutching hunks of cheese and bread in the other, 'the school does little to prepare children for any occupations. As far as I can tell, the future mechanic or agricultural worker learns hardly anything of a practical nature from his classroom lessons. Hardly anything!'

'In the grammar schools it's not a whit better,' said Thomas's father. 'Boys emerge with stunted minds because they're fed with dry husks of ancient learning when they should be taking sound food from modern discoveries. What worth is there in scraps of Latin and Greek for the children of our middle class? How can such things help them understand their social position? Their prospects? What they need, surely, is a knowledge of political economy to guard them against fanatics and knaves, and a study of modern history to show them the progress of civilisation.'

Ralph nodded, wiping beery froth from his whiskers with the back of his thick hand. 'And more than that,' he responded, 'they ought to be learning how to apply science to everyday wants. Especially chemical and mechanical science. If their schooling fails to provide a proper scientific foundation, where will our needful army of engineers and architects and surveyors come from? Apprenticeship is all very well, but unless it can build on something solid, it won't equip the most talented of our young lads for all the opportunities they'll encounter.'

'I place some faith in these new mechanics' institutes,' said Henry. 'Large membership, from what I hear, in both the Liverpool institute and the Manchester one. Strong emphasis on self-improvement through lectures on mechanical science and engineering, along with debates, and plenty of library books.'

Thomas listened intently to his elders as their conversation rolled along through the evening, fuelled by beer and tobacco. Exhaling smoke like steam engines, they discussed the merits and limits of technical training for young apprentices; an expected decline in the use of canals for transporting goods, now that roads and railway tracks were improving so rapidly; the relative advantages of brick and stone and iron for different kinds of bridge construction; the remarkable but risky growth of large-scale business ventures; the foundry's financial management under Charles Tayleur; and the imminent return of Robert Stephenson, Tayleur's junior partner in this enterprise and son of the eminent inventor.

Hanging on their words, Thomas imagined illustrious careers for himself in the world that was beginning to be born. During a pause, he felt bold enough to declare his ambition. 'I'd like to design a railway and bridges and things. One day. Like Mr Stephenson.' He meant it to sound like a well-considered decision, demonstrating maturity, but it came out squeakily.

His father looked at him askance. 'Off to bed, Thomas,' he said with a derisive snort.

But a fortnight later Henry Browne made an announcement that startled his son. 'Time for me to return to London, Thomas,' he said. 'I intend to leave on tomorrow's coach. You'll be staying on here. I've arranged for you to be an apprentice at the foundry, under Mr Stephenson the younger. Your uncle will keep an eye on you while you're at work, and you'll continue to live in his house.'

'For how long?'

'For as long as it takes you to learn all that an apprenticeship can teach you.'

'But that could be years, Papa.'

'It will be. It will be.'

'When will I see you again? And Mama, and my sisters?'

'Not for some while, probably. You can't tie yourself to your mother's apron strings, Thomas, or expect me to be always looking after you. You've had enough cockering. You'll need to learn independence. How to stand on your own feet. How to make your way in the world. You're young, but not too young to get started. If you apply yourself diligently here in Newton and show some self-discipline, an apprenticeship may become a pathway to profit.'

Thomas licked his lip to disguise its quivering. He felt… excited, yes, but queasily apprehensive, too. Cast loose. Nearly orphaned.

∞

*'You haven't done what I told you to do!' The huge burly shape, robed in black, looms over him like a giant and seizes him by the arm. Thomas tries to speak but makes only a gurgling sound as he is shoved into a barred cage. Its door slams shut. 'Fool!' shouts the ogre. 'You'll never learn!'*

*'But I don't know what I haven't done.' The words are so heavy, squatting on his tongue, that Thomas cannot squeeze them out past his lips. Seeming to hear what Thomas is failing to utter, the tall black judge roars a reply: 'To be ignorant is to be guilty!'*

And then Thomas did release a terrified cry, rising to a shriek that became louder and louder until he woke, his face streaked with sweat.

∞

The months went past at a gallop. There was no leisure to indulge in pining and self-pity. He had to be at the foundry, a half-mile walk away in the darkness, no later than six o'clock every morning from Monday to Saturday. Ralph Browne strode along energetically, Thomas skittering beside him to keep up. The weather was often unpleasant, and many a time Thomas would be wet and shivering by the time he passed beneath the fierce frown of Vulcan at the iron gateway.

'You're a lucky lad,' Ralph told him as they hurried to the works together on one of these murky mornings, 'and I hope you know it.'

'Being able to lodge in your home, you mean? I'm truly grateful for that, Uncle Ralph.'

'No, no – I mean lucky to have this opportunity to learn the rudiments of draughtsmanship. Especially with Mr Robert Stephenson to guide you. Very timely. It'll equip you well for employment in the years ahead.'

'Then why isn't cousin Edmund working in the foundry too?'

'Just doesn't have the noddle for that kind of work,' said Ralph with a regretful shake of his own grizzled head. 'He'll make a good enough butcher but he's not a clever lad, alas. So that's another aspect of your good fortune: you're quick-witted enough to pick up knowledge wherever you look, and make the most of it.'

Thomas beamed at this avuncular recognition of his aptitude. It would make all the long weary days worthwhile. He couldn't remember any words from his father, not ever, that acknowledged he might have any talent at all.

At first he'd been puzzled to see how much busy activity continued to fill the foundry, day after day and week after week, keeping nearly a hundred men occupied. It was more than two years since the Liverpool and Manchester railway had opened, and nearly a year since it was joined just west of Newton by the line from Warrington. So what were all these things being produced for now? He asked his uncle about it.

'Well, for one thing,' explained Ralph Browne, 'there are pieces of engine and sections of rail that break or wear out. Boilers explode, tracks buckle – so there's always a demand for replacements. Some other bits just don't work well enough, so they get redesigned. All sorts of little adjustments. And besides, there's a couple of new companies just established, one they're calling Grand Junction that intends to link our railways with a new line down to Birmingham and another that will run from Birmingham into London. Both colossal schemes. Our foundry should get plenty of business from them. Locomotives and all their parts – pipes and pistons and cylinders and the rest. Wheels, wagons, rails. One way and another, we'll have our hands full for a long while yet, you can be sure of that!'

In the following weeks Thomas spent long hours at his little window-side workbench in a cold and musty room at the back of the foundry, faithfully executing the many tasks of technical copy-drawing that Robert Stephenson set for him: plans and elevations and shaded perspectives display-ing in meticulous detail various parts of machines, station buildings, tunnels, bridges. It was fastidious work but gave him great pleasure, this process of taking a blank sheet of paper and inscribing an arrangement of fine lines upon it until gradually an elegant image appeared.

Once or twice a week Mr Stephenson would stop beside Thomas's bench and inspect what he had produced, usually saying little. A nod of approval was encouragement enough and a raised eyebrow would suffice to prod Thomas into even more diligent efforts. He knew that until his mentor was thoroughly satisfied with his skills as a copyist there would be no progression to the stage of drafting original designs.

He was in great awe of Stephenson. They all were. 'A brilliant young man,' said his uncle, who regarded the ambitious engineer with a deference nobody else elicited from him. 'Just thirty years old, and what achievements already!' Everyone at the foundry knew how much 'The Master' had accomplished. How, showing even greater ingenuity than his famous father, he had swiftly devised improvements in all the vital components of a steam engine, from angled cylinders to robust boilerplates. How he formed the world's first company for constructing locomotives. How he went off to South America to get engineering experience in the gold and silver mines there. How he came back to England in time to design the acclaimed Rocket engine for the Rainhill trials. How he'd now been appointed chief engineer for the grand London-to-Birmingham railway project.

Robert Stephenson had an imposing physical presence combined with an air of preoccupation: tall and broad-shouldered, he wasted no words and never seemed fully attentive to those around him.

'Absorbed in his own ideas and schemes, I suppose,' said Ralph Browne when his nephew asked why their master was so taciturn. 'Always thinking. Little time for chitchat.'

But there was one memorable occasion when Stephenson became almost talkative, not long before he began to spend most of his time in London to coordinate the planning of the big north–south line. He'd paused beside Thomas to appraise some drawings of pistons, but then picked up a thin book from the corner of the bench.

'What's this?' he asked, flicking it open.

Thomas flushed. 'Just some little sketches of my own, sir. I did them around Newton before starting my apprenticeship.'

'Aha. Here's our viaduct.' Stephenson examined the page closely. 'Hmmm. Very precise. And well composed – a nice balance here between the spandrels and the piers. I like the way you've caught the play of light on different surfaces, the projecting bands of stone on the brick jambs, and the cornices – delicately hatched. Those shadow lines beside the pilasters, too. You've got a keen draughtsman's eye, m'lad. Keep working at it. Good foundation for the craft of an architect or an engineer, especially if you look beyond the appearances to consider the function of each component. For instance, those ledges inside the arches – they may seem merely ornamental, but can you guess why they were put there?'

Thomas shook his head.

'They supported the massive wooden arch formers when the building was going up. So whenever you're observing the structure of something impressive, think about the process of designing and making it.'

Stephenson put a large encouraging hand on the boy's thin bony shoulder. It rested there for a moment, and Thomas felt its warm pressure long after Stephenson left the room. Deep inside him there was a yearning to respond somehow.

# 4

# Newton,
# January to April 1834

It was not only his father who unnerved him. Whenever thoughts about his mother crossed Thomas's mind he would feel less certain of himself. Though her attitude never seemed quite hostile, he was troubled by her way of pursing her lips as she inspected him. Even in childhood he'd felt her scrutiny. When he reached the age of six, she decided the youngster was not turning out in a manner that matched the name they had given him.

'You're not what I thought a Thomas would be,' she mused, head cocked like a bird considering a worm. He raised his face, pudgy and puzzled, to meet her dissatisfied gaze. 'I'll have to think of something else,' she added, stroking her cleft chin.

'Stephen!' she announced with sudden conviction at the dinner table that evening.

Her husband looked blank. 'Mmm? Who is Stephen, m'dear?' said Mr Browne, his tone expressing no curiosity but only a disdainful resignation that reflected long experience of his wife's whims and fancies.

'This child!' she yelped, pointing with her fork to the cowering boy. 'That's who he's going to be from now on. No more Thomas. I've spent time enough trying to make him grow into that name. I want him to be a Stephen.'

So she began, for a while, to call him Stephen. Whenever she used this strange descriptor the boy would frown with confusion. What did the change mean? Did he look somehow different from before? Leaning over a bucket of water, he stared at his reflection. Was that Stephen looking back at him, or Thomas? Neither name seemed to fit him properly now.

His sisters and father continued to call him Thomas, so after about a year his mother gave up her attempt to discard his original identity and impose a new one on him. From then on, she seldom addressed him by any name. He began tentatively to think of himself as Thomas again. But he carried that other potential self with him as he grew up, a shadow at his shoulder. He was especially conscious of it now that he was trying to find a place for himself in this new setting, a long way from his London home. It unsettled his sense of where he really belonged.

∞

Some four months after Thomas came to Newton, another youth arrived at the foundry as an apprentice. Shaking hands with Daniel Gooch, Thomas watched him warily: this new-comer was much taller, a year or two older, surely, with a self-confident manner and a prepossessing smile.

'I heard that Mr George Stephenson is a friend of the Gooches from his Northumberland days,' Ralph Browne told Thomas. 'Daniel's father was in the Bedlington ironworks there at the time. The boy already has a good deal of practical knowledge, so I'm told. Wheel-moulding, pattern-making, things like that. His father died recently, so the elder Mr Stephenson encouraged Daniel to work here for a while. He's lodging at the Houghtons' farmhouse – the place that Mr Stephenson uses as his headquarters when he's in this neighbourhood.'

The two apprentices had benches alongside one another. On Daniel's first day he picked up a handful of Thomas's drawings, looked at them cursorily, nodded, and dropped them back on his draughting board without comment. In the weeks that followed he showed scant interest in Thomas's background or aspirations. Full of his own stories about the things he had done, he regaled Thomas with diverting accounts of various experiences and escapades: riding a recalcitrant donkey to school, falling off it and breaking a collarbone; spending Saturday mornings underground at the colliery pit near his home from a tender age; learning to turn fancy objects on a lathe when he was only ten years old; observing the manufacture of a new and stronger kind of rail at the local ironworks; and playing pranks on the village folk.

'One time I caught a little frog and used it to tease and tickle some of the girls, and Jenny Birkenshaw was laughing with her mouth wide open so I slipped the frog into it. The slimy thing went straight down her throat, and she ran off screaming. Silly wench. There was soon a hue and cry after me.'

Thomas gasped at such bold and shameless mischief-making.

'I liked to amuse myself,' Daniel went on with a smirk, 'at the expense of a bad-tempered old crone in the cottage next to ours. I remember one winter's evening I filled a cow's horn with old tar-rope, and then put a hot cinder in it, and inserted the small end of the horn into the keyhole of her door, and blew at the large end to drive smoke into the cottage. You should have heard the commotion!'

As winter turned towards spring and light-green tufts began to fledge the willows around the town's lake, Thomas came to feel ever more subordinate to Daniel. He admired and envied the older boy's handsome bearing, sinewy forearms and casually dominant manner, his ability to converse in a smooth and nonchalant way with grown men. Daniel seemed to be regarded with particular favour by Mr Charles Tayleur, who not only let him spend time in the fitting shop, helping to put machinery together, but also permitted him now and then to get away from the factory for a day so that he could ride with foremen on the footplate of engines and hobnob with locomotive superintendents at both ends of the Liverpool and Manchester line.

Once, as they stood side by side, Thomas was startled to feel a sudden yearning to be touched by Daniel, to be embraced. Hastily he dismissed that thought from his mind.

His moods fluctuated. Bursts of energy would propel him forward excitedly for days on end, with increasing momentum, so that he sometimes felt like a cartwheel spinning downhill faster and faster, out of control. And then he would come to a sudden halt, exhausted, lapsing for a long while into a kind of melancholy trance.

In contrast, Daniel's temperament appeared to be calm and steady. As far as Thomas could see, his fellow apprentice exhibited neither great excitement nor any sign of despondency. Although there were times when he worked with intense concentration, he always seemed equable.

That made it all the more surprising when, in midsummer, a kind of languor came over Daniel. Drooping, he fell sick and was confined to his bed. 'They say he can't even keep down a bowl of bread and milk,' Ralph Browne reported. Thomas wanted to help in some brotherly way, but for a couple of days he couldn't think what to do. Then he began to work on a shaded drawing of one of the new locomotives, and after hours of painstaking effort he took it to the farmhouse where Daniel was living. Miss Houghton showed him into the invalid's little room.

'I did this for you,' he said, shyly approaching the bed and holding out his sheet of paper. 'A present.'

Giving it the merest glance, Daniel nodded, put the drawing aside, and closed his eyes. He seemed to slip immediately into a half-dormant trance. Thomas stood there for a few minutes, wanting to bathe the sleeper's pale forehead and hear him talk. But the room was silent except for Daniel's noisy breathing. Thomas walked slowly home, feeling...What did he feel? He couldn't give it a name. It was almost like being spurned, but to blame a sick person for seeming unfriendly wouldn't be fair. So he tried to push the shapeless emotion into a nook at the back of his mind.

As he came around a bend in the path he saw a rabbit ahead of him, sitting timorously still. In a sudden fury he grabbed a handful of pebbles and flung them at the stupid little beast, chasing it and yelling wild curses, and then sank to his knees and moaned without knowing why.

A week later Daniel returned to the foundry looking wan and thin.

'I'll be leaving Newton shortly,' he told Thomas. 'Need to get my strength back. Spend a while with my mother, and then look for work when I feel better. Perhaps there'll be an opening for me in one of the new railway companies.'

∞

One evening, soon after Daniel's departure, Thomas did something impulsive and furtive.

The foundry had closed its operations for the day an hour earlier than usual because of an ugly accident in the boiler room, and instead of going straight to his uncle's house he decided on a sudden whim to walk up to Castle Hill. He met nobody on the road. By the time he'd made his way there and climbed to the top of the high mound, daylight was wilting and dusk had begun to settle over everything. At this hour it was a gloomy spot. A gust of wind whooshed over the hillock. The big trees, indifferent, shrugged at him through the murk. He shivered. Putting his hand to his groin, he rubbed himself rhythmically. Then he lowered his trousers and stepped out of them. The cool air caressed his skin, and he looked down to watch his tingling pendant rise stiffly to attention. Leaving his trousers on the ground and descending the slope, he broke into a run and didn't stop until he had completed a circuit around the base of Castle Hill. By now the darkness had thickened and he felt damp with his exertion and the misty air on his body. He pulled his trousers on and walked back down the road. It took a long while for his excited flesh to subside.

# 5

# London, May 1839

Navvies laboured within a lustrous cylinder of light cast from the great shaft far above them. On a narrow platform a man with a basket of rubble was rising, irradiated, towards the top of the cylinder, part of a slow ascent that would take him on through the shaft to the distant surface. At either side of the illuminated central space, the tunnel's brick-lined walls glowed orange as they curved up to the Gothic peak of its tall roof. Harnessed horses waited wearily to haul their next load. In the foreground of the enclosing darkness was a glimpse of the reason for all this toil – the railway track itself, with pools of water glinting beside it.

'He's captured something elusive here, don't you think?' Thomas tapped his finger on the lithograph. 'There were moments that did feel like this on our Euston-to-Camden project – brief moments that had...well, almost a serene quality, when the noise and tension seemed to recede. I suppose it may have been like that for you, too, sometimes, on the Great Western?'

Daniel Gooch gave a little nod but remained silent as he poured himself another glass of wine and looked around the room. There was something disappointingly reserved in his manner, or detached – perhaps a kind of aloofness. Thomas had expected their conversation would flow more easily. After more than four years since their last meeting, engaged for much of that time in their different but comparable railway construction ventures, he'd looked forward keenly to this rendezvous, to an exchange of stories, perhaps to a deepening friendship. When Daniel agreed to meet him over a meal, Thomas began to make a mental list of topics he'd like them to talk about. And he'd brought this fine book along to impress – especially because the picture lying before them now on the tavern table evoked perfectly, he thought, one of those quiet scenes of surprising splendour that occasionally lit up the arduous project, now concluded, on which he'd worked with such anxiety for so long. *Drawings of the London and Birmingham Railway*: it was astute of the artist to arrange for such a handsome collection to be published soon after the line had opened. Of all John Bourne's drawings, the one that most appealed to Thomas was this luminous image he was now showing Daniel.

Wanting his own appreciation of it to be acknowledged and shared, he read its caption aloud: 'Working Shaft, Kilsby Tunnel, 8 July 1837' – and added, 'but the tableau belies that prosaic description, doesn't it? I mean…the men here appear to be…well, if you ask me, it's as if they're almost *transfigured*. By the heroic scale of their efforts. No one would guess, from looking at this, that the tunnel caused far more trouble than any other part of the undertaking.'

Trouble, he thought, was much too mild a word for all the misfortunes that had nearly thwarted that whole herculean enterprise of excavation. Just a few weeks after he'd joined the London-to-Birmingham project as draughtsman for an architect on another part of the line, Thomas had heard about the work beginning on the Kilsby Tunnel. Before long, almost everyone knew what a gigantic task it had become. Even if things hadn't gone badly wrong it would have been extremely difficult to dig out such a high and wide passage that extended well over two thousand yards, and with all the other practical problems, not least the challenge of ventilating spaces so far underground. People said it should never have been necessary to build this, anyway. But those obstinate Northampton landowners had forced Stephenson to change the line's direction so that it would pass at a distance from their town, which meant constructing a tunnel all the way through Kilsby Ridge. Then came the disastrous deluge when, soon after work began, the roof collapsed, nearly drowning the navvies in that part of the tunnel. A vast expanse of waterlogged quicksand, deep below the bed of surface clay, had gone undetected during preliminary surveys. It took many months to pump out the water from above with mighty engines erected over each shaft.

Thomas remembered well how stories about Kilsby had spread rapidly along other parts of the line, through the contracting offices and among the legions of labourers. There were valiant feats, as when an engineer rescued a group of navvies from the swirling flood by getting them onto a raft and towing it to safety as he swam with a rope in his mouth. And reckless acts, too – none more idiotic than when a trio of numbskulls, drunkenly celebrating their escape from inundation, died one after the other as each tried to jump over the mouth of a shaft in a game of follow the leader.

Daniel stretched back languidly, thumbs hooked into armpits, and inflated his broad chest. To Thomas he epitomised manly self-confidence. 'On the Great Western line,' said Daniel, fondling his newly cultivated and enviable whiskers, 'we've faced nothing so dreadful as the Kilsby debacle. Not that it's all been smooth going – the Box Tunnel will take a couple more years to complete, and our board is making a fuss about the wide flat arches on the Maidenhead Bridge – but Brunel takes it all in his stride. I haven't had to give much thought to the construction work. My job has just been to get suitable locomotives ready and keep them operating efficiently. Stephenson's *North Star* engine serves us fairly well, though I reckon I can improve its blastpipe.'

'I admire Mr Stephenson greatly,' Thomas said, eyes shining. 'To have designed a new class of locomotive to suit your railway's special needs at the same time as he was coordinating all that work on the Birmingham line – amazing, really. I don't know how he held our project together. Twenty-nine contractors, each with a few miles of the track to manage, and he not only kept the whole chain of them up to the mark but also intervened to solve problems when anyone ran into trouble. The Kilsby Tunnel was the most difficult case, of course – after the roof collapsed the contractor seemed to be paralysed with indecision, and Mr Stephenson earned respect right along the line, believe me, for the resolute way he took command of that task. He almost lived on the line for more than a year. I doubt anyone else could have completed the work successfully against such odds.'

'Clever man, all right,' Daniel conceded, clasping his hands behind his head and half suppressing a yawn. 'But no more so than Brunel. An absolute genius, Brunel is. Even younger than

Stephenson, remember, and look at the range of what he's designed: ingenious bridges, dockyards, stations, the broad-gauge railway to Bristol – surveyed every mile of that route himself, y'know – and now he's created a giant steamship to take passengers right across the Atlantic!'

Thomas made no comment. While he could recognise the brilliance of Isambard Brunel, his own loyalty as a hero-worshipper lay with Robert Stephenson, the exemplar to whom he owed his employment. Having been appointed on Stephenson's recommendation at such a young age to the role of an assistant architect on the London end of the line, from Euston up to Camden, he could hardly believe his luck. It meant he'd been able to learn from close, regular contact with an outstanding architect, Philip Hardwick, a man who compelled respect, and through him with the equally eminent structural engineer Charles Fox. And now he himself was an associate of the Institution of Civil Engineers. He wanted to talk about the work he'd been doing, but Daniel was showing no interest.

Thomas drained his wineglass. 'You look well, Daniel,' he said. 'When I saw you last there wasn't much colour in your cheeks.'

'I'm in pretty good health now. Fine fettle. Marriage suits me.'

'Married already, are you? I didn't know.' Taken aback, Thomas tried to repress a disconcerting image that came to him instantly – of Daniel folding a woman in an intimate embrace.

'Last year. My wife Margaret hails from Sunderland. Perhaps you've heard of Henry Tanner – the wealthy shipowner? It's his daughter. Comely and sweet-natured. I can recommend the wedded state, Thomas.'

'I need...' Thomas coughed and cleared his throat. 'I need to strengthen my financial position before I can think of marriage. And find an agreeable young lady, of course.' He kept to himself the rest of the truth, a half-acknowledged awareness that what he felt drawn to most strongly was the company of men.

Daniel took out his fob watch. 'As late as that!' he exclaimed.

Outside the tavern they shook hands. 'I hope we can meet again soon,' said Thomas.

'Ah – difficult for me, I'm afraid. Very busy in the months ahead, very busy. And my wife expects my company in the evenings. Perhaps I can make contact with you later in the year.'

The tone was so indifferent that Daniel's words stung Thomas like a slap. He watched as the man who would plainly never become a friend to him strode off, all too self-sufficient, into a sulphurous fog.

On the long dark walk homewards Thomas recalled in detail a previous occasion, some eighteen months earlier, when a longing for male closeness had consciously disturbed him.

## 6

# Kilsby, October 1837;
# London, May 1839

He had travelled by coach with Charles Fox up to Rugby, and from there they walked the five muddy miles to the Kilsby tunnel entrance, where digging and pumping had proceeded apace for several months. At Robert Stephenson's invitation, Mr Fox was there to see for himself what kind of engineering challenge the tunnel presented. He'd asked Thomas to go along with him and make some sketches, notes and technical drawings.

As they approached the site, Thomas was astonished to see a massive camp, a makeshift town of turf shanties and tents, hundreds of them sprawling across the bruised hillside. Slatterns slouched in doorways and ragamuffins were playing raucous games, but it was the menfolk who caught his eye, making their way in a noisy herd from the tunnel mouth up towards their ragged settlement. It had just gone midday, and they'd downed tools to take time for eating and drinking.

Charles Fox gestured towards them. 'A rough band of heathens, eh?' he murmured to Thomas.

'Such numbers! Is there food enough for all of them?'

'Oh, the victuallers keep them pretty well fed. Every workingman here gets two pounds of beef each day, and a gallon of beer to wash it down. Some of them drink a lot more than that, of course. Not much else around here for them to do with the good money they earn. So it's wild carousing, mostly. And fighting and fornicating, of course.'

The throng came closer. Thomas could smell their rankness, hear the ribald banter, see the sooty grime on sweat-streaked faces. Their clothing was distinctive: most of the men wore canvas shirts, square-tailed coats, hats of felt or sealskin with the brims turned up, and muddy moleskin trousers gathered in with string below the knee. There were incongruous splashes of colour – a few gaudy handkerchiefs protruding from breast pockets, and a couple of rainbow-hued waistcoats.

A group at the front of the crowd passed within a few yards of the two onlookers, led by a tall hulking fellow who carried himself with all the self-confident swagger of a powerful warrior chieftain. His gaze fell on Thomas, in whose eyes he seemed to detect something submissive. With a knowing grin, he paused to peer down insolently at him and then gave an ironic stooping salute. Thomas looked away, trying not to think about the giant's uncouth vigour, the sheer size of him.

But an image of the man came back to him, disquietingly, that evening on the return journey to London – an image of towering bulky masculinity. Thomas could almost feel his presence and detect a sweaty odour, as if standing close beside him. Conscious of his own small stature and thin frame, he felt a pang of something like envy as he pictured the animal strength of those who hefted barrow loads, wielded shovels, swung heavy picks. With their meaty forearms and thickset bodies, they belonged completely to a world of brawn. In the eyes of such men he himself must be a ridiculous milksop.

Stories about navvies were legion. Thomas had heard details of their living conditions, and it was easy to imagine that the hovels on this hillside were nests of squalor. People said that a small room with four beds would often need to accommodate as many as sixteen lodgers – two to a bed, and two shifts of eight-man squads exchanging places for their rest and their exertion alike. To Thomas it seemed an appalling way to live. On the job it was all mud and danger and backbreaking labour, while extreme discomfort marred what should have been their hours of respite. But there was something exhilarating, too, about this kind of existence – he could see that, and he hankered after it. What had pulled these men away from the northern coalfields, from the farmlands of Lancashire, and from across the Irish Sea was not only the lure of better money but also the sheer exuberance of working together strenuously on massive projects. Self-displaced, they showed no inclination to return to their former work as miners, mechanics, harvesters and haymakers, or to the quiet comforts of their home villages.

∽

Remembering now that encounter with the Kilsby navvies, and the tales he'd heard of the way such men lived, Thomas tried to reason with himself as, having parted ways with Daniel Gooch, he trudged towards the family home in Islington. Yearning covertly for an amicable connection with ruffians like these was foolish, he knew that. Any prospective companions should of course be sought within the professional field in which he'd begun to establish himself – among young men who shared his particular enthusiasms and his aspiration to shine as an engineer or architect. Yet so far nobody of his acquaintance was congenial enough to form a close bond with him. He'd hoped that Daniel might become a kind of elder brother, at least, but that had turned out to be a foolish dream; there was no place for him even at the edge of Daniel's attention. Older men such as Stephenson, Hardwick and Fox could hardly be regarded as friends; they were on a higher plane in the priesthood of their profession, mentors whom Thomas keenly wanted to serve as an acolyte, and strive to emulate. He could only apply himself sedulously to the tasks they allocated, waiting for the day he might feel less subservient and less alone.

It was unclear what his next professional step should be. Now that the Euston Station was open – the first mainline terminus in a capital city anywhere in the world, with its superb entrance featuring the largest Doric arch ever built – he could share in the pride of that colossal achievement, though he knew his personal contribution had been insignificant, notwithstanding the kind words of approval that came his way.

'Excellent draughtsmanship, Browne,' Hardwick had said, nodding approval. 'Well done.'

In truth, Thomas himself was pleased with the drawings he'd produced so painstakingly as the plans and calculations were revised countless times during the project. And now he could look with a just satisfaction at the finished work – the great stone structure in its splendid Greek-revival style, supported on four columns and four piers with bronze gates placed behind them and lodges on either side of the arch. A wonder of the modern world had taken shape before his eyes.

It was gratifying that the project in which he'd played a role – an inconspicuous role, yes, but still he did his bit – could claim other notable successes as well. They developed an electric telegraph system for the Euston section of the line. They used a stationary steam engine to cable-haul locomotives from the terminus up the steep incline to Camden. And their own particular triumphs on their part of the line had merged with all the other things achieved by the London-to-Birmingham railway venture – which in turn was just one part of an expansive national network, incorporating many kinds of innovative designs and construction materials. In order that powerful machines could run in all directions on smooth wheels and smooth rails, city and country were being transformed by countless embankments, drains and other earthworks; by bridges across rivers and valleys; by tunnels through hillsides; by grand station buildings. It had become a great and exciting industry, just as his father had prophesied.

With characteristic immodesty, Henry Browne made a point of reminding Thomas about his foresight. 'Would never have turned out like this if I hadn't taken you to Newton to get some training – right place, right time,' he remarked when his son gained a position on the Euston-to-Camden project. 'Told you so,' was his only comment when *The Times* ran an article on the growing prestige of the Institution of Civil Engineers.

Thomas's thoughts always came back anxiously to his father, the embodiment of complete manhood, who knew everything that mattered, who exuded self-confidence, whose approval his son could never wholly obtain and from whose thraldom he could never escape. Thomas, like both his sisters, still lived in the family home. It was hard even to imagine an independent existence, let alone achieve it. When Henry Browne spoke, his stentorian voice reached into every corner of the household. Its timbers trembled; its members quailed.

By the time Thomas reached Islington the fog was thickening into a drizzle that made the ground sticky. As he cleaned his mud-smeared boots noisily at the scraper beside the entrance porch, the house door opened unexpectedly and their manservant hurried out, looking more lugubrious than ever.

'Evening, Grice,' said Thomas. 'Anything amiss?'

'Yes indeed, sir, sorry to say. I was watchin out for you. Very grave news. It's your father, sir. Barely an hour ago. Stood up from the table and toppled back like a log. I run for the doctor to come quick, which he done too, but no elp. Pronounced im dead as…well, completely dead. Seems the heart just went bang all of a sudden and that was it. Your mother's in such a state. And the young ladies. They need you to take charge right away. You're the man of the family now, sir.'

# 7

# Islington, November 1860

As he'd done every Sunday afternoon for a long while now, Thomas crossed at this same corner to the best side of Richmond Avenue and made his way towards the semi-detached villa in the most respectable part of Islington. The house still proclaimed prosperity; Papa had been a good provider.

These regular visits to his widowed mother always gave him a hammering headache. The filial obligation itself was painful enough, requiring him to walk for hours through cold and often muddy streets so that he could sit quietly with clenched teeth while Mrs Browne performed her familiar rituals of self-conceit, and his father's sternly reproachful apparition aggravated the misery.

Each time Thomas drew near the imposing doorway of his childhood home, the same feeling came over him, almost a hallucination: it was as if his father's ghost loomed over the threshold, blocking out the light. With all the intimidating bulk of authority he stood there frowning implacably, like a judge poised to deliver a damning verdict. Though it was now more than twenty years since his coffin, glistening with rain, had descended into the dark Highgate soil, he still seemed to withhold from his son any benediction.

Old Grice, his manner morose as ever, took Thomas's hat and coat, showed him into the parlour and went off with a sigh to apprise Mrs Browne of her son's arrival. Thomas stood stiffly, hands clasped behind him.

As she came into the room, leaning on a stick, she gave a perfunctory greeting before adding in her usual tone of brusque reproof, 'Really, Thomas, you should try to look a little more cheerful when you come here. Your face is nearly as gloomy as Grice's. Look in the mirror! More doleful than a bloodhound that can't find a scent. What's the matter with you?'

'To be frank, Mama, there are so many things troubling me at present that it would stretch your patience to hear me recite them.'

She raised a stern eyebrow at him as she settled herself in an armchair. 'Are you suggesting that I treat you less forbearingly than you deserve?'

He could see it was going to be another of those conversations filled with snares and quicksands. Plainly she was in a contrary mood – no doubt because, caught off balance by her censorious gambit, he had impulsively mentioned his own state of mind instead of inquiring immediately about hers. Perhaps her teeth were aching again, or her hip joints. Or perhaps his mere presence pained her. He was sure she had never really liked him.

'Less than I deserve? It's not for me to judge what my just deserts are, Mama. But I don't think you like any of us, any of your children, to talk about our difficulties and disappointments. And besides, I really haven't come here with the purpose of unburdening myself.'

'Then why do you pay me these visits, Thomas?' Her voice sounded harsh and rejecting.

He paused, choosing his words with care. 'Because I'm your eldest child. Your son. My sisters can't call on you; you know their situation. So it's my duty – and my wish, of course – to...'

She pounced. 'Aha! Duty? Duty? So you feel *obliged* to make your way here from time to time, do you?'

'You're twisting my meaning. I come here to show my affection and concern, you must know that. I suppose there's something dutiful about it too, but only in the sense that, since Papa passed away, I have a natural responsibility to make sure you're well. And contented.'

He knew she would never be contented. Despite the fact that her late husband had left her well off, her comfortable circumstances had evidently brought her no pleasure, evoked no sense of gratitude, and given her no twinge of conscience about her children's urgent need for some of the money left in her charge. She had closed her ears to their predicaments.

'But *you* are not contented yourself, Thomas,' she said. 'You tell me your life is full of troubles. I can't imagine why that should be so.'

*No*, he thought, *imagining how someone else feels and why – you're incapable of that. Heartless.* But he didn't say it.

She wouldn't let it rest. 'Well? What's on your mind?'

He suppressed a sigh. 'Things are hard for us these days. For Eliza and me. Financially. With seven young mouths to feed, and...'

'So who's to blame for the number of children, Thomas? Eh? And besides, feeding them shouldn't be a problem. You're a trained engineer – thanks to your father's foresight in arranging that apprenticeship for you. You should be earning a good income, surely. You've been practising here in London for – what is it? – six years now, after all that time in Manchester getting established. Are you telling me you're failing in your profession?'

'Not failing, Mama – of course not. But I don't think you understand how many obstacles and uncertainties one faces in civil engineering projects. All sorts of things can go wrong. Delays, for instance, in the supply of materials and labour – they mean that money doesn't flow. There are good reasons to be anxious.'

'No doubt. On the other hand, from what the newspapers tell me it seems there are plenty of opportunities for engineers to become wealthy and famous. That man Fox, for one – you worked with him on the railway to Birmingham many years ago, and look how well he's done for himself. Designing the Crystal Palace, and getting a knighthood.'

'But it's not fair to compare his fortunes with mine. Sir Charles Fox is several years my senior, so he was able to get an early start with his career. Gained experience on the Liverpool-to-Manchester line before I'd even started my apprenticeship.'

'The Gooch fellow, then – he was there in Newton with you, wasn't he? Began about the same time. And yet he's been very eminent for a long while, hasn't he?'

'I don't believe,' said Thomas petulantly, 'that Daniel Gooch is more talented or hardworking than I am, Mama. Sheer luck plays a big part in determining who meets with public acclaim and financial reward. Anyway, it's not helpful to hold up these illustrious exemplars. I've been trying hard to succeed but the miserable fact is that I can hardly cope. My household ekes out a very modest existence, and I can barely support my family or keep up appearances in the business world. To be frank, I'm fearful of ruin.'

'Oh, Thomas – you always exaggerate. You like to see yourself as a character in a drama.'

∞

Later, walking home to Camden Town through the rain to save the cost of hailing a cab, he asked himself fretfully whether his mother's accusation that he habitually dramatised his situation carried a grain of truth. Perhaps it was indeed a silly overstatement to say that fortune had passed him by and favoured others. Perhaps he was magnifying conceitedly his own merits as a defence against admitting that, after all, men like Fox and Gooch really were uncommonly clever, seizing their chances and deserving whatever recognition they received. It was Fox's genuine mastery of structural ironwork that had led to his being engaged to build that wonderful edifice for the Great Exhibition. It was Gooch's exceptional shrewdness that equipped him to improve the exhaust system on locomotives on Brunel's Great Western Line. In contrast to the adventurous spirit that those two had repeatedly shown, he allowed himself to be shackled to a medium-sized machine-making business in Manchester when he should have been making a name for himself. And since then, back in London, he'd watched his career prospects shrink.

Anyway, the days seemed to have passed when brilliant inventors and entrepreneurs – heroic figures like Telford and the Stephensons and Isambard Brunel, all dead now – could dominate the industrial world and profit from it on a grand scale. In recent times, civil engineering had given itself a formally professional structure, with regulated membership, a subscription threshold, a set of examination standards and the like. Such things, it seemed to Thomas, had placed constraints on individual initiative.

There was something else, too, that held him back. Something concealed. His mother had put her finger on it: 'So who's to blame for the number of children, Thomas?' It wasn't easy to admit the truth of this to himself, even to glance surreptitiously towards it, but he half guessed that his begetting of child after child was a compulsive way of insisting that he *could* copulate with a woman, whatever other forms of physical intimacy he might still furtively imagine. How he'd come to wed Eliza in the first place was a question on which he didn't like to dwell. He hadn't thought much about marriage beforehand; it was just something expected of a young man, part of the business of demonstrating normal adult status. Eliza was the quiet sister of a lawyer with whom Thomas had become acquainted through the railway project, and not long after being introduced to her he found that a sort of involuntary momentum seemed to develop; their families implicitly encouraged the couple to see their paths as convergent, and somehow decisions eventually emerged without much apparent deliberation, until they were man and wife. Then, as the years slipped by, Eliza had a succession of confinements, and he himself began to feel confined, shut in. So this was wedlock.

Beyond the ordinary little domestic transactions, they had little to say to one another. He'd hoped for a wife who would take pride in the things he was accomplishing as a young engineer, but Eliza showed scant interest in his work. Scant interest in anything much, apparently. In the early days of their marriage he used to read newspaper items aloud after dinner and try to discuss them with her. The potato famine in Ireland. The first propeller-driven steamship. The repeal of the Corn Laws. Cholera epidemics. But she seldom made any response. *Almost devoid of animation*, he thought one evening as he watched his wife bent over her lace knitting in the parlour chair where she spent so much of her time.

As the family kept expanding, her lassitude was even more obvious and she became inattentive to the children and to the need to rein in expenditure. Thomas had to keep reminding her of the simplest financial practicalities. They were paying more rent than they could well afford; the cost of food, clothing and general household supplies was mounting; and unless his earnings very soon increased it would be necessary to replace their two servants, the nursemaid and the cook, with a maid-of-all-work. But irritating though Eliza's inertia was, he could hardly blame her for their situation. The painful truth was that, unlike his father, he himself had not turned out to be a good provider. His father's dismissive attitude to his problems, he admitted to himself ruefully, would have been no different from his mother's. Thomas could imagine all too readily how scornful Henry Browne would have been of his son's lack of success.

By the time he reached his front door, the chilling rain had soaked through his trousers and into his boots. His legs ached and the hand that had been holding his umbrella felt lifelessly numb. But it was as if the coldness that had begun to move in from his extremities towards his heart was more than physical – as if professional disappointment and personal trouble alike were draining the blood from his veins. Lack of money was the most conscious source of distress. If he was going to find a way out of his financial worries, sooner or later he might have to do something drastic.

# 8

# Bermondsey, March 1861

The pleading message from Jane a few months later came at a painful time. His own cares were already vexing enough. Keeping up the rent payments, keeping up appearances, trying to inculcate some sense of thrift into his obstinate wife, feeding and clothing the seven children, with another now on the way — all of it had been filling his mind with desperate phantoms of anxiety and shame. Jane's situation was yet another thing to fret about.

He had done his duty towards his young sister as best he could during the year since she was so cruelly widowed. Walter Burstall, hardworking and sober, had looked after her with conscientious concern despite his paucity of talents and skills. The violent fever that carried him off suddenly, along with an infant daughter, left his pregnant wife in a sorry plight. Wanting to help, Thomas made a few modest contributions, but his meagre savings had now dwindled alarmingly. He looked again at Jane's letter, murmuring some of its phrases as he read.

a good brother to me…grateful for all your kindness… distresses me to seek this further assistance…wit's end… doctor says both my little tykes are getting weaker with the croup…bad air, and a lack of proper nourishment… everything costs so much now…weeks since I was last able to buy any scraps of meat…cannot afford more physic for them…they look so wan…think I shall go mad…the only work I can get pays the merest pittance…dreadfully alone… would be a comfort just to see you…Believe me, I would be too ashamed to appeal to you like this if I could bear my burden unaided…futile, of course, to approach our mother after the previous rebuffs…cannot find the words to convey how distraught I feel.

The notepaper had an unpleasant smell and her handwriting was cramped and crabbed, tilting unevenly across the page with ugly blotches where the nib had sputtered. He could picture her shaping the words laboriously, hunched over them in that dark little room in the lodging house at the end of an alley. Bermondsey being such a very long walk from Camden Town, he had gone to see her only twice since Walter's death. It was nauseating. He remembered how the whole district stank abominably – a rank stench that blended the acrid odours from stagnant backyard cesspools, the sulphurous tanneries nearby and mounds of sooty slush.

This time, as he made his way in her direction, it seemed even worse. The thoroughfares and side streets pullulated with rowdy people, and to be caught up in such a teeming mass made him feel short of breath and sick at heart. There were so many of them, calling out raucously, accosting him, shoving past him or hemming him in: donkey-cart costermongers, sellers of sprats and cockles and herrings, hawkers of half-repaired toys and damaged provender, dog-breakers, bird-catchers, watercress vendors, street singers and sweepers, doormat-makers, cadgers and beggars, loungers and skulkers, scavengers and vagabonds, felons and outcasts. It was like being trapped and trampled in a lurid nightmare.

By the time he had reached the southbank slums a feeble sun was setting, and in the filthy labyrinth of alleys beyond the reach of gaslight he soon lost his way. Trying to retrace his steps, he took another wrong turning and found himself in a dark smelly lane enclosed by broken walls through which fetid matter oozed. In a yard to one side was a giant-sized dust heap, and among the cinders and ashes he saw a dead cat, scraps of vegetables, crockery shards, whelk shells, oddments of metal, and rag and bone.

Children were playing leapfrog near the rubbish. He asked them where to find his sister's street. 'Fellmonger's corner,' shouted one urchin, pointing, 'and ven you turn away from v'river and you'll see it.'

Pieces of horse dung and shreds of decaying cabbage leaves stuck to his boots as he walked up to the vaguely familiar ramshackle house and pushed open the sagging door. It was just as putrid inside the building as on the street: a grime-blackened honeycomb, riddled with narrow passages and a warren of small rooms. More than a dozen people, apparently from several families, were huddling in the first space he glanced into. Some slept on straw or shavings; others rested in a sitting position against the wall, with children on their knees. The faces nearest the door showed the signs of a wasting fever – cheeks flushed hectically, eyes sunken and glassy with dark circles around them.

*It's like a foul corner of hell*, he thought, and was uncertain for a moment where to find her room. 'I'm looking for Mrs Burstall,' he announced. Someone pointed to the staircase. He climbed until he saw her through a doorway, sitting on a stool, the air thick with a mist of fur that had whitened her clothes and hair.

'Thomas!' She tried to say more but a fit of wheezing stopped her.

He went over to her and put a hand on her shoulder. As a gesture of comfort it seemed absurdly ineffectual. Looking around her squalid little room, he saw that the bed was strewn with rabbit skins and the floor littered with small bones. Paper bags stood on the floor, ready to receive the scrapings from the skins. So she had come to this. A fur-puller. The pungent animal smell from the skins was overpowering, and he caught a whiff of something else, too – a chamberpot stink.

'Sorry,' she said in a husky voice after clearing her throat noisily. 'The down gets into my nose and mouth. Makes me breathless. Sometimes I feel half-choked.'

'This is dreadful, Jane. You're harming your health – I can see it. Can hear it.'

'What choice do I have? Many women hereabouts have to eke out a livelihood now by fur-pulling. It's nasty work, and the pay isn't what it used to be – just a shilling now for five dozen skins. People tell me the rewards were better at the time of the Crimean War, when there was a great need for skins to be stitched inside the coats of soldiers.'

With a mirthless laugh she added, 'Having to spend hours every day rubbing reeky skins with a blunt knife to remove the loose down – no wonder they call this kind of existence *scraping along!*'

'Only a shilling for sixty skins, you say?'

'That's right, though there's a few extra pence for odds and ends. Nothing's wasted. We even cut open the tail to extract the little bone – they use pieces of tail fur to make cheap blankets and hats.'

From a dark corner of the room there was a sudden bark and a groan that turned into crying, and then a second hoarse voice joined the first. They began to cough and gasp in loud harsh unison. Thomas had forgotten momentarily about her children, the twins born after Walter's death.

'I was hoping they'd sleep a bit longer!' Jane exclaimed. 'The poor mites have been so miserable these last few days. Their throats are on fire. All this furry dust afloat in the air sets them off yelping like dogs.'

From a tin jug she poured some water into a cup and hurried over to the narrow cot where the two small boys lay.

'It may be a long while before I can settle them,' she said apologetically to her brother. 'Not a good time for us to be talking much. Anyway, you'll need to be on your way home, Thomas. It's a long dark walk to Camden Town. Good of you to come here to see me.'

'It wasn't just to *see* you, Jane. I want to help as best I can.' Wiping away the down that was clinging to his whiskers, he crossed the room and drew money from his pocket. As she looked up at him and took it, she flushed.

'There's a quarrel in my breast,' she said in a low voice, 'twixt gratitude and shame – to say nothing of the bitterness I feel towards Mama, who could so easily give substantial help but refuses. It's the same with Charlotte – there hasn't been even a letter from her, let alone a visit, since poor Walter passed away. I know you have your own children to think of, Thomas, and I wouldn't have written to you, believe me, if...'

'Ssshh!' He put a finger to his lips. 'No need to say it. Your situation's desperate – I can see that plainly. I wish I could do more. Our mother...' His voice trailed off, and he shook his head at the thought of that selfish parental aloofness. As for his other sister, Charlotte seemed to have forgotten or discarded her siblings and become absorbed in the little world of a rustic Dorset parish where her husband the vicar reportedly spent much of his time studying Roman antiquities.

Holding back his feelings as best he could, Thomas took his leave of Jane. The image of his prematurely frail sister, bent anxiously over the little cot and breathing in that deadly powder of fur, would stay with him for a long time. And he knew there were many thousands of others like her in London, prisoners of poverty, poisoned by the city's decay, forced to inhale its foul vapours, oppressed by its injustices, enveloped in a miasma of social misery. As he walked he felt gripped by a dismal sense that the whole civilised order was as precarious as a rickety bridge over a huge malodorous cesspool.

# 9

# Camden Town, July 1861

'Pardon me for saying so, Mr Browne, but you don't look altogether happy these days!'

'What is there to be happy about?' replied Thomas irritably. Fenner was always poking his snuffly nose into another person's state of mind, obsequious in his pretence of sympathy. Whatever he could prise out of you he would soon be gossiping about to everyone else in the office.

'Oh, it's quite understandable you'd be feeling down in the mouth, Mr Browne. They haven't given you much to do, have they, since the bypass line was opened? You did a fine job of supervising that project, if I may say so, a fine job – not an easy task, not easy by any means, to take the railway from Camden around through Kentish Town all the way across to Willesden Junction, and you must be disappointed that your talents have lain idle these last few months. Such a shame. But that's the North London Railway Company for you!'

Thomas shrugged, affecting indifference – but, annoyingly, he couldn't deny that Fenner was right. To have been employed as chief engineer for the bypass project, to have seen it through to a successful opening despite real challenges, and then to have your wages cut – it did indeed feel galling. And it wasn't as if the industrial conditions were unpropitious for suitable further work. Several joint stock companies continued to build railway arches, viaducts, stations and new lines at astonishing speed all around London, in contrast to the various public works that still dragged on and on with their scaffolding and hoists and cranes obstructing pedestrians for years. Private enterprise was thriving, no doubt about that, but it didn't follow, alas, that well-qualified and experienced professional men such as he would all share in the prosperity.

It was demeaning that the company now expected an accomplished architect and engineer, who had given them solid service, to spend his time compiling inventories, monitoring the loss of stock through theft, and reporting the details to a mere clerk like Fenner.

Shrewdly, Fenner read his thoughts and amplified them. 'It's impudent, isn't it, sir, the way blackguards are pilfering goods from our wagons here? Hardly a night passes without more provisions being taken – wine hampers, silk parcels, drapery boxes and the rest.'

Thomas nodded, lips pursed.

'But the odd thing,' Fenner went on slowly, with an air of rumination as if surprised to discover this item in the cud of his half-digested thoughts, 'is that we're required to pay such close attention to petty theft, and keep an inventory of every item that's stolen, and yet the company ignores the fact that those who handle its finances on a daily basis have opportunities for fraud on a much larger scale.' As if leaving it at that, he turned back to his desk for a moment – but then resumed his theme. 'Senior officers, you see, often know little about bookkeeping. There's no reliable way to keep orderly accounts – partly because the task of recording financial transactions is being placed into the hands of many different people, and partly because of course money takes several forms nowadays, not just coins but banknotes as well, and bills of exchange and the rest. Documents can be forged. Records manipulated. And there's no thorough audit procedure, either. So nothing's easier than to rob a company!'

Thomas glanced at him sharply but Fenner was looking out the window, whistling, having – it seemed – already forgotten what he had been chewing over.

The conversation lodged in a corner of Thomas's mind, chafing like a small stone inside his shoe. What worried him increasingly was that the money he was earning no longer seemed adequate to the family's basic needs. He couldn't understand why they were finding it so hard to cover their food and clothing and general expenses. Meals were scantier these days, and the children sometimes whined about going hungry. Despite the cut in his wages, the amount he set aside regularly for Eliza to apportion to their household items should still have sufficed, but apparently didn't.

One evening when he came home earlier than expected, his wife was admiring herself in the mirror, wearing a fashionable dress of expensive green silk.

'What's this, Eliza?' he said in alarm. 'Surely you haven't bought it? You know we can't afford such finery! It's hard enough to make ends meet.'

'I don't see why I shouldn't have a few nice things.'

'A few? That dress must have cost a royal fortune. Don't tell me you've got more.'

Her sullen silence confirmed his anxiety. He strode to her wardrobe and flung open its door. Half a dozen ornately embroidered gowns hung there. Cheeks pale as whey, mouth a gaping oval of incredulity, he turned and stared at her, appalled.

'How do you suppose we are to pay for all this...this lavishness?' His voice was a horrified croak.

She clamped her lips in mute defence and defiance.

Then on the top shelf of the wardrobe, secreted behind cushions, he discovered other things – elegant bonnets, soft kid side-laced boots, satin reticules, beaded bracelets.

'Good God, Eliza! How can you be so profligate? Have you gone mad?'

Gradually he extracted details from her. The situation was dire. In addition to the cache of costly clothing and accoutrements, she had hidden away in a locked cabinet two full sets of fine bone china plates from the Staffordshire Potteries and an assortment of ornate silverware. She just didn't know, she told him, what had compelled her to make all these extravagant purchases. She admitted to an accumulation of large debts, and confessed that the shopkeepers were pressing her aggressively for payment.

Thomas felt trapped in a small hell of desperation. In law, her creditors would hold him liable, but he had no way of settling the debts quickly. Trying to sell everything she'd so stupidly bought would take time, unless he resorted to pawnbrokers, who wouldn't put up enough money anyhow. There was no father to rescue him, and begging his coldly contemptuous mother for any assistance would be not only humiliating but also quite futile. Nor could he look to either of his sisters. He was stuck fast; retribution was inescapable.

The following week exhausted him. Night after night he lay sleepless for hours on end, feeling ill and fearful. During the daytime he sat listlessly at his desk, scarcely able to attend to anything. He knew Fenner was watching him closely.

'Nothing amiss, I trust, Mr Browne?' the clerk asked with unctuous concern. 'You're looking poorly.'

Thomas shook his head, trying to avoid Fenner's inquisitive gaze. But at the end of one afternoon, when they were alone in the office, he cleared his throat and gingerly broached the matter that had been preoccupying him.

'I'm sure you remember our conversation about the company's lax accounting procedures,' said Thomas in a low voice. Sweat shone on his pale lined forehead.

Fenner leaned forward, eyes glittering.

∞

It did not prove difficult to make false entries in stock registers as a mask for the regular appropriation of inconspicuous amounts of money. Even forging banknotes was a fairly simple matter. Fenner provided the necessary clerical subterfuges in return for half the proceeds, and months went by without detection.

The temporary financial relief brought Thomas no contentment. Dread of eventual exposure never left him, but it was not only that. He had become obsessed with a feeling that menace pervaded the whole city: the hydra-headed menace of pestilence, of violence, of poverty, of political and social instability. These evenings as he walked back through Camden Town from his office, the yellow fogs were even thicker than before, impregnated with the sickly effluvium of bad drains and seeping graveyards. Rank corruption seethed beneath his feet, floated in the air he breathed. His thoughts were continually invaded by a bizarre story someone had told him about monstrous black swine living in the sewers of Hampstead. He kept imagining their filthy snouts, their ferocious grunting.

His arrest and swift conviction came in May 1862, just after Fenner suddenly absconded, vanishing without a trace. Sixteen months later, in the company of 269 other prisoners and eighty-nine passengers including guards, Thomas Browne left Portland on *Lord Dalhousie*, a transport bound for the Swan River Colony. The journey would take ninety days, and for most of it he would be sick in body and at heart.

Surging through him like a fever, his anguish fed on several different emotions. Often during the voyage he tried to picture each of his children, whispering their names to himself one by one, but whenever they were in his mind he was filled with self-disgust at what his reckless actions must be inflicting on them: bewilderment at his sudden removal from their home, shame at learning about his crime, physical distress at having to depend now on charity for food and shelter. How would his wife cope alone with such an acute need to take care of them? He couldn't imagine it. Towards Eliza herself he felt a swirling mixture of feelings, remorseful and angry; yes, he'd brought scandal to the family's door, and probably penury, but that was because her own foolish behaviour had made him desperate. The greater blame was hers. She had undermined him. When he thought of what his professional colleagues would be saying about his dishonourable conduct, especially former mentors such as Fox and Hardwick, he alternated between loathing himself fiercely and wanting somehow to justify what he'd done. If only they knew how he'd been driven to it by his wife's extravagance, and the company's failure to remunerate him properly...If they knew how Fenner had tempted him, and then treated him so treacherously...If they knew how coldly his mother had dismissed his appeal to assist him and her widowed daughter...

Although he'd written to his mother from prison, begging her to make provision for his children and his sister Jane's, he had little hope that she would do anything about it. He'd written to his wife as well, asking her to go to his mother and plead for help in person, but nothing, he feared, was likely to come of that. In prison he hadn't been permitted to receive either letters or visits, so he would never know whether everyone had turned their backs on him. Thank God his father hadn't lived to witness his disgrace.

∞

He had never forgotten his mother's brief attempt to impose a sudden arbitrary change of name on him when he was a young boy. It continued to rankle. Ever since then, he had insisted tenaciously on the use of his proper name in its full form. If anyone tried to shorten it to Tom, he wouldn't respond. Cousin Eddie had tried teasing him with Tomtit, but he ignored that. Other nicknames, too, were shrugged aside and had always evaporated. Until now.

Early in the wretched voyage to Western Australia, as Thomas tried to subdue his disgust at the smelly privations and coarse vulgarities that hemmed him in during the long hours of confinement below decks, a waggish gap-toothed fellow convict coined a new name for him, and it stuck.

At first he was more puzzled than annoyed. 'Satan?' He screwed up his face with incomprehension. 'Satan? What's this about?'

The men around him laughed rudely. 'Prince o darkness, eh?' exclaimed one, and there were more guffaws.

He felt indignant at their obscure jesting. There were vicious malefactors among the riffraff, hardened criminals, and it was impudent of such people to call him a name that was a byword for evil. Several days later, after much 'Good morning, Satan!' and 'Fine weather, eh, Satan?' and 'How d'yer do, Satan?' from all and sundry, the gap-toothed lag enlightened him: 'We jeer at yer, see, because of ow yer hold yerself apart – as if you're better'n us. It don't pay to be too proud. All bad boys togevver, ain't we?'

And then as an afterthought his informant added, 'But it started wiv yer air.'

'My hair?'

Gap-tooth grinned at him. 'Ow often do men your age ave such black air? Like jet. Looks devilish.'

So the gibes continued, and Thomas remained Satan except in his own eyes.

# Alfred

# 10

# Great Baddow, October 1848

Head inclined to one side, Alfred would lift and stroke the fabrics slowly, put his cheek against them and listen to the subtly different sounds they made when he ran his fingers across their textured surfaces: the squeaky rustle of the satin weaves, the muffled whisper of twill, the way the pile on smoothly tufted velvet would purr under his caress.

Their variegated colours, too, gleaming and glowing as he watched light nestle into the folds, gave him such intensely voluptuous pleasure that he felt himself drifting into a blissful trance of contemplation. Iridescent taffeta, shining like a mint beetle. Heavy russet-hued brocade with its rich raised patterning of twisted gold strands. Coarse dark fustian, its nap seemingly soaked in shadow.

After working for months now in Mr Bell's shop, Alfred still marvelled at his luck. What could be more fortunate than having gained employment here at a time when the big spinning mills were producing an astonishing quantity and range of tight-threaded textiles on the new Lancashire looms, and smaller specialised manufacturers like Courtauld in Braintree were flourishing nearby? Surrounded every day by all these bolts of cotton, linen, silk and woollen materials, so variously woven and dyed, he luxuriated in a little fibrous world of quietly sensual delights.

And this morning, leaning contentedly against the counter and watching a pale patch of autumn sunlight as it inched across the floorboards, Alfred was conscious of the further gratification afforded by something that he alone knew about – his upstairs secret.

The shop door rattled and opened, dispelling his happy daydream. Basket on arm, a woman entered with a simpering expression.

He smiled back as he greeted her. 'Ah, Mrs Rolfe! Good day to you.'

'And t'you, Mr Letch. Good to be out of that sharp wind for a minute or two. The sun seems alf-arted this morning – no warmth in it. You ave some things ere for me to collect?'

'Indeed I do.' Reaching beneath the counter, Alfred drew out a pair of parcels wrapped in brown paper. 'You'll find the cloth has a beautifully smooth finish,' he said, handing her one of the parcels. 'Use the same pattern and measurements as before, please. In this other package' – he passed it to her – 'are the items we agreed upon, except that I've added a few more candles because the quantity of tea-leaves is a little smaller than last time.'

Nodding to confirm acceptance of the terms, she placed the two parcels in her basket, covering them with a shawl, and turned to go. He walked quickly to the door and opened it for her, glancing up and down the street as he bade her farewell.

'I'll be back Friday with the finished garment,' she said as she left.

It was a relief that Hannah Rolfe had not wanted to linger. Alfred was anticipating a visit from William Black at some point during the day, and things could have become awkward if both the dressmaker and the tailor had been present together for their similar transactions. There was always a possibility, too, that tiresome old Mr Bond would stop by unexpectedly with further excuses for his delay in repairing the viola's cracked pegbox. Best if these informal little business matters were kept private, and separate from his dealings with ordinary customers.

In the course of a day the comings and goings were usually sporadic. The door might open only a dozen times from morning until the end of the afternoon, or even less often, and most of those who entered would be seeking only little items from the grocery end of the shop. But a few ladies would come in from the more substantial and discerning families in the vicinity – notably the Bacons, Bullens, Parkers and Wistocks – to make regular drapery purchases, often expensive, and the most enjoyable part of his job was discussing with these people the finer points of different fabrics for different purposes. He supposed they could see that he had knowledge and taste beyond his years. They trusted his judgement – he was sure of that – and indeed he trusted it entirely himself. Alfred was confident that his business acumen warranted an ambition to establish his own drapery shop. It would take time and money, but he would achieve it. Undoubtedly he would.

Meanwhile, it was irksome that his wages were so low. Was it wrong of him to want a better return for his efforts?

Had he become avaricious? He dismissed the thought. No, no – rather, he believed simply that those who had genuine talent deserved the resources necessary for it to thrive. Besides, nobody could call him selfish; he was just as keen to help his siblings as to help himself, and felt frustrated that his means were so limited. With young George's wedding coming up so soon, Alfred wished he could do more for his irrepressibly cheerful but incorrigibly thriftless brother, though there was plenty of satisfaction in having contributed to the furnishing of George's newly rented house in readiness for his bride.

'I shall always be grateful, Alfred,' George's letter had said, 'for your kindness. You're a truly generous fellow. And the whole family is mightily proud of the way you've earned Mr Bell's trust. He must hold you in high regard – deservedly so – to be leaving you so often in charge of the store.'

Alfred had felt a jab of conscience when he read those words. George was such a ninny that he always thought the best of everyone, but the family's pride would turn to utter dismay if they knew what Alfred was up to, and how it was that he had the wherewithal to assist them and give them presents. Apparently the question hadn't occurred to them; they assumed he was well paid.

Still, resentful thoughts prickled. Receiving lower remuneration than he surely merited was only part of it; he also remained dependent on Mr and Mrs Bell for board and lodging, and it seemed that in little insinuating ways his employer contrived occasionally to remind him of his subservient position.

That evening, after dining with the Bell family as usual above the shop, he excused himself from conversation and climbed the narrow squeaky back stairs to his attic bedroom.

Lifting a candlestick and standing close to the mirror, he looked at himself steadily. Regular features, though the pock-marks didn't enhance them. His brown eyes were set a little too close together. Quite unlike his brothers, he had dark hair and a complexion that was almost swarthy. While the Letches had always treated him as if he were a full member of the family, his sense of being a cuckoo in the nest persisted. He didn't want to be merely a recipient of their charity; he was eager to achieve something remarkable that would earn their admiration.

It would take some while, and in the meantime he must be patient. But Alfred consoled himself with the thought that certain things stowed away in the large chest and wardrobe would eventually do much to equip him for an independent and affluent future. He took out the three elegant waistcoats, each with its shawl collar and six bright buttons, and laid them on the bed to contemplate. Then he picked up one of them, holding it against his body as he gazed again at the mirror. Yes, he would keep one for his own use; but the others would fetch a good price, as would his growing collection of dresses, petticoats and bonnets.

∞

He smiled often, and others thought him cheerful, but much of the time it was not quite what he felt. Although he would hardly have regarded himself as discontented, there was an uneasy sense of lack. Knowing confidently where he really belonged: that sureness eluded him.

Vague doubt about his proper place in the world had first come to him as a young lad when he was looking at the

Letch family Bible. There in his father Edward's immaculate hand was a list of the boys' names with their birth details. All five of his brothers were born in Finchingfield; Alfred's place of origin was another village, Braintree, some nine miles to the south. He saw, too, that Charles was only a few months younger than he. He'd wondered about these things but didn't like to ask. The family's only connection with Braintree, as far as he knew, was that his father's sister – another Mary – lived there, a spinster. It was a good three hours' walk each way, so she could seldom pay them a visit in Finchingfield, but when she did she would always place her small hands gently on either side of Alfred's face, look at him lingeringly, and then give him a warm squeezing hug.

Aunt Mary's demonstrative affection, or perhaps the fact that it was glimpsed so intermittently, had disconcerted him as a boy. When he was old enough to guess why the nature of some relationships might need to remain tacitly conjectural, he'd felt a tinge of embarrassment in her occasional presence. Since his move to Great Baddow to work for Mr Bell, he'd neither seen her nor let any conscious thought of her cross his mind. So it was startling to receive a note from his father telling him of her sudden death from pleurisy, and to find enclosed with the message a small wrapped keepsake that she had left specifically for Alfred: a black enamel brooch with silver filigree. 'We didn't know she owned such a thing,' said his father's note, 'but she was particular about wanting you to have it.'

*Pretty enough*, Alfred thought, turning it over in his hand, *but not much good to me. Should fetch a good price; I could do with the money.* When next in Chelmsford he sold it.

# 11

# Felsted,
# April 1842 to December 1844

For the Letch family, life had been good in Finchingfield. As the village miller in a district whose fertile land was mainly put to arable use, Edward prospered. Alfred adored their home: the mill cottage was large, two-storeyed, comfortable, and on sunny days its white walls looked radiant under the neat thatch. Most evenings, music filled the living room. His father patiently taught him how to coax melody from the flute, while Charles and George fingered their fiddle strings with increasing dexterity, the other boys sang in harmony and Mrs Letch played for them on the pianoforte. On Sunday, before bedtime, they would all join their voices in sonorous hymns. 'Time, like an ever-rolling stream,' they intoned solemnly, 'bears all its sons away...'

Edward owned other cottages, too, and a farm on which Alfred worked happily with two of his brothers, George and Charles, after they left school. Nobody for miles around had earned more respect than their father. They were proud of his standing, not only as a man who had worked hard for his worldly success but also as superintendent of the Sunday School and a deacon in their Congregational church. In the eyes of the family and the villagers, he epitomised decency.

Farming work kept the adolescent boys occupied much of the time. There was always some chore to be done – scything the grasses, pitching hay through the hatch into the barn, repairing wall timbers of the cart shed or the cattle shelter, mucking out stables and spreading the mixture of threshed straw and manure on the fields, cutting drains, feeding and grooming the horses and checking their harness fittings, preparing the soil for wheat and barley by ploughing in bean stalks, and penning the sheep within hurdles for fold-dunging.

'He's conscientious enough, young Alfred, with any tasks he's asked to carry out,' remarked his father one evening as the parents retired to bed. 'More diligent than our George, I'll say that. But he doesn't seem to have his mind fully on the farm work the way Charles does.'

Mrs Letch nodded and sighed. 'A bit of a dreamer, is Alfred,' she said.

It was true enough. He would often pause, leaning on shovel or pitchfork, and linger in a sentient reverie as the sounds of different seasons soaked into him. Bees murmuring to bramble flowers in summer hedgerows. October breezes lisping across the stubble. The snuffling breath of cattle as misty skits of rain tickled their hide.

When Alfred was nearly nineteen his father told him the time had come to leave home and take on some paid work. 'I hear old Mumford, the harness-maker in Felsted, wants a young fellow to assist him. It's a useful trade to pick up. Bed and board with it, and a few shillings in your pocket.'

So he presented himself to Samuel Mumford, who looked him up and down silently for a tense minute, before nodding and setting him to work at once. Over the ensuing months Alfred was assiduous in learning the craft. Before long he knew all about selling tack and could shape a saddletree nearly as quickly as Mumford himself. He showed uncommon skill in working and finishing the leather for collars and straps. He became deft in the use of stitching awl and waxed hemp thread, of clam and punch and round knife.

Although there was a simple satisfaction in the work he did for Mumford in Felsted, Alfred's greatest pleasure came every Sunday morning when he would set out early on the path back home to join his family for chapel worship. For most of the three-hour walk to Finchingfield, and on the return journey in the late afternoon, he drifted into a contemplative trance more serenely absorbing than the devotional decorum required by the church services. Birds went flickering through the blackthorn and bullace that fringed the fields around him, and their chirrups were in tune with his mood. Listening to them, he recalled and recited lines from a poem his father often used to read aloud:

*And hark! how blithe the throstle sings!*
*He, too, is no mean preacher:*
*Come forth into the light of things,*
*Let Nature be your Teacher.*

As he walked through the woodlands, they creaked with the movements of leafy branches and small shy creatures. The soil underfoot had a pleasant aroma, faintly damp, that was redolent of brewed tea-leaves and made his nostrils twitch.

Oxlips trembled in the breezy meadows that sloped down to the river near Great Bardfield. Alfred felt himself to be in a kind of pastoral heaven.

∞

Nobody in the village knew whose carriage it was, though evidently it belonged to a person of substance. It had come to a halt in Felsted only because of a mishap: one of the main harness straps had snapped and needed urgently to be replaced. A smartly liveried coachman appeared at the entrance to the little saddlery, flustering old Sam Mumford, but Alfred stepped forward with a deferential nod and a confident manner, quickly ascertaining what the driver wanted and helping him select a suitable bridle piece. The transaction didn't take long. Alfred went out to the carriage with him and fitted the replacement efficiently. Only as he stepped away from the horses did he see that the two passengers had alighted. While the gentleman conferred with his coachman about arranging payment, Alfred's eye was dazzled by his companion, a young woman of proud bearing, attired in a blue silk brocade dress embossed with bronze flowers. He thought he had never seen anything so beautiful. Only when she became conscious of his gaze and met it with a disdainful expression did he look away. The carriage soon moved off, watched from several windows.

'Shouldn't stare at a fine lady, Alfred,' said Mumford. 'It's ill-mannerly for the likes of us to peer so keenly at such a one.'

'A cat may look at a queen,' said Alfred, unabashed. But his eye had not been on the woman herself; it was what she wore that entranced him. In later years he would remember that little incident with perfect clarity, and especially the blue silk dress with its bronze floral motif, as the origin of his abiding interest in textiles.

With the help of his cousin Joan, Alfred soon obtained copies of two monthlies popular in the cities – *The Magazine of the Beau Monde* and *The Ladies' Cabinet of Fashion, Music and Romance*. In the evenings, by candlelight, he turned their busy pages. The assorted stories, poems and articles were diverting, but his chief enjoyment was the variety of fashion plates, many of them coloured, and the accompanying reports on London and Parisian fashions.

'Richness in colour and costliness in the material,' he read, savouring the words, 'are more than ever characteristic of the fabrics now in vogue. The modern materials have this advantage, that a greater degree of pliability is now gained by our manufacturers than was formerly deemed attainable. The texture of some of our magnificent satins and of the *satin de laine* is most beautiful. These exquisite stuffs fall gracefully into folds, and adapt themselves admirably to every variety of costume, whether close-fitting or in draperies.'

Alfred began to amuse himself by adapting the patterns illustrated in these magazines, sketching men and women in fashionable clothes of his own design. One Sunday he took a few of his small ink-and-watercolour drawings home to show his brothers. As he was sitting with George in the parlour and proudly handing one of the sheets to him, their mother came into the room and snatched the drawing.

'What's this, then?' she demanded to know. 'Who's the fine lady? Why are you making a picture of her? It's not proper!'

'Not proper?' Alfred wrinkled his forehead, bemused. 'But it's no particular person, Mama. It's just showing some fashionable styles.'

'Nonetheless, it's not a suitable thing for a young man to draw.' She handed it back, mouth tightening sourly, and left the room.

Alfred's cheeks reddened – though not because of the painting itself, which simply depicted an elegant but demure young woman in a walking dress. There was nothing unseemly about the figured cashmere cloak, the double velvet cape, the wide sleeves, the muslin collar with blond edging, the high oval satin hat with a feather ornament. His sudden blush came from remembering what had crept into his head when he was creating the sketch with pen and brush. As the stylish female form took shape on his page, rounded at the shoulders and becoming very narrow at the ceinture, he had let himself picture what such a person would be wearing under her gown: a corset, a knee-length chemise, and layers of flounced petticoats. And then, pruriently, he had imagined her at the end of an evening, removing the garments one by one before drawing a flimsy nightgown over her naked flesh and retiring to bed.

The months slipped by. Daylight hours were largely occupied with meticulous leatherwork and dominated by the pungent smells of horses and hides; in the quiet evenings he would pore over fashion magazines and become absorbed in making his own careful sketches of fine clothes. The fashioning of fabrics, he began to feel, was his true vocation. He learnt everything he could about the newest preferences in costume: skirts were getting fuller, bonnets deeper, men's frockcoats tighter-fitting, their cravats wider.

It was only after Alfred had spent three years at Felsted, his mind increasingly on things other than harness-making, that he gained a position in Mr Bell's general store in Great Baddow as drapery assistant. This move, so earnestly desired and joyfully celebrated, would shape the rest of his life in ways he could not then foresee.

# 12

# Chelmsford, January 1849

Piled on several tables at the front of the Quarter Sessions courtroom, in full view of everyone, was a strange assortment of items: candles, tobacco, tea and many different articles of clothing – all of them loudly proclaiming his crimes. Mortified, Alfred hung his head. He could not bring himself to look straight at his brothers, though from the corner of his downcast eye he had glimpsed them all sitting together as he was led into the large crowded room.

He remembered distinctly, as he was sure they would too, the candid and contrite letter he had written to his mother and father more than a month earlier, the day after his arrest.

My dearly beloved parents,

You will know with distress the situation I am in. My guilt is clear; my shame you can imagine. You have often told me to take care of my money, my character and my soul. I have given you sore proof of having paid too little attention to your words. Money lost, character ruined, and soul trifled with. I now know well, but too late, the value of freedom and a good name. If they are ever returned to me, I trust to use them right.

My hope is that you will still love me as your son. The police will not permit us to see each other while I am remanded here, but please write to me as cheerfully as you can, for I am in need of it.

Your unworthy but affectionate son,

Alfred

The response that came to him in Springfield Prison from his father was sorrowful but not as sternly judgemental as Alfred had feared. Indeed, Edward had reproached himself for the young man's lapse: 'I am searching my own heart to uncover the failings that must somehow have contributed to these things you have done. If I have unwittingly neglected to provide needful guidance, may God be merciful to me – as I pray he will be to you, my son.'

Reading those words, Alfred had sobbed remorsefully. A few days later his anguish became more acute when he learnt that his parents would themselves be brought to trial on a charge of wittingly receiving stolen goods from him. He knew they were blameless but the legal machine was inexorable. Even if their innocence could eventually be proven, their humiliation would meanwhile be assured. He had not only disgraced himself, he had stained their good repute.

And now the day of the trial had arrived. His parents would be led into the courtroom later, when the charge that concerned them was introduced. Alfred could imagine all too well what a painful moment that would be for them both – and what an ordeal the court process would also be, whatever it might involve, for the others who in turn would be arraigned with him.

He was unsure how a trial such as this would be conducted. He had heard that a chairman presided at Courts of Quarter Sessions, that chairmen sat with a jury and were seldom formally qualified in legal matters, and that they were reputedly inclined to pronounce more severe sentences than were handed down at the Assizes. Apart from that, he knew little.

Light snow had fallen, and on his long walk under guard to the Chelmsford Courthouse the bitter chill made him shiver uncontrollably. But inside the austere tall grey building the air had a stuffy warmth, and sweat started to leak from his pores. He felt short of breath. As he waited with squirming conscience for the formal proceedings to begin, he looked quickly towards the Rolfes, who sat just a few yards away from him, heads bowed in misery. Apart from that stealthy glance he kept his face lowered, but knew that neighbours and acquaintances from Baddow and Chelmsford, from Felsted and Finchingfield, would also be present. The place was crammed, every seat taken. People lined the walls and jostled in the doorway, shoulder to shoulder and cheek by jowl. Others peered in at the windows. In the few minutes since Alfred had been led to the dock, the whispering had swollen into a noisy babbling. James Cotton, the trial chairman, was doing his best to quell the hubbub but with limited success until he began to bang his fist repeatedly on his desk.

As silence fell, Cotton cleared his throat and read out the first charge. 'Alfred Daniel Letch, you stand accused of stealing several articles of drapery and haberdashery, and a quantity of tea and sugar. Charles Rolfe and Hannah Rolfe, you stand accused of receiving the same goods. To you first, Mr Letch: what answer do you make to the charge of larceny?'

'I wish only to state, sir,' responded Alfred quietly, 'that neither Mr nor Mrs Rolfe had any knowledge that I was transacting business in an illicit manner.'

Murmurs rolled around the room, and the chairman rapped his desk again.

'So you absolve them of blame entirely?' Cotton asked.

'I do, sir.' Feeling light-headed, he tried to steady his breathing.

'Then let us be quite clear: you are confessing that in your dealings with Charles and Hannah Rolfe you alone are culpable?'

'That is correct. I am. I misrepresented the situation to them.'

Tears were running down Hannah Rolfe's ruddy cheeks. When it was their turn to be questioned, she kept her head lowered and her husband spoke for them both. They had no reason, he insisted, to think that Mr Letch had come by the goods dishonestly.

James Cotton frowned, cleared his throat and made some summary remarks. This, he said, was a matter in which it was not obvious what share of responsibility each party should bear for what had occurred. Indeed, he felt obliged to observe that it had been injudicious of Mr Bell, whose business assets were valued at about five thousand pounds, to have neglected to take stock for several years, thus leaving himself open to depredation. Regarding the charge, he added, members of the jury would need to consider whether the prisoners seemed truthful in claiming that Alfred Letch alone knew that the dealings were illicit, or whether remorse had prompted him to take the full blame upon himself.

After brief deliberation, the jury returned a verdict of guilty against all three prisoners, with a recommendation that mercy be shown to the Rolfes.

As the room became loud with prittle-prattle, two well-dressed young ladies rose from their seats and made their way haughtily to the door, casting scornful looks in Alfred's direction. To his great chagrin he saw that they were Emma Parker and her younger sister Sylvia, a pair of pretty customers he had done his best to flatter during their regular visits to Bell's store. They had been susceptible to gallant compliments, and he had sought to ingratiate himself with them by offering each a fine bonnet at an unauthorised 'special price'. Though apparently impressed then, they were plainly disgusted with him now.

And repugnance was so plain on other faces in the room that he could almost smell it. Had he hoped to earn some forgiveness by making a clean breast of his crime and exculpating others? If so – and he couldn't be certain of his own motives – the attitude he'd shown had apparently failed to mollify public opinion.

The second charge, chairman Cotton announced, was against Alfred Letch for stealing certain items, mainly of high-priced silk and satin, and against Mr Edward Letch and Mrs Mary Letch for receiving them.

Once again, Alfred stood in humiliation with his hands clasped and jaw clenched. It was stifling in the courtroom now. A few yards to his left, his parents rose unsteadily to their feet, a picture of vulnerability. His father stared at a spot high on the opposite wall. His mother, biting her lip, clutched her husband's arm. The colour had drained from her face.

'Evidence has already been presented,' intoned Cotton, 'that other acts of larceny by Alfred Letch were premeditated, and he has not contested that fact. The court is now to consider whether the further articles of property discovered at his family's home were knowingly accepted as stolen goods by Mr Letch the elder and his wife.'

As Cotton uttered the words 'his wife' there was a low moaning sound from Mary Letch and she fell forward in a faint, striking her forehead with a loud crack against the railing in front of her. Gasps and cries of alarm erupted from the crowd. Edward Letch knelt beside his wife, raised her gently to a sitting position and used his handkerchief to dab at the blood that trickled from a cut on her brow while supporting her with his other hand. A large woman, their neighbour Moll Higgins, rushed up to her with smelling salts.

Alfred had tried to move towards his mother too, but Cotton made a restraining gesture and he could only watch, stricken, as she slumped against his father's arm. To Alfred it seemed that he himself had inflicted this injury as surely as if he had raised a savage fist against her. Weeping quietly, he hid his face in his hands.

'Mrs Letch,' said the chairman when the commotion subsided, 'you can remain seated while the case proceeds. Also your husband, if he wishes.'

During the next half-hour, as Alfred stood there abashed, his mother sat bending forward, handkerchief held to her eyes, like an allegory of sorrowful reproach.

Many testified to his parents' integrity and upright character, providing details about the good standing of the whole family in the community, about their civility, their piety, their kindness to others, and much more. A few people ventured to remark that Alfred's fall from grace was all the more difficult to comprehend since it could hardly be attributed to any deficiency in his upbringing.

The jury, after deliberating for a mere ten minutes, returned their verdict: 'Guilty against the principal, Alfred Letch, and not guilty against the receivers, his parents.'

Loud cheers broke out.

The chairman held up a stern judicial hand. 'I quite concur,' he said solemnly, 'in the decision of the jury; for although Mr Letch the elder and Mrs Letch may have acted with insufficient caution, there is no likelihood – let alone proof – of guilty knowledge on their parts. They may leave the court without any blot on their characters.'

This remark was also applauded.

Alfred's mouth felt dry, and he ran an anxious tongue-tip over his lips. Cotton's voice, summoning George Bond, had a strange echo, like a church bell muffled by mist.

White-haired and fidgety, Bond wore a bewildered air. He looked about him with a frown of puzzlement, seemingly astonished to find himself in this place.

'Mr Bond, you employ yourself in the High Street as a seller and repairer of musical instruments?' the chairman asked.

'That's my main occupation, yes, though there's not much regular work in it nowadays, so I supplement my earnings with a little business as a tea merchant.'

'Ah, tea merchant. And what is your response to the charge of receiving twenty-four pounds of stolen tea, along with other articles, from Alfred Letch as his accomplice?'

'Well, you see, Mr Cotton, I just didn't know anything was stolen. I've never been involved in any wrongdoing in my life, as far as I'm aware. Young Mr Letch comes from a very musical family and when he brought along a viola that needed its pegs fixed, offering to pay me in tea and candles and the like, I didn't think anything of it.'

'So you saw nothing strange in being offered tea as payment for your work?'

'Well, no, I assumed he'd bought it from Mr Bell or been given it in lieu of wages.'

'And you now, Mr Letch: do you agree that Mr Bond was perfectly innocent of any knowledge of the way the property in question had been procured?'

'Yes, sir, you may be sure he is guiltless.'

The jury soon came to the same conclusion, and the trial then proceeded to the final charge, which linked Alfred with William Black the tailor as partners in misconduct.

Black was a portrait of distress. Skinny as a beanpole, and so stooped that the thin stalk of his neck protruded almost horizontally from between his collarbones, he had always looked unwell and unhappy, but being arraigned here seemed to fill him with as much dread as if summoned from his grave by the last trump. He made small pitiable mewling sounds, shook his head tremulously, and kept wiping his nose with the back of his hand.

Feeling the contagion of Black's suffering, Alfred recognised contritely how much he himself had contributed to it. The haggard tailor, while not free of fault, had been led into temptation and would be unable to withstand any onerous punishment. Black's crime was hardly more than having asked no questions about the miscellaneous bits of cloth from which he had stitched a few garments at Alfred's behest.

The chairman's exchanges with the two men followed the same pattern as for the previous charges. The jury found both prisoners guilty but recommended that mercy be shown to Black, as Letch was the instigator. At this verdict, Black wept like a child.

The chairman rapped on his desk to quieten the crowd before passing sentence.

'Alfred Letch,' he said grimly, 'you have been found guilty of four separate indictments of robbing your master. Under the law you are liable to fourteen years' transportation on each indictment. I am not disposed to make the sentence cumulative, but the court would not be performing its duty if you were suffered to remain in this country after the harm you have done not only to Mr Bell but also to others whom you encouraged to participate in the offence. Accordingly, the sentence is that you be transported for the space of fourteen years.'

Flinching, Alfred closed his eyes like someone who did not expect he would ever be able open them again.

'I hope,' James Cotton added, 'that you will, during this period of punishment, reflect on your conduct and endeavour to make some amends for the injuries you have inflicted on our society. As to you, William Black, though I am willing to believe that you have been led astray by Letch, it is my view that you had a real guilty knowledge that these articles were stolen. You would therefore be liable to transportation, but given the jury's recommendation of mercy, and the enticement put in your way, the sentence is that you be confined for six months, and kept to such hard labour as the medical man thinks you can perform, the first and last week in solitude. I trust you will become truly penitent, and will never be brought into court again. The trial is now concluded.'

While the room was slowly emptying, Alfred remained in the dock, head drooping, shoulders hunched. He stared sightlessly at his boots. The public recitation of his misdeeds had suffused him with dishonour; the prospect of long years of punishment and exile tormented him.

As the guards led Alfred out through the stony portal of the courthouse, he heard reviling words from the crowd gathered near the entrance – 'Shame on you, Letch!' 'Treacherous young rogue!' But none of this contumely wounded him as much as the sight of his family's stricken faces while they stood with linked arms, silently watching him shuffle away through the grey slush with his dour pair of escorts.

# 13

# Chelmsford, April 1849

Angling the sheets of paper up towards the scant light from his small window, he re-read what he had so laboriously written.

Springfield County Gaol
Chelmsford
18 April 1849

My dear parents,

It is now three months since I was incarcerated here, and you will doubtless be aware that my gaolers have not permitted me to receive any visits or exchange any letters during this lonely time. But in recognition of good behaviour I have now been granted the use of quill and paper, and thus I inscribe these pages in the hope of being able to send them to you eventually – though this may not be possible until after another two or three months have elapsed, by which time I expect to be in Millbank Penitentiary, in London, awaiting transportation.

Millbank is said to be formidable, yet it will offer something not available to me here: an opportunity to develop a few practical skills that may eventually be useful in the new country to which we are to be taken. Tailoring, for instance, is reportedly taught there to selected prisoners, so I hope to be permitted to learn more about that craft. Perhaps it will stand me in good stead if I am ever able to resume work in a drapery business.

Meanwhile, it is difficult to convey some impression of how hopelessly confined my life has become here within Springfield Gaol. I shall try to describe the conditions in this fearful place, beginning with its physical structure. Two extensive corridors radiate from the central hall, each containing more than one hundred cells, arranged in three tiers on each side. Every cell is fitted up with a water tap, water closet, a hammock and bedding, and – mercifully! – a few good books. (I have lately been reading the poems of William Cowper – with profit, I trust. His mood is seldom cheerful, so it matches mine. Do you know The Castaway?) We are allowed an hour's exercise in the morning and afternoon, in the small airing yards, of which there are twelve for the men and twelve for the women. From a semi-circular lodge, officers can see into every yard through small bull's-eye windows without being observed by the prisoners. You may have heard reference to the 'Separate System'; well, this means that each of us is in an individual cell, where we remain most of the time with the exception of visits to the chapel, or for exercise. We may not see or to talk to another prisoner.

I mentioned the airing yards, where we exercise. Usually this opportunity to get outside for a while and warm our limbs with some brisk walking is welcome, because our cells can be achingly cold. But last week, just two days after Easter Sunday, we were sent into the airing yards for another purpose: to witness the piteous spectacle of an execution. I cannot shake it from my mind.

They had placed the scaffold and drop above the entrance lodge, which is flanked by a brick boundary wall about twenty feet high with thick stone columns at intervals.

The condemned man, we were told, was a murderous ruffian who had throttled one of the warders to death in a fit of anger. But what provocation may have led him to his crime one can only guess. At any rate, it was a terrible thing to see him hanged. The prisoner, hands tied in front of him, was taken up some steps to the black platform high above us at the top of the gateway tower. His agitation was plain to see: his limbs trembled violently. A chaplain read to him from a prayer book and the executioner placed a hood – just a white bag – over the poor wretch's head before putting the noose around his neck and adjusting it. Suddenly the bolt was drawn and the trapdoor opened. For three or four minutes he twisted convulsively, as if his soul were straining to wriggle free of its pinioned body. And then he became a limp carcass.

Since that moment, the dreadful scene has stayed with me night and day. What haunts my thoughts is the brute fact – so starkly dramatised by this abrupt punishment – that a sentient human creature can be at any time just a short step from extinction. No doubt I should console myself by finding a salutary moral lesson in such a grim truth, but for the time being I can only feel the utter cruelty of it.

Enough of that. A warder here has told me I shall be dispatched before long to Millbank. I alluded earlier in this letter to the fact that Millbank, these days, is – as you probably know – a holding depot for convicts prior to their being assigned for transportation. I am likely to be held there for a few months, still in solitary confinement and restricted to silence; and eventually to be taken thence to Portland Public Works Prison in readiness for boarding the ship that will carry me to the other side of the world – if I do not perish on the journey, like Cowper's 'destined wretch'. It is hard to avoid despair at the prospect.

Your affectionate son,
Alfred

He put the letter aside, gloomily reflecting that it expressed nothing of his acute sense of deprivation – nothing about the many cherished things that were now lost to him except when called wistfully to mind. He tried to remember the smell of summer warmth nestled in fibres of cotton and wool. The spectacle of oxlips in the meadows near Great Bardfield. The harmonies of flute and strings and pianoforte in the old family home. But pressing down on all such sensuous fragments was the heavy knowledge that he had damaged irreparably not only his own life but also the lives of others. It came to him now with numbing force that he would never be free of this weight of misery. Never. His stupid criminal acts had brought consequences that were irreversible, inescapable, just as surely as if he'd been washed overboard into stormy seas, or swung at the end of a throttling rope, heart and lungs and brain about to burst.

That afternoon the prison chaplain paid one of his regular visits. Reverend Charles Ogden seemed the epitome of dullness, but Alfred was glad of their conversations because inmates were not permitted to talk to anyone else. Being able to exchange even a few trite words made a session with the chaplain seem valuable, though usually it would consist of little more than a soporific reading from the scriptures, a formulaic prayer and some predictable admonitions. This time it was different. No sooner had the stooping figure of Ogden entered his cell than Alfred began to spill tears of self-pity.

'Now, now, pull yourself together, young man,' said Ogden gruffly, sitting down beside him on the narrow bed. 'The pain of remorse can be severe, but it shows that God is exerting a beneficial pressure on your soul.'

'It isn't just remorse,' said Alfred. 'It's also that I feel bereft of consolation. To be so solitary, so permanently separated from my dear family, and to be expelled, too, from the countryside that's been like an Eden to me – I can hardly bear the thought of it.'

'You'll just have to accept your sense of loss and isolation as inevitable. I'm sorry to be so blunt about that, but it will fade with the lapse of time, assuredly. You should expect other things to become less acute, too, and you'll feel the better for it. Your shame will eventually subside after you've left this district where many people know you well. Departure to distant places will allow you to walk in the paths of righteousness without such a burden on your shoulders.'

'But I'll remain guilty forever, that's the truth of it. What can I do about the permanence of my guilt?'

'You'll learn to live with it.'

The chaplain stood, walked over to the little plank of shelving on the opposite wall, and took down one of the books.

'Do you know Milton's mighty epic, *Paradise Lost?*'

'Only in part, Mr Ogden. I began reading it but found the going difficult.'

'Difficult, yes, because it treats of difficult themes, like transgression and punishment. All the more reason to give it your fullest attention. I want you to hear a few solemn lines from its last section. This is the passage that brings the poem to a close. It describes the moment when our first parents are leaving their first home. I thought of the lines just now when you said you regarded your Essex countryside as a kind of Eden. A paradise you've lost.'

Ogden cleared his throat and read aloud:

*Some natural tears they dropped, but wiped them soon.*
*The world was all before them, where to choose*
*Their place of rest, and Providence their guide.*
*They, hand in hand, with wandering steps and slow,*
*Through Eden took their solitary way.*

Shutting the book and looking over his spectacles at Alfred, he said earnestly: 'There's a wider world before you now, young man. It will doubtless be a sad world for you much of the time, but you can choose to see it, if you lift your eyes to the horizon, as a place where it's possible for you to redeem yourself through honest and diligent effort. Never forget that.'

# Amelia

# 14

# Ashton-under-Lyne, May 1862

After the chapel service, as the tall dignified-looking man stood apart for a moment at the edge of the crowd outside to light his pipe, she found the courage to approach him. Something kindly in his countenance softened the obvious differences between them – differences of age, class, bearing and attire.

'Begging your pardon, Mr Mason, sir.' She smoothed the front of her skirt with a nervous hand, and wished she knew how to speak like gentlefolk.

He doffed his hat and nodded courteously. His considerate manners, even towards working people such as herself, were widely known. She'd heard many appreciative comments. *He awlus treats folk with respeck, that Hugh Mason. Daycent man for a boss. A jannock fella, well liked when he were Mayor of Ashton.*

Mason's response posed a gentle question. 'Good morning, Miss…?'

'Amelia French, sir. Employed as one of the weavers at your mill these last four year.'

'Ah. Forgive me for not knowing your name, Miss French. It's a large workforce. But I did think your face looked familiar.'

'You may think it's too bold of me to speak to you like this, Mr Mason, but I want to ax your advice, if you please. There's no one else in our town can tell how these bad times will turn out, and what someone like myself should do.'

'Not too bold, no' – he shook his head, and his smile was heartening – 'though I'm unsure what help you think I can offer…'

'Nobut a word of guidance,' said Amelia quickly. 'I don't seek more'n that, sir, truly. Everyone knows you've already been generous to folk hereabouts since the cotton famine began. Refusing to cut our wages, and giving large sums of money to the borough relief fund.'

Mason made a self-deprecating gesture. It's nothing worth mentioning, said his eyes.

'But I see what's happening at other mills,' she went on, 'and I'm afeart for the morrow. All those smokeless chimneys – I've never known the air so clear, and it's worriting. People say you cannot go on much longer yourself, sir, dipping into your own fob so some of us can stay in paid work. My old uncle – it's in his house I'm living – he reckons if this continues beyond end of year we'll all be frabbing paupers.'

'What of the sewing classes that the churches provide in the evenings, so that women will have other skills in case they're needed?' Mason asked. 'You attend those, and find them useful?'

'Well, sir, I don't mean to sound ungrateful, and there's comfort in the company of other young women, right enough, as we learn our stitches and Bible lessons and such like. But charity ain't real work. To speak plain, it's nobut shaffling. Pretending to be busy. At any rate, what I want to ax you about is somethin my Uncle Harold has heard. The Australian colonies are offering free passage for young women from these parts, and I should emigrate, says he, while I can. My parents...'

She paused for a moment, clearing her throat to disguise the sudden quaver at the edge of those words. *My parents.* Back into a dark mental cranny she pushed the painful traces of a night eight years ago. Mr Mason, she could see, was watching her closely as she resumed.

'My parents, they've passed away, y'see, and I've no siblings, so it'd be a fairly simple matter to leave. But I'd need to make up m'mind without delay, and I feel too addle-headed to decide for certain. So I'm hoping you can tell me frankly, Mr Mason, how long you think the present troubles will last. If there's no end in sight...I've a horror of being reduced to begging, or being cooped up in a workhouse – it'd be better to take my chances now on t'untherside of the world.'

Knitting his brows, he nodded understandingly. 'I see, I see. Well now, Miss French, it's prudent of you to contemplate that idea. I wish I could reassure you about a quick return to prosperity in the cotton industry, but you ask me to be plain about the facts and so I will. To speak frankly, I have to say that things could get worse before they improve. The problem, I'm sure you understand, is this ongoing civil war in America. We'd all hoped it would be over swiftly but that looks most unlikely now. So we still have no prospect, you see, of getting the baled cotton that our mills so desperately need. First it was a boycott from the southern states that interrupted the imports, and then a

Union blockade...Anyhow, the famine of raw cotton will persist here for as long as their conflict continues. I'm afraid this means that unemployment will probably spread much further yet, and an increasing number of our citizens will depend on Poor Law relief, meagre as it is. If you can face the uncertainty of a long sea voyage, Miss French, and the challenge of finding your feet in a strange remote place – your bravery may perhaps bring happy rewards, though there can be no guarantee of that. I've scant knowledge of the Australian colonies, to tell the truth. Have you been told much about Australia yourself?'

'No, sir, naught. Where it is, even. Very far away, Uncle Harold says, *farther than you could imagine* is how he put it. *Too far to come back if you don't like it.* I heard they send convicts, along with respectable folk. But surely they'd find good work for me there, the people who arrange the emigration?'

'I'm confident they'd do their best, yes. Of course, it wouldn't be the kind of work you're used to doing – you have to bear that in mind. There are no textile mills operating in any of the colonies, to the best of my knowledge. Nor, probably, any other industries where you could find a ready opening. Domestic service is your most likely employment; it's mainly why colonial governments are offering these assisted passages, after all. Do you consider yourself well equipped for such work?'

'I believe I am, Mr Mason. Cleaning and cooking and ironing, and setting a fire in the hearth – I can do those things right enough, and for whatever else I need to know I'll be a willing learner. I can read and write, too.'

'Good, good. Mind you, I can't say what the wages would be. But in time you should be able to establish yourself comfortably. The simple fact is that there's a shortage of women in Australia, so if you develop your skills diligently as a household help and maintain an upright character you'll be well placed, I expect, for marriage.'

At his mention of marriage Amelia glanced at the black crape armband he wore; everyone in the town knew that not long ago he'd been widowed for a second time. She blushed and thanked him, apologising again for her presumption. As she turned away, he put his hand to his hat's brim, wished her the best of luck, and gave her a warm smile that made her heart bounce. She would always remember it.

On the way home she hummed quietly to herself the tune of the sewing class song she and her friends liked to chant, and as the words of its final verse rose now to her mind they seemed more apt than usual:

*Come lasses, then, cheer up and sing, it's no use lookin sad,*
*We'll make our sewing school to ring, and stitch away like mad,*
*We live in hopes afore so long to see a brighter day,*
*For the cloud that's hanging o'er us now is sure to blow away.*

That evening she went to see Lucy Smeddles, her freckle-faced but comely friend who worked alongside her at Mason's mill.

'Well, I screwed up m'courage,' Amelia told her, 'and axed Mr Mason for advice about emigrating. He were real kind to me, and spoke gentle, and the upshot is, I'll be going to Australia just as soon as I can – leastways I'll go if you come with me, Lucy. Will you?'

Within minutes the venturesome decision was shared. They would put forward their names together for the emigration commissioners to consider. The process, they'd been told, was straightforward.

Amelia lay awake in her narrow bed, hugging her knees to get warm and trying to imagine the unimaginable. She could hardly peer beyond the simple prospect of imminent departure. 'A brighter day!' Lucy had exclaimed with a giggle, and they both yearned to sail away to a new life that would be luminously happy. But for Amelia this expedition was not only a search for employment and companionship: there was more to it than that, an unspoken motive, a deep-seated ache. Neither Lucy nor any of Amelia's other friends – nobody at all, except perhaps Uncle Harold, who was careful never to allude to this – knew of her fervent hope that by leaving her homeland behind she might eventually free herself from the continual haunting memory of how she had become an orphan. Nightmare images of that grievous event still clung to her like greedy leeches, sucking, sucking.

## 15

# Fremantle, October 1862

Gusts of wind, uncomfortably warm, plucked at the shifty powder that seemed to form an unstable ground surface everywhere in this strange environment. Where were ordinary soils, like the muddy peat and dark silty loam of the district where she'd grown up? Nowhere to be seen. With her back to the fitful wind and to the almost boundless sea over which she'd voyaged for three months, it seemed to Amelia that the expanse of open land stretching out before her, much of it bare to the wide bright skies, was hardly less desolate than that vast ocean. Consternation clutched her. The soft sand underfoot made her yearn for the solidity of familiar living spaces in her forsaken homeland. The sunlight's dazzle, reflected from limestone buildings and gritty roads, stung her eyes.

As if stupefied, whether by the merciless heat or the sheer bleakness of their new surroundings or the realisation that this alien place was their chosen substitute for home, the women stood together in their black skirts and bonnets, silent and motionless. To Amelia it felt like a funeral of the hopes that had brought her here.

Urged on by the redoubtable Miss Mowbray, their big-boned matron and moral supervisor, they followed the taciturn man assigned to conduct them to the immigration depot. Their luggage accompanied them in a pair of carts pulled along despondently by bony horses. For nearly half an hour the group trudged on under the stabbing sun, sand swirling against their ankles and sifting into their boots and the hems of their skirts. Flies clung to sweaty faces. The hot air carried an odd mixture of smells: horse dung had a familiar odour, and food scraps too, but these mingled with whiffs of salt, smoke and parched grass, and with the pungent tang of some plant the women couldn't recognise.

'Here y'are then,' their guide announced phlegmatically, gesturing with a parsimonious thumb.

So this beggarly little building was where they would be quartered! They stared in dismay. And the hostel's interior, they soon found, was even more depressing: cramped, dingy, sparsely furnished.

'Hardly better than a gaol,' Amelia murmured miserably to Lucy Smeddles. They rolled their tired eyes at each other.

Miss Mowbray clapped her hands, a pair of fat pancakes, to get the group's attention. 'Well, it's no palace, you can see that clear enough,' she conceded. 'But we have to make the best of it, young ladies. This is where all of you must wait until employers come along to offer you a situation. I'll be staying here with you in the meantime. Same rules as on the ship, mind you, so don't do anything foolish.'

This reminder of shipboard rules produced some half-suppressed groans. Not that her charges had resented Miss

Mowbray's authority – in fact, most had particular reason to be grateful during the voyage for the firm way she'd protected them from the coarse drunken advances of Surgeon-Superintendent Bristow, and all had felt at one time or another the benefit of her little acts of gruff kindness. It was simply that they wanted to be less trammelled now that they were ashore. Yes, discipline and constraint had been necessary until now, they saw that, and looking after their welfare was her job, after all. So without much complaint they had spent the whole ninety-day period in a compartment at one end of the partitioned ship, with single men at the opposite end and a buffer of families in between. They had slept two to every hard narrow bunk. They had put up with lice and fleas, sickness and soreness. They had obeyed meekly when the matron laid down the law, such as a strict time limit for any dancing on the deck in the evenings. They had listened to her forewarnings about the need to avoid moral and physical danger once they reached land and began to disperse. ('Some of the men you meet will be disorderly,' she had said, 'so be on your guard. And keep to the coastal towns if possible. Anywhere else the living will be very rough.') But now they itched to be free of her precepts and prescriptions.

Utter tedium pervaded their next few days at the hostel. The food was insipid, the inactivity excruciatingly dull, the water insufficient for washing skin or clothes properly. All the women had to loiter indoors every day from seven o'clock in the morning until an hour past noon, on the off-chance that someone would arrive seeking their services.

'And there's to be no picking and choosing,' the matron insisted with an admonitory frown. 'Whatever situation comes up first for you, it's to be taken promptly. And with gratitude.'

Lucy, the prettiest among them, was hired first. A ruddy-faced, snaggle-toothed, heavy-breathing man, announced by Miss Mowbray as 'a landowner, Mr Brough', inspected the whole group slowly and wordlessly before pointing to Lucy and beckoning her outside for a muttered conversation.

'I'm to be a cook, far up into the hills,' she told them as she came back inside. Amelia embraced her tearfully. 'When you're settled y'self, let me know where you are,' said Lucy. 'A message to Brough's farm, near York – that'll find me, he says.'

'It's hard to part after so long together,' said Amelia, wiping her eyes. 'But crying'll do naught, will it?'

One morning about a week later, Amelia sat by an open window singing a ditty her uncle had taught her:

*Some folk can lie till the clock strikes eight;*
*Some folk may sleep till ten,*
*Then rub their eyes and yawn a bit,*
*And turn them o'er again;*
*Some folk can ring a bell in bed,*
*Till the servant brings some tea;*
*But wet or dry, a factory lass*
*Must jump at break of day!*

She tapped her foot rhythmically to the tune, as she used to when sitting at the weaving machine in her wooden-soled clogs. It made her smile to recall how she and all the mill workers had worn clogs to steady their footing on the factory floors, which had to be kept wet so the cotton would remain moist enough to be pliable. Clogs! They'd never be needed in this arid new place, surely.

*But wet or dry, a factory lass*
*Must jump at break of day!*

As she finished her song now, it was not a factory worker who appeared in her fond thoughts but a factory owner, Hugh Mason. Again she pictured his understanding smile, and smiled back at the memory of it.

A loud peremptory knock at the hostel door brought her swiftly out of her reverie. Moments later Miss Mowbray was standing in front of her in the company of a well-dressed middle-aged man, stoutly built, with a pockmarked but pleasant face.

'This is Mr De Leech,' explained the matron. 'He asked me to show him who was singing just now when he arrived.'

Amelia stood and inclined her head deferentially. 'Good morning, sir. Amelia French is my name. I didn't know anyone were listening.'

'You have a beautiful singing voice, Miss French,' said the man. 'And music gladdens the heart.'

She blushed, unable to think of any response. Long afterwards she would often recall how the idle impulse to sing that song at that moment had shaped so much of the rest of her life.

He was looking at her intently. 'Well now,' he said. 'I own a store in Perth, you see. Drapery and other business. My house is attached to the back of it. I'm in need of someone to cook and clean for me. Can you do that? And some needlework?'

She nodded. *De Leech: an impressive name. Sounds more like a doctor than a draper. Not short of a penny, by the look of his clothes.*

'Standard wage. The servant's room is comfortable. All meals provided, of course.'

'I'd be happy to work for you, sir. Thank you.'

'Good, good. Very good. All settled, then. I'll send a carriage tomorrow to collect you and your things.'

As soon as he had left, the other women clustered around Amelia. 'A *carriage*!' cried one of them, clapping her hands gleefully. 'He looks a real gentleman, don't he?' said another. 'Just look at your smile, Amelia! Ain't she a lucky one!'

Through the window she watched him walk away, his head jerking forward slightly with each step. *Like a bantam,* she thought. *But seems a genteel bantam. With that foreign-sounding name, perhaps he'd come to the little colony from somewhere like…Well, who'd be able to say where from?* Back in her part of England, you always knew – or someone else knew and could tell you – what a person's background was. 'Amelia French? Oh yes,' folks would say, 'she's the lass whose parents died in that terrible way when she was little, poor thing; put in her uncle's care after that; her forebears were handloom weavers in Ashton-under-Lyne for generations back. Lucy Smeddles? Well, the Smeddles have lived in these parts since Adam was a boy; big family, and she's the youngest; her pa and all her brothers work in the Fairbottom coal pits. Hugh Mason? We all know Mr Mason. Born in Stalybridge, he was; then, after his schooling, he worked in the local mill that his father managed; got himself elected Mayor of Ashton three years running; married one of those Buckley girls, and when she died in childbirth he married her sister, and after a few years she died too…'

But out here, she supposed, it was different. Perched at the edge of a strange land, everyone – not counting the blacks, of course – had come recently from other places, and seldom knew much about one another. There might well be little mysteries around many of them. The places and families they'd come from. What they were doing before they came. It would even be possible for some people to re-create themselves entirely. With little difficulty you could invent a new identity and leave your old self behind, buried out of sight. Who would know?

# Polly

# 16

# Finchingfield,
# June to October 1867

The little harmonium began to creak and croak and whine. With a scraping of chairs and a shuffling of boots, the Sunday School class stood to sing. Polly glanced across again at Arthur Ridgen. As they were the two oldest in the room, she could see him clearly over the heads of the others without seeming to lift her eyes. For a young lad, fifteen like herself, he was already solidly muscular, with broad shoulders and big strong-looking forearms.

Now he caught her observing him, and nodded towards her in a sly way, smiling his lopsided smile so that it seemed to imply a wink of shared amusement. He bellowed out the hymn, and his startlingly strident voice dominated the piping trebles around him so that the words of Dr Watts resonated with particular vigour:

*How doth the little busy bee*
*Improve each shining hour,*

*And gather honey all the day*
*From every opening flower!*

*...*

*In works of labour or of skill*
*I would be busy too:*
*For Satan finds some mischief still*
*For idle hands to do.*

Arthur gave lusty emphasis to those last two lines, staring across at her with a wicked look and grinning. She blushed and looked down at her own nearly blameless hands.

A few days later it happened that Polly's mother sent her down the Bardfield road to fetch a rabbit for their evening meal from Ridgens' farm, as she had often done before.

'Oh, yes, m'dear,' said Mrs Ridgen, taking the money. 'Half a dozen handsome little carcases in the shed, and you can choose any one of them. Arthur! Show young Polly where they're hanging.'

So Arthur took her to one of the outbuildings. As they walked he began to hum the familiar tune about busy bees and opening flowers, looking at her meaningfully with his head at a tilt. She found herself thinking about idle hands.

The rabbits were suspended in a row, headless and hulked.

'You can choose your cony presently,' he said, 'but I've got something I want to show you first.' He gestured to a large cask in a corner of the shed, and she approached it with him.

Arthur turned a spigot and held a wooden cup underneath it. 'Try this,' he said, with that crooked smirk of his. 'Strongest cider in the county, they say. Don't just sip, swallow it down.'

He quaffed a draught of it himself. 'Good, eh? Let's each have another'n.'

So she drank again, quickly. It made the back of her throat tingle, and she began to feel giddy as a peg-top. Arthur stood closer to her, his warm breath redolent of apple juice. He reached his hand down and lifted her dress. He pressed his big body against her. She wanted to say something but couldn't quite think of the right words and her tongue had become heavy. His hand was rubbing the front of her thigh, and now the inside of her thigh, in a slow rhythmical way, and then his mouth nuzzled at her neck and slid slowly down towards her trembling titties while his big fingers fumbled with buttons.

'Nmnmnm,' she heard herself blurting with alarm and excitement. 'Nmnmnm.' When she tried to push his hand away, his mouth became more insistent.

'There's plenty of soft straw up in the loft,' he said, pointing to a ladder with his thumb. 'Let's lie down for a while. C'mon Polly. C'mon.'

But she shook her head, pulling back from him and holding up a hand as if to ward off temptation. 'I must get home right away,' she told him. 'I really must.' And she turned quickly to go.

'Wait, Polly! Your cony! Choose one and I'll hock its hindlegs for carrying.'

'Can't stay for that,' she said, grabbing the nearest rabbit and tugging it off the hook. 'I'll take it just as it is.'

'Don't be in such a pucker, Polly Letch! Let me wrap the carcase for you. It's gory.'

'No, no.'

With a half-sobbing hiccup, she ran out of the shed and on down the road full pelt to her home, heedless of the splashes of blood on her dress.

∞

After that, whenever she saw Arthur she avoided talking to him or looking at him. But she couldn't banish from carnal memory the feeling of his hand and mouth. It troubled her every bedtime, no matter how valiantly she tried to shield herself with prayers. Before she fell asleep she found that her own hands always wanted now to move over her body, as if they were someone else's.

Many months later, at the Bardfield market with her father, she saw Arthur in front of a vegetable stall. His thick arm was around a buxom young woman with a braying laugh.

'Who's that in the bright dress, cheek by jowl with Arthur Ridgen?' she asked her father.

'The noisy redhead? Ah, that's Moll Seccombe. Her family's from over Braintree way. A flackety lot, they are. She'd be a couple of years older than young Arthur, and a step or two ahead, I'd say. She's got a certain reputation. The way she's playing up to him, I wouldn't be surprised if the Seccombes have got their shrewd eye on the Ridgens' farm. Arthur may look like a bumpkin, but it'll be his farm eventually, so whoever hooks him will get a fine property.'

Property, she knew, was never far from her father's thoughts. She often heard him talking about it with her mother, and their conversation usually followed the same pattern.

'But I'm quite content with this little house, George,' Caroline Letch would insist. 'Truly. Our family is well provided for. We don't need anything more.'

'It's not that I covet a grand estate,' he would respond. 'You know that, m'dear. I just can't forget how many of the comforts we have about us here, furnishings especially, came from my brother's generosity. Alfred did some things he shouldn't have done, and for that he's paid a severe penalty, but he was big-hearted, wasn't he? Did so much to set us up in this house. Without his help we could hardly have started our married life. I wish I'd managed to build up some assets since then, acquire a piece of property, so I could repay him. But it's harder than ever to make a living hereabouts, isn't it? Let alone prosper. In the last ten years every second person from these parts has moved to the big towns or cities. And there's Alfred in a little colony on the far side of the world, making his fortune! Whenever one of his letters arrives, we find he's acquired some new buildings. Perth seems to be a go-ahead kind of place. Being transported there has brought him great opportunities. Perhaps we should consider emigrating, m'darling. Join him under southern skies, as he keeps urging us to do.'

Although her uncle had been shipped away before she was born, Polly knew well the story of his fall and rise. Formerly a source of shame to the family, now a source of pride, he had become the very epitome of a redeemed sinner. Self-redeemed, apparently.

When Uncle Alfred's name next came up at the family table, and her father again spoke speculatively of emigration, Polly asked the question that in her eyes was obvious, though it seemed not to have occurred to George.

'Surely it can't be the case that everyone who goes to Australia becomes as successful as your brother?'

'Well, I suppose not – but...' Her father looked nonplussed.

She let it rest there. George Letch was a dear old nincompoop, and Polly doubted that he could flourish anywhere in the world, let alone in some little colonial outpost. But she didn't want to make him feel silly; he had always been an amiable papa. Besides, the idea of moving far away from here did have some appeal. She had begun to find her life in Finchingfield much too quiet. Every year the number of farm workers diminished further, and that meant less activity in and around the village. Market days no longer bustled as they used to when she was a child. Even in the surrounding district there were not many people of her own age, and none of them interested her much – apart from Arthur, who'd now been snared by that blowsy creature Moll Seccombe.

Attending chapel with her pious family had become tedious, stifling. Her younger sisters immersed themselves as eagerly as her parents in the numbing conventional routines of worship services, but she couldn't share their zeal. Week by week their preacher had been making his inexorable way through the traditional list of cardinal vices. As she tried to stop herself yawning, Polly recognised impenitently that she had been touched by most of them. Pride? She was pleased with the shape of her ample breasts, and liked to take the weight of them in her hands when undressing for bed. Gluttony? Her appetite for almost any kind of food was proverbial in the family. 'You'll eat us out of house and home,' said her father. 'You'll need to let out the waistline of that dress,' said her mother. Sloth? She was the last one out of bed in the mornings. Lust? No biblical word brought greater imaginary pleasure than that – except 'fornication', which always made her think of Arthur Ridgen's ox-like body rubbing against hers.

It was a relief when the time came to walk home from church. Polly sniffed the wind coming up from the mown pastures, and took off her bonnet so that she could feel the sun's warmth on her cheeks. Perhaps, she thought, if her papa did eventually decide to move the family to a new country, and somehow managed to make it happen despite his usual ineffectiveness, there'd be more room for her to spread her wings. Even meet an agreeable and affluent gentleman. Someone who, at least, knew how to be merry. Would that be too much to ask?

# Runty

# 17

# The *Hougoumont,*
# October to December 1867

Discovery could mean death, without a doubt. The men around him would be enraged if they found out his true purpose and identity. Some of them were burly brutes with menace in their eyes, quite capable of beating him savagely with their fists, or stringing him up, or kicking his head to a pulp – all too easy in the darkness below decks at night. The risk of being unmasked was real enough. Many of the prisoners were from London; perhaps someone among them could have encountered him there in his previous role. Unlikely – checking the list carefully before going aboard, he had recognised none of the names – but still possible. Or the convenient fiction of his trial in Stafford might lead to some awkward questions. Most of these convicts liked to probe for details of each other's criminal background. He was gambling on the probability that his intimate knowledge of the Potteries would stand him in good stead if anyone from that locality turned up and wanted to talk about it.

There was comfort in the fact that only Captain Cozens knew his real identity. To everyone else, including the warders, he was just one among the 280 convicts on the voyage. But if anyone guessed the truth it would soon spread and he'd be done down. Safety depended on blending in, acting the part well. From the moment he boarded this Blackwall frigate at Sheerness he'd been discreetly observing the mannerisms of the lags around him. Noting how they used certain physical signs to communicate – the wry lift of an eyebrow, a finger tapping the nose bridge, the artificial puckering of a cheek – he casually incorporated some of these into his own repertoire. And after listening to their muttered conversation on the few occasions when talk was permitted, he filched a few tics of speech to season the cant terms he knew already.

The *Hougoumont* stopped at Portland to bring more prisoners aboard. Among them was a second group of Fenians, bringing their total number to more than sixty – almost one in four of all those under guard.

'You'll need to be damned cautious, Rowe,' the chief commissioner had said when briefing him. 'Most of the prisoners are the usual sort of ruffians, so you know what to expect from that lot. The Irish agitators will be less predictable, and keeping an eye on them is your primary task now. Some of those Fenians are smart devils. Schoolmasters, clerks, writers. Cunning and plausible. They shrug at the charge of treason – see themselves as patriots, not criminals at all, and in some quarters there's sympathy for that view. Be that as it may, you're there to find out whatever you can about them: whether they're hatching any trouble, who takes the lead in their plans, what differences emerge between them, anything like that. If you get wind of a serious threat to orderly conduct, let Captain Cozens know immediately. Otherwise, not a word to him during the voyage. Anyway, make sure you're unobtrusive. Don't let anyone catch you spying on them, unless you want a dewskitch, as they call it.'

'A merciless drubbing – I know, Sir Richard. I'll watch my step.'

'Trust no one, Rowe. Killers and rapists may not be the most dangerous. Before setting sail the captain will show you – surreptitiously, of course – a full list of the prisoners: names, ages, crimes, occupations. They'll be from many walks of life. A few of the ordinary rascals, mind you, could well have family links with Ireland, and be supporters of the Fenians, so perhaps someone will mention something useful in your hearing.'

Commissioner Mayne had been right about the range of occupations. The ship's manifest listed labourers, miners, tailors, carpenters, grooms, butchers, coopers, hawkers, horse breakers, potters, puddlers, masons, shepherds, bricklayers, boot closers, boilermakers and many others. But knowing what kind of work a man had undertaken before the law tripped him up told Rowe nothing about political allegiances. So during the early weeks of the voyage, he spoke no more than necessary, keeping on the fringe of conversations whenever he could, listening quietly without seeming to take much notice of what was being said.

Even so, avoiding the belligerent attention of shipboard bullies was sometimes difficult.

'Hoy!' A hefty hackum swaggered towards him. 'Reg'lar Tom Thumb, ain't ya? Not lean, but the shortest man on board, I reckon. What are you – barely five foot, eh?'

'Around that.'

The big man leaned over him and pushed a fat finger against his chest. 'Runty,' he guffawed, 'that's ya new name.' To those around them he bellowed, 'Mark him, lads, this little fellow here's gunna be called Runty now!'

There could be no gainsaying the nickname. Others took it up gleefully, and with repetition it stuck.

∞

By the time they had been a month at sea, Runty was feeling fairly secure in his disguise and confident he could judge which prisoners were likely to be reliable sources of information. During the long nights below hatches, none of the mutterings and curses that thickened the fetid air ever revealed much. Daylight afforded better opportunities: in good weather there were several hours when, after completing their assigned chores of cleaning and scrubbing and washing, those who chose not to play cards could amble around the deck or slouch against the rail to smoke and chat. From two of the talkative older men, Sam Slack and Jack Hampshire, friendlier than most and near his own age, he picked up stray bits of gossip about some of the others. But the person with whom he could talk most freely was a Scottish clerk, Alex Carey, whose crusty manner belied a shrewd intelligence.

'Strange bunch, those garrulous Irishmen,' Carey said, sucking hard on his clay pipe as Runty stood with him and gazed out at the ship's wake. 'Swollen with sentimentality.'

Runty nodded. 'It's loud and clear in the concerts they put on in the hatchway – full of nostalgic ballads that make their homeland sound like the Garden of Eden.'

'Mixed up with their religion, if you ask me,' rejoined Carey. 'The earnest way they give voice, you'd think their patriotic songs were hymns to the Almighty. Or to that bloody pope of theirs. They're just as much Roman as they are Irish. A priest hovering around all the time to feed their superstitions with his hocus-pocus. Delaney, their chaplain – I call him the witchdoctor – I'm told he supplies them with paper and ink, too, for their newspaper.'

'What galls me,' said Runty, hoping to prise out any information Carey might have acquired, 'is the way they hold themselves apart. When they talk of "convicts" they mean only the rest of us. They're proud of being political prisoners. In their eyes we're just ordinary riffraff while they're champions of high ideals, unjustly victimised. Maybe there's some truth in that. What d'you think?'

'I'll admit some of the paddies are men of talent,' said Carey between puffs. He watched the coils of smoke drift away. 'And political argument seems to be in their blood. Have you heard O'Reilly speak? Or Cashman? Damned eloquent.'

'That pair, they'd be the ringleaders, you reckon? Couple of rabble-rousers?'

'Could be. Along with that fellow Flood, I suppose, the one who edits their newspaper. But they all seem to egg each other on.'

Runty wasn't finding it easy to carry out his secret commission of surveillance. He had no way of knowing what the Fenians discussed at night, because they slept in a separate hold. During the daytime they generally kept to themselves. The concerts they often put on in the early evenings were open to all, and displayed their attitudes plainly: in defiant songs and maudlin recitations they defended their cause and encouraged one another, confident of being able to surmount adversity through mutual support. But he suspected there might be more details about their opinions, more hints about their plans, in the magazine they compiled every week – *The Wild Goose*. Although everyone had heard of this, only the Irishmen themselves knew exactly what it contained. Seditious ideas? According to Sam Slack there was just a single handwritten copy of each edition, which the editor would read aloud to the group when they gathered in their own hold after nightfall. Father Delaney, reportedly, had charge of all issues produced so far.

Runty contrived to have a seemingly casual conversation with the priest, and then spoke with him again at greater length a few days later, turning the topic towards families.

'My own da's folk came from Dublin,' Runty lied. 'A fervent republican, he was. Used to talk passionately about the terrible injustices inflicted by the English. He died when I was young, so I don't know as much about the politics of it all as I should, but I'd like to understand more, Father. I've heard there's a mettlesome little newspaper your men have been writing, and that you're the keeper of it. D'you think I might have a look at it?'

'To be sure, to be sure,' Delaney nodded. 'It's a spirited production, so it is. You'll enjoy the reading of it. Five issues to date. I can't let you borrow them, of course, but you're welcome to sit in my cabin this afternoon and look at the papers.'

After thumbing through the editorials, articles, poems and snippets of advice for half an hour, Runty could already see that *The Wild Goose* was actually a very tame fowl. There were sentimental verses, like John Boyle O'Reilly's piece on remembering a quaint old clock in the classroom of his boyhood. There were jokes, like the notice of items 'to be sold by public auction on the forecastle deck: a few secondhand paper collars, the property of a gentleman who has no shirt'. The only expressions of disrespect for the British legal system were harmless enough to bring a smile to Runty's lips:

This great continent of the south, having been discovered by some Dutch skipper and his crew, was in consequence taken possession of by the government of Great Britain in accordance with that just and equitable maxim, 'What's yours is mine; what's mine is my own.' That magnanimous government, in the kindly exuberance of their feelings, has placed a large portion of the immense tract of country called Australia at our disposal. Generously defraying all expenses incurred on our way to it, and providing retreats for us there to secure us from the inclemency of the seasons...

This mildly sarcastic tone suggested that there was little to fear from the Fenians. He would remain watchful, lest the apparent good humour masked something more devious, but it seemed unlikely he'd uncover anything noteworthy to report later to Sir Richard Mayne.

He continued his conversations with Father Bernard Delaney, attracting quizzical comments from Alex Carey.

'Seems you're getting friendly with the witchdoctor. You'll be caught in his papist snare,' said Carey.

'No chance.'

'What do you find to talk about with someone like that?'

'Ah, things beyond the ken of a mere Scot.'

'C'mon, you whippersnapper, tell me!'

'Well, this morning, for instance, we had an earnest debate about distinguishing between what's illegal and what's immoral. To the Fenians there's a fundamental difference. They're bold enough to break the law when it's in conflict with principles they hold dear – especially the principle of Ireland's right to national independence, even if that requires armed rebellion.'

Carey sniffed at this. 'So he's softened you up, the witch-doctor? Ready to join their cause, are you?'

Smiling, Runty shook his head. 'Haven't quite reached that point yet. But the conversation did stir a few thoughts. I may be just a rough old lag like you, Carey, but I told Delaney I've got my own sense of right and wrong, regardless of what lawgivers decide. So where's it come from then, he asks me. Not from any court or church, says I, but from my parents. Good people, they were.'

Carey raised a languid eyebrow. 'Not good enough to keep you on the straight and narrow, eh?'

'Both dead for many a long year. Can't blame them for my mistakes.'

Even his feigned mistakes. Runty tried to imagine what his mother and father would say about the situation he was now in if they knew: a police officer disguised as a convict, on his way to a country almost as distant from his Staffordshire origins as a man could ever go.

# 18

# Tunstall,
# July 1841 to September 1842

When Runty was still Tommy, he had spent much of his boyhood in man-made clouds. Smelly, low-hanging clouds, thick with coaldust, that loitered in the valleys and drifted slowly over the hill slopes. Shawls of smoke wrapped themselves around the red-brown shoulders of the squat brick chimneys and bottle-shaped kilns. Reeky wisps made their way into noses and throats so that everyone continually coughed, hoicked and spat. Nobody who lived in the Potteries took breathing for granted.

From the age of ten, Tommy would make his way before dawn every morning except Sundays through the dark uneven alleyways. The noisome clouds were moist, their wetness left grimy streaks on his clothes, and it felt as if the damp had seeped into his aching bones. As soon as he arrived at the factory he had to stack kindling in the big stove, coax a flame from it with the tinder, and then choose the right moment for shovelling lumps from the coal-bin to feed the hunger of the quickening fire. Within an hour the cramped shelf-lined room they called the drying-stove was almost unbearably hot, the iron stovepipe in the middle of it glowing red. Tommy's face was a matching blaze as he sprinted to and fro, anxiously dodging the other mould-runners. Runnels of sweat dripped into his eyes, down his back, around his armpits.

Hour after hour he was at the beck and call of his master, Big John Turpin, gruffest and most impatient of the muffin-makers, who on the boy's first day had tersely explained the whole process to him.

'This set of plates over ere, see?' Turpin growled. 'Just a small portion from yesterday's work. We ave to produce piles and piles of em every day. Now, as to ow I make a muffin – that's our word for a plate – ow I make it is like this, look: I spin the plaster mould on the disc ere with one and, then I press clay into it with t'other. This is where you come in, boy, now that you're to be my mould-runner. I need you to carry the plaster casts, quick as lightning, from my bench to the drying-stove down along there, so the soft clay can bake. You place the moulds on the shelves, leaning em against the walls to let eat come nice and even on their surfaces. You need to be nimble on the stepladder, and don't let t'other runners hold you back. And b'God, you'd better be swift and bloody careful at the same time. If you drop a mould I'll thrash you, I will!

'Now listen well. When they're alf-dry, that's usually after about twenty minutes, you bring em back to me, fleet-foot, mind you, and I smooth the surface of the plate and shape its foot-ring, y'see, for it to stand on later. And then you urry back with em, one at a time, to the stove room for more drying before the mould gets shelled off. And last, you gather the plates into buckets, a couple of dozen in each bucket, and fetch em ere, and elp me to fettle em, that's when we use a knife to scrape off the casting seams and clean the ridges.

'And tween times there won't be any sitting around. You can wedge clay for me, to make it pliable. I'll be showing you ow. That's real work, that is. Takes muscle to do it right. It'll make a man of you, if it doesn't kill you first.' Turpin's whinnying laugh was lined with horsey yellow-brown teeth.

∞

Sundays had always been different from the rest of the week. The Rowe family spent them quietly at home except for attending worship services at the Wesleyan chapel. The hours moved sluggishly. Tommy's mother often used to while away the time by telling him stories about the just and the unjust, about how Robin Hood or Dick Whittington or King Arthur surmounted misfortune and set things to rights.

One cold drizzling Sunday afternoon when he was nearly nine years old, Tommy was in a sulk. Cuffed and angrily rebuked by his father for cracking a windowpane through careless play with a large taw, he lay on his bed and scowled at the ceiling. There was a knock at their cottage door, and he heard his mother greet his young cousin.

'Jimmy, lad! This is a surprise. Come in and warm yourself at the inglenook. You look clemmed. What brings you all this way here in such weather?'

'A message from Mum, Aunt Margery. She says to tell you her eyes are much worse and she can't see well to do the stitching now, so she's sorry but she won't be able to finish that big blanket she promised to knit for you.'

'Ah, bless her – she shouldn't be worriting about that when she's proper poorly. Let me get you a bowl of broth before you set out on the road back to your village.' As she drew the visitor in from the doorway, she called: 'Tommy! Come and see cousin Jim, walked here on his own.'

There was no response.

'Tommy! Did you hear me, Tommy? I'm getting young Jim some broth. Want a bowl yourself?'

Silence.

Mrs Rowe went to find her son. 'What's this, then? You've got a face like a smacked arse. Come and greet your cousin Jimmy.'

'Don't want to.'

'Why on earth not?'

'Don't feel like it.'

'This is no time to lozzock around and be peevish.'

Tommy turned his face away, pouting, and would not budge.

'It's your cousin! Your friend! He's walked miles in bleak weather to bring a message to us, and the least you can do is talk with him while he warms up.'

'Don't want to talk to nobody.' He knew there was no point to his petulant defiance, no good reason to snub Jimmy, but now that he'd begun to act pig-headed he felt stubbornly that he had to keep it up.

'You should be ashamed.'

He heard the murmur of her apologetic words to Jimmy, and then the sound of the closing door as his cousin left to walk the long wet road back home. An hour later his father returned from a neighbour's house, was told about the obstinate rudeness, and summoned his son.

'Your hangdog face speaks plain enough, Tommy. You know you've done wrong, don't you?'

The boy nodded.

'Look at me and say it.'

The boy raised his head slowly. He'd never felt more like a dwarf. As his father's brown eyes stared down into his own blue eyes, Tommy mumbled, 'I've done wrong, Dad.'

'Why wouldn't you greet Jimmy?'

'I don't know.'

'Hasn't he always been friendly to you?'

'Yes.'

'So it was just meaningless spite, because you were in a bad mood?'

'Yes.'

'You disappoint me, Tommy. Now you think I'm going to thrash you, but I'll not do that. It's enough for you to punish yourself by never forgetting − I'm sure you won't − your foolish unkindness towards Jimmy, and always ruing it. Imagine what his feelings were as he trudged back to his home in the rain, knowing that you'd refused to greet him. For no good reason! That lad used to look up to you, but in the future he won't. You let him down, son. And let yourself down. And disgraced your family. To reject someone who deserves your loyalty − that's a serious crime in the eyes of God and man. D'you understand that?'

Yes, he understood. His tears flowed.

'Never forget it,' said his father grimly.

∞

It was a relief to have been castigated. To have had a precept laid down so clearly. To be reminded that his father was an authoritative custodian of the rules of right behaviour.

Tommy was in awe of his father and proud of his accomplishments. Everyone knew that only brave and skilful men could be leggers in the Harecastle Tunnel, and nobody could leg a barge through that long dark tunnel faster than Hector Rowe, whose speed earned him extra bread and cheese each time, even though the effort would often leave him red-faced and gasping. It was a low and narrow passage – no room for a towpath – and the length of it was a wonder: nearly three thousand yards to link the waterways between Kidsgrove and Tunstall, taking raw materials to the Potteries and bringing back the finished ware. Their backs resting on planks of wood, the leggers had to lie on top of the boat so that they could propel it along by pushing at the roof and sides of the tunnel with their feet.

Just before Tommy's tenth birthday a barge his father was legging stopped in the tunnel and emerged only when the boat travelling behind it managed to nudge it along to the exit. Hector's lifeless body lay there as if on a moving bier. His heart had given out, the doctor said.

Almost the only thing Tommy would remember in later years about the funeral was how the minister dwelt on a biblical text familiar to the townsfolk – 'But now, O Lord, Thou art our Father; we are the clay, and Thou our potter; and we all are the work of Thy hand' – and how, clutching the pulpit and licking the edges of his bushy moustache, he laboriously developed this image.

'Wet clay can be crafted with ingenuity,' he said, 'pressed this way and that, but it's nothing without a flame to fix it firmly into a durable shape. So in times of sorrow, when we feel the fierce heat of life's afflictions, it may be consoling to imagine that God has placed us in a drying-stove or kiln, to make us sturdier vessels.' To Tommy the thought of being baked hard carried no comfort at all.

A few weeks after the funeral, both he and his mother found work at the potbank. While Tommy learnt the arduous routine of a mould-runner, Margery Rowe was employed to hand-paint fine china. Her pay was little more than his: eleven shillings and eleven pence for a fifty-three-hour week, added to his eleven shillings and twopence, was barely enough to make ends meet. But Tommy knew there was no choice. Unless they could eke out a living on those wages, they would have to face the shame of the workhouse at Chell.

In the evenings the two of them would sit exhausted by the fire, talking quietly until sleep beckoned. Their small home seemed a refuge from disorder. Outside in the rowdy streets there were coarse women smoking cutty pipes and men yelling drunkenly.

Repetition of her stories soothed him. 'Tell me again about the place you came from,' he asked his mother. 'And how you met my dad.'

She put down her knitting. 'You've heard talk of Tameside. That's the district where I grew up. Near Manchester, it is. Our little town was called Dukinfield. We lived in Dewsnap Lane, just along from a hatting factory – my father worked there – but a lot of folk worked in the mills. Some of them had a hard time of it and there were often troubles in the town, especially after the coming of the power looms. I remember weavers' riots when I was a girl, and the cotton workers' strike later. How did I meet Hector? Well, he'd brought a barge along the Trent and Mersey cut, and after unloading a cargo of pots canal-side he thought he'd look around our district for a while, just curious at first, hadn't been away from the Potteries before, you see. So he got some navvying work on the final stage of the Macclesfield canal, and found lodging in Dukinfield, and then he chanced to see me one day as I was coming out of a shop in Town Lane, and we got talking. Hector was a fine-looking young man, a bit shy at first. Anyway, we took a fancy to each other. He was in our town for a few weeks and we met up as often as we could. It didn't take him long to put the question to my dad, and I was already keen to leave home anyway, so everything happened quickly.'

'Why were you already keen to leave home?'

'Oh, one thing and another, Tommy. I had a bit of a falling out with my sister Rebecca – I won't go into the whys and wherefores – and she was set to marry a local fellow, a weaver, Will French. Very plausible, he was, quite a charmer. But not a good man.' Margery fell silent and stared into the fire.

'Mum?'

With a slight grimace she shook her head as if to rid it of something unpleasant.

'I lost contact with my family after I came here,' she said.

'Why?'

'None of them could read or write. I didn't learn any letters myself until Hector taught me. And we were all too busy for visits.'

∞

Having no siblings, and hankering after companionship, Tommy was keen to ingratiate himself with other boys. As he left the factory one evening to walk homeward, weary and hungry, two of his fellow mould-runners came up beside him – Harry Woodcock and Judder Buttle. They'd seldom spoken to him before, but seemed friendly now. 'Ay up, surry!' Buttle greeted him. 'How'd ya like a juicy sweet apple?'

He nodded, feeling the saliva rise from under his tongue. He'd had nothing but a couple of oatcakes since breakfast.

'Come along here with us,' said Woodcock, beckoning. 'Around this corner.'

Tommy followed them, and Woodcock pointed to the street cart of Hibbins the toothless old coster. 'Hungry? Take one of Hibbins's russets, then.'

'Can't. Got no money to buy it.'

'Then don't pay,' said Buttle. 'We'll start talking to Hibbins, and while he's distracted you can just grab an apple. He's so slow-witted he won't notice.'

'But I don't want to steal from him.'

'Ah – don't be a little girl,' hissed Buttle contemptuously. 'If you're too feeble and fearful to pilfer an apple, we don't want you as one of our friends.'

Goaded, Tommy went with them to the cart. While they kept old Hibbins talking, he snatched a russet. But at once, to his horror, they rounded on him and loudly denounced him.

'Thief!' shouted Judder Buttle, pointing at Tommy. 'Look! He's taken one of your apples, Mr Hibbins!'

Tommy turned and ran, flinging the apple on the ground. The pair of false friends pursued him with spiteful merriment as he sprinted home and scurried through his doorway.

They stood outside, shouting raucously, until Margery Rowe emerged to rebuke them.

'Shame on you for hounding him like curs! Get away from here!' Heads down, hands in pockets, they shuffled off along the street.

'They caught me in a snare,' Tommy told her tearfully as he confessed his misdemeanour. 'They pretended to be my friends.'

'Let's have no more self-pity. What do you think your father would have said to you about this incident? What would he want you to learn from it?'

He wiped his puffy eyes. 'Not to be so trusting.'

'And?'

'Not to be treacherous, the way they were towards me.'

'And?'

He thought for a moment. 'Dunno what else.'

'To make amends, my lad. Those boys wronged you, but you wronged the poor old coster. So take this' – she held out a coin – 'and give it to Mr Hibbins with an apology, and beg his pardon. Go to him right now.'

In later years, thinking about what shaped his sense of justice and led him eventually into the Metropolitan Police Force, he would often recall her words about the stolen apple, along with his father's reprimand over the snubbing of his cousin.

# 19

# Fremantle,
# January to February 1868

The *Hougoumont* dropped anchor half a mile from shore. As they crowded against the deck rail and stared across the pale-green coastal waters, shielding their eyes against the glare, they could see plainly a large walled structure, chalk-coloured, that spread along a ridge above the town.

'That's your new home up there,' said one of the warders, pointing. 'Its official name is the Convict Establishment. Local people call it the limestone lodge.'

Barges came alongside to take the convicts to a small jetty. From there they marched in single file through the sandy streets of Fremantle up to the long white fortified gaol building. Two pentagonal towers framed its gateway, jutting out from the high wall of limestone blocks. Set into the classical pediment that joined the towers was a large black-faced clock with gilt roman numerals. Its chime, announcing noon, resounded as they approached.

Once inside, the men were mustered in the quadrangle and informed about prison rules and various practical matters before being taken off to their allocated cells. Then, as he'd anticipated, Runty was called aside and discreetly escorted to the office of Superintendent Lefroy. Despite his unprepossessing appearance – big ears, baggy eyes, scruffy beard – Lefroy had an authoritative and self-assured manner. Over cigars, he asked about the voyage.

'Those Fenians you were watching – any trouble from them?'

'None at all, sir. I suppose you could regard a few of their songs as mildly provocative, but really there was no warrant for alarm.'

'Which of them do you reckon we should keep a weather eye on here? Who's the most likely to stir things up?'

'Well, there's a young fellow called O'Reilly stands out – John O'Reilly. He's got a furnace in his heart, and honey on his tongue. They all look to him and want to know what he thinks. Has the makings of a natural leader, that one. But it's only fair to say he caused no ructions on the ship. None that I could see.'

Lefroy pondered this information for a moment. 'Here's how we'll deal with Firebrand O'Reilly. It'll be a simple matter to have him assigned to duties in the prison library for a good part of each day. The Roman chaplain, Father Lynch, can supervise him there. That'll curb O'Reilly's opportunities for any rabble-rousing he may have in mind. Now, about your own situation: I want you to retain your guise of a convict for a while yet, Rowe, so I'll arrange for you to work in the library too. That way you can continue to observe O'Reilly, get to know him, find out whether he's planning anything.'

Dismayed, Runty shook his head. 'But that's not what I was told to expect,' he said. 'Sir Richard's instructions were that I should send him a report when the ship reached Fremantle, and then join the police ranks here.'

'The situation isn't quite as simple as the London chief commissioner seems to have imagined,' said Lefroy firmly, stroking his whiskers. 'The fact is, Rowe, the role you've played during the voyage – valuable though it may have been – presents us now with a difficulty. This new lot of prisoners hasn't settled into the routine here yet. They've had a fairly easy time of it on the ship. Adjusting to the discipline we impose, and to the heat and the flies and the rest of it, is likely to make them tetchy enough. If they find out that someone who's been travelling among them is actually a government spy, we could have trouble on our hands. So it's necessary to keep up the pretence.'

'For how long?'

'Oh, a few months should suffice. Then we'll quietly transfer you to somewhere up the country.'

'With all due respect, sir, that's not what was agreed when I accepted the commission.'

'It's for your own good, Rowe, as much as for the sake of peace in the prison.'

'So I'm to languish in a cell, like a criminal?'

'No alternative, I'm sorry to say. It's only for a limited period, of course.'

'But won't it raise suspicion anyway, if I'm given a soft job in the library?'

'I've thought of that. In addition to a few pleasant hours in the library each day, we'll put you on night-cart duties. That'll show you're not being favoured.'

Runty's protests were unavailing and he was set to work at once. As his shit-shovelling task became known among the lags, a few of them – those he'd befriended on the ship, like Slack and Hampshire and Carey – muttered casual words of condolence, while others laughed stridently and made a fastidious pantomime of holding their noses whenever they were near him. He kept quiet about the library work.

∞

Day after day the air was scorching. He'd never imagined that summer heat could be so fierce. Twice a week the convicts were sent in small groups to South Bay so that they could bathe in seawater. Their loose clothing – jacket and trousers of duck – was cool enough inside the gaol but they sweltered in it after a few minutes' walking in the full sun. White sand and limestone buildings reflected the glare. By the time they returned from the beach the sun had reddened their stinging skin.

'This bathing only exposes us to more heat,' they grumbled.

'It's to keep you clean, not cool. To wash the sweat and dirt and lice away.'

Despite the inescapable sun, Runty was glad of this ritual bathing. To him the seashore was still a strange place. Until the day he'd boarded the *Hougoumont* his life had been entirely landlocked. Now the ocean's edge was bringing simple sensual pleasures that caught him by surprise. The tickle of waves, flecked with foam and grit, as they curled against his flesh. The sight of them too, flung down like a toss of dissolving dice, and the long exhalation as they hissed across the sand.

The water enlivened everyone. Each time the men waded into the tumbling surf they became boys again for a while, as if the water could rinse off more than layers of grime. Grinning at each other, they smacked the surface with playful fists and a few of them broke into snatches of song.

But when they returned to the limestone lodge, nobody remained lighthearted for long. For most prisoners the daily routine of heavy labour was made more onerous by the merciless weather. Many had to spend long hours toiling in the open, scarcely protected from the sun. A gang known as the strong party went out daily to Cantonment Hill to quarry blocks of stone, and some groups were carted further afield to work on roads, bridges and public buildings such as the Perth Town Hall.

Each morning as he began his quiet routine of light work in the prison library, hearing the clink of leg-irons, Runty would look out the narrow window to see a line of chaingang members shuffle through the gatehouse towards their allotted labours.

'Have you felt the weight of those irons?' O'Reilly asked him angrily on the first day they were sorting books together. 'Forty pounds or more riveted to your body – it's bloody degrading. You've seen what bruises and calluses and sores they cause?'

Runty nodded, and O'Reilly took this as sufficient encouragement to continue: 'It's a cruel place, fiendishly cruel!'

'Oh, I've seen worse prisons back where we came from,' said Lynch, the chaplain responsible for the library.

'Besides,' Runty interjected, 'not everything's bad here.'

'Tell me what's good.' There was a pugnacious edge to O'Reilly's question, and the eyes, deep-set beneath his thick dark brows, stared out intently. His gaze was an auger, drilling into Runty's mind.

'Well, you can't complain about the food, can you? Better than I often had as a boy. Plenty of bread and treacle with sugared tea for breakfast and supper. Fair helpings of meat and potatoes for dinner. Soup a couple of times a week. Lime juice, vinegar, vegetables. No one goes hungry.'

'But surely you don't think it's out of the goodness of their hearts? Far from it. They feed us up so they can work us harder, that's what it is. Why have we been transported here, eh? I'll tell you: it's merely to rectify the colony's lack of a drudging class. They mean to build a comfortable outpost of England for themselves by the sweat of *our* brows, not theirs. Providing us with necessary nourishment is a piddling price to pay for exploited labour.'

Conversations of that kind were frequent, with O'Reilly relishing any opportunity to wield his rhetoric provocatively. But in Runty's hearing he said nothing that could be construed as downright bellicose. Mischievous derision was his usual mode. When he wasn't waxing oratorical, O'Reilly liked to sing, and since arriving in Fremantle he'd expanded his repertoire with topical ditties picked up from other prisoners. One of their favourite targets was the acting comptroller-general of convicts, appointed in a blatant act of nepotism by his father, the unpopular Governor Hampton.

*The Governor's son has got the pip,*
*The Governor's got the measles,*
*For Moondyne Joe has given em the slip:*
*Pop goes the weasel.*

'Enough of that, young man,' remonstrated Father Lynch half-heartedly. 'It's not for the likes of you to make fun of the Governor and his family. Or to turn that reprobate Joe Bolitho into a hero.'

'Anyone who can escape from custody repeatedly, and who's been on the run for a year this time, deserves my admiration,' said O'Reilly. 'No wonder Moondyne Joe's exploits are on everyone's lips. We'd all like to cock a snook at the authorities as nicely as he has.'

'I hope you're not entertaining foolish thoughts of escape yourself,' the priest cautioned him. 'It'd only bring more retribution on your reckless head, because you'd surely be caught if you didn't perish. That fellow Moondyne Joe is probably dead. There's nowhere to go from here. Inland it's all barren desert, and to the west there's the menace of that vast ocean. Nature walls you in on every side.'

'Don't worry about me, Father,' said O'Reilly. 'I'll be a model prisoner. Exemplary, that's me. A thoroughly reformed character.' He winked broadly at Runty, who would recall this conversation when O'Reilly later became notorious, the talk of the town.

∞

Violence, though seldom erupting dangerously, was never far below the surface of prison life. Runty well understood how important it was for him to be circumspect, and felt glad he could spend part of each day in the library, out of harm's way.

The fact that the prison did have a library, albeit a small one, showed considerable optimism of the part of the administrators. For the many convicts who were illiterate, or nearly so, the presence of Bible and prayerbook in every cell conferred no practical benefit, and the notion of looking beyond those ubiquitous items to the shelves of a library never crossed their minds. For the few who were equipped to find some solace in reading, the library offered no great variety. Runty soon became familiar with its holdings, which included numerous tomes of sermons and pious essays, weighty historical works such as Gibbon's *Decline and Fall of the Roman Empire* and Macaulay's *History of England*, a handful of such edifying manuals as Smiles's *Self-Help*, and some anthologies of poetry, along with novels by Scott, Dickens and other writers deemed morally safe.

At certain times of the week, prisoners were permitted to come to the library – by arrangement and under guard – to select reading matter to take back to their cells. Most of the Fenians often availed themselves of this opportunity, but there were few other frequent visitors. One person who did turn up there regularly was an unpopular shifty-eyed fellow called Robert Green. Runty knew two things about Green: that he declared himself eager to read and re-read all the novels of Charles Dickens, and that he was shunned by most of the other inmates because of his reputation as a sodomite – not the only one among them, but the most impudent. On the voyage to Fremantle he'd been flogged for trying to force himself on one of the younger prisoners. Since then there had been a few incidents where a group surrounded Green in the prison yard and treated him with rough contempt.

'That filthy bugger seems to regard our library as a refuge,' said O'Reilly to Runty one day as they watched the pariah scanning the shelves. 'While he's in here he's not going to be kicked and cursed and spat on and shoved around.'

'Reading can be a sort of refuge too, I suppose,' Runty remarked. 'I'd say Green uses books to take his mind off this place for a while. It makes good sense. I ought to do more reading myself.'

O'Reilly curled his lip. 'Reading books won't make Green and other mandrakes less repulsive.'

'There are worse vices than his.'

'It's against nature, what he does. Disgusting to God and man. He deserves every thrashing he gets.'

Runty shrugged and made no further response, but the exchange left him pondering. What was it that made most of these men, inured as they were to all kinds of depravity, treat so ferociously anyone who displayed this particular predilection? Was it like a kind of exorcism? Did they need to dispel from their midst any lurking impulse of lust for each other's bodies? Punish the loathsome thought?

A couple of weeks later, as they were all returning to their cells from a chapel service, Sam Slack sidled up to Runty and whispered: 'D'you know that someone's nobbled Green properly this time?'

'He's been hurt bad?'

'Killed. In his cell's what I heard – so musta been a warder done it, or turned a blind eye.'

Runty soon learnt the details from Father Lynch in the library. Someone had bashed Green over the head and then suffocated him, tearing pages from Dickens's *Bleak House* and stuffing them into the man's throat and nostrils until he stopped breathing. On the swollen protruding tongue, his assailant had placed a large dead cockroach.

# 20

# Fremantle,
# January to February 1869

A role that matched his expectations: not until a full year after his arrival in Fremantle was Runty entrusted with that. By then it was some four months since Police Superintendent Gustavus Hare had intervened to release him from his irksome duties at the prison and from the pretence of incarceration there.

'Glad to have you working with us out in the open now,' Hare had said, shaking his hand vigorously. 'And no doubt you'll be glad to put your work for the Convict Establishment behind you. We're hard-pressed and short-handed, so between now and Christmas we'll be calling on you to provide backup for several of our one-man stations in the districts out beyond the town. Not easy work, but it'll give you a fair idea of the rougher side of life around the colony. If you keep your wits about you there's a good chance you'll still be in one piece come the new year, and then we can bring you back to Perth.'

So Runty had moved around from one country location to another as an all-purpose assistant constable. In Northam, in

Williams, in Champion Bay, for a few weeks in each place, he did what he could to relieve pressure on the incumbent officers by undertaking miscellaneous tasks, some difficult, some dull: dampening tensions between settlers and blacks about disputes over missing stock, dealing with routine episodes of assault and drunkenness, covering general duties for a constable injured in a fall from a horse, responding to diverse complaints from local residents, helping to repair a shed attached to a lock-up after it was damaged by fire. Much of the time he felt listless, without quite knowing why. Perhaps it was partly because of the savourless food. Perhaps it was the unsheltering landscape, too – drab and arid, so unlike anything he'd known in England. Perhaps it was also that nobody smiled at him or seemed to take any pleasure from their lives in the bush. Probably, more than anything else, it was an inner isolation that weakened his morale: Runty's wife and young children would not be emigrating until he'd gained a sufficiently settled position to allow him to lease a cottage that could become the family home. He yearned for their company.

His spirits lifted when a letter came from Gustavus Hare early in January asking him to report without delay to the police headquarters in Fremantle 'in order to be assigned to an important role' – which was explained as soon as he arrived.

'It's no secret,' said Superintendent Hare, combing white cloud-like whiskers with his fingertips, 'that the Duke of Edinburgh will very soon be making his first visit to this colony. You've seen the newspaper reports?'

'I have indeed, sir.'

'So you're aware that the precise time of his arrival remains uncertain, though it's likely to be just before the end of the month. A few official ceremonial events can be expected, of course. The Acting Governor will receive the Duke at Government House, and a ball's planned for the banqueting room there. That sort of thing. But the advice we've had is that this is to be a short informal sojourn. The Duke would like to mix socially with a number of prominent citizens. He's keen, we're told, to be shown around some of the public buildings in Fremantle and Perth. There's talk of arranging a cricket match for him to watch. And unless the weather is unpleasant, there may be an excursion into the hills, perhaps as far as York, where his party can look over a pastoral property or two. Anyway, it may prove difficult to keep everything orderly. His ship, you know, will be the biggest ever seen here, so there'll be hundreds of sailors disembarking. The streets will be crowded and some of the local people are probably going to get overexcited. Now, I suppose you can guess why I'm discussing this with you?'

'Presumably, sir, the police will be responsible for safe-guarding His Highness, and you'd like me to assist with some precautions.'

'Exactly, Rowe, exactly. After what happened to him in Sydney last year —'

'The assassination attempt.'

'Yes — and because it was a mad Irishman who shot him, and there are more than sixty treasonous Fenians in custody here in Fremantle, we must be fully alert to the dangers. Prisoners do sometimes escape – that cunning rascal Moondyne Joe is still on the loose after nearly a couple of years, some others have been getting away lately, so people are anxious. Imagine the consequences of a big breakout while Prince Alfred is with us!'

'So you'd like me to...?'

'Just keep a lookout without being noticed, and report at once directly to me if you learn of anything suspicious. Unobtrusive surveillance, the kind of work you've done before. There'll be a formal escort, of course, plenty of mounted police in attendance from the moment he disembarks from the *Galatea*, but I want you to operate behind the scenes before he arrives and throughout the visit. Civilian clothes. Hang about and watch and listen. Get in thick with warders at the gaol and try to find out discreetly whether those Irish prisoners have anything brewing.'

∞

After more than a week of listening at dusty corners and skulking in shadows, Runty uncovered no information, no plot, nor even any idle talk of trouble. He'd quietly followed the official party wherever it went, including the tiresome expedition to York. He'd stood inconspicuously in the background as the royal visitor mingled with the Perth citizenry and charmed them. The Duke came and went without serious incident. The sole mishap was a slight one, swiftly transformed from a potential embarrassment into a display of cheerful allegiance when the steam launch carrying the official party down the Swan from Perth at the end of the visit became grounded on a Fremantle sandbank – whereupon a score of convicts from a road gang nearby plunged into the river and soon succeeded in freeing the vessel. Perhaps a genuinely patriotic impulse devoid of conscious irony, thought Runty, but even so they were shrewd in seizing the opportunity; each man immediately received a twelve-month remission of his sentence.

When the *Galatea* sailed away, Hare expressed great relief that nothing untoward had happened, but Runty felt vaguely disappointed. Afterwards he could remember little from those watchful wary days except the relentless heat, the sweat soaking his felt hat, the flies tickling his sticky face.

'Highness': it was a peculiar appellation, Runty thought, for any human creature. That honorific phrase 'His Royal Highness' had titillated the colony before the Prince's arrival, but in person he didn't seem remarkably elevated. Just a pleasant young man with hesitant side-whiskers and a shiny uniform. While the colonists were duly respectful, and expressed – doubtless sincerely – the requisite sentiments of loyalty, Runty sensed that out here in Australia what a man accomplished in his own right mattered more than his lineage. Comments during the visit suggested that for some local people the most impressive thing about this royal visitor was his reputation as a competent naval captain. In Runty's hearing, one wag had said that Perth already had its own Prince Alfred in the town's most notable self-made businessman, 'Alfred De Leech – the potentate of St George's Terrace'.

And then, barely a fortnight after the royal frigate *Galatea* left Fremantle bound for Adelaide, the town was suddenly abuzz with news of Fenian audacity. Being based at Fremantle, Runty heard what had happened before it became general knowledge. Sub-Inspector Timperley, the hapless officer in charge of the Bunbury district, sent a dispatch rider to the Fremantle station, where Sergeant Furlong let out a furious shout when he received the message.

'God help us! Look at this, Constable!' Furlong flung the letter across his desk, and Runty skimmed through it.

regret to advise that Prisoner 9843 John Boyle O'Reilly has bolted from a road party here…whole thing appears to have been cleverly planned…group of Fenians who arrived yesterday from Fremantle to work on road construction made trouble from the start…refusing to be split into separate parties…I had to call on all district police to take them to the lockup cells…ensuing rumpus…no doubt a deliberate distraction…O'Reilly made a swift escape… acknowledge my responsibility…search continues…keep you informed…

In a further message the next day, Timperley reported that he had boarded two Yankee whalers anchored off Bunbury and offered a five-pound reward for any information about O'Reilly, though with little hope of assistance from that quarter. Their captains seemed disinclined to cooperate. Another whaler had sailed the day before, but O'Reilly could not have reached it in time because a warder had spoken with him a considerable distance from the port at about 10.30 the previous evening. It was suspected the rogue might still be hiding somewhere in the sandhills around Bunbury, said Timperley, and police were checking that possibility. But it was also likely that plenty of local sympathisers would readily shelter an Irish fugitive until an opportunity arose to get him away on a ship.

It was to be a full seven months before the police discovered what had happened to O'Reilly, and more than seven years before Runty found himself at the centre of a famous sequel to that Fenian's escape.

But just a week after O'Reilly absconded, a long-lost bolter returned to public attention. Police in the Swan Valley seized a thoroughly inebriated Moondyne Joe in the cellar of Houghton's Vineyard. Runty chuckled at the news; an alcoholic slumber was as near to liberty as some lags would ever get.

∞

'You could look at this place differently, Constable,' said Philip Furlong, 'and to be frank I suggest you should. Instead of whingeing so much about the heat and the flies and the sand, why not see our little colony as full of opportunity? A man can do some thinking here. Clear skies, clear head. Natural to be homesick, especially when you're still waiting for your family to come and join you, but don't forget what a miserable existence most people have in London. Nearly always cold and dirty. Thick with clutter. Those crowded streets – remember the smell?'

Nodding, Runty poured more tea into their mugs and reached for another oatmeal biscuit. Only midmorning, and already their office was uncomfortably hot.

'Back there, everyone's stuck for life in the station they're born into,' Furlong went on. 'All that grinding poverty – no escape from it for those who stay in England. My brother and sister are still in Southwark, where I grew up, and it's a kind of hell. What about you, Rowe? I know you were in the Metropolitan Police Force but you don't sound like a Londoner.'

'I come from the Potteries,' Runty told him. 'It was a hard life there, too, and I wouldn't want to go back. So I admit you're right – out here in the colony we've got every chance of shaping a better life for ourselves.'

'The future's as big as the horizon. With a bit of luck and effort, a reformed lag can set himself up comfortably and do business with free settlers. Women who were factory drudges can leave that wretchedness behind and turn themselves into ladies. Almost anything's possible here if you put your mind to it.'

It was true enough, Runty thought. Fremantle, Perth and all the rudimentary settlements in the vast hinterland – these little places with their unclouded skies were waiting to be made into whatever people might want them to become.

# Amelia

# 21

# Fremantle, June 1869

Although pride was supposedly a dangerous emotion, surely on an occasion like this there could be no harm in feeling so proud of her husband's humility? The size of the crowd that had come to listen testified to his standing in the community, yet he spoke in such an unassuming way that she was confident no one would think him too pleased with himself. Sitting at the back of the Congregational Chapel, she saw that almost every pew was full. Sunday worship services seldom attracted such a large attendance as this. Joseph Johnston's idea of holding a series of public lectures here on Wednesday evenings, promoted through the newspapers and the Fremantle Workingmen's Association, had been drawing appreciative audiences, but this evening's was the best-attended lecture so far.

Reverend Johnston himself had introduced the speaker effusively. 'Ladies and gentlemen,' he said, 'we are gathered together to hear about "Success" – a topic of great importance to our flourishing colony, and one on which nobody amongst us could speak with more authority than our lecturer this evening, Mr De Leech. In less than two decades since arriving here in difficult circumstances, he has established himself as a prosperous and highly esteemed exponent of commercial enterprise. Most people present will be well aware that, among other achievements, Mr De Leech has developed a thriving drapery and grocery business in St George's Terrace; he has bought and sold land in the Avon district and elsewhere, conducting some of these transactions in association with prominent free settlers such as Mr Shenton; for several years he operated a daily cart service for passengers to Guildford, replacing it recently with an omnibus coach; and he continues to handle government contracts for mail between Perth and Fremantle...'

The minister's laudatory recital of her husband's deeds had continued at some length, but what she found gratifying was not so much this extensive reminder of all that he had done; rather, it was the modest and contrite spirit with which Alfred himself then addressed the audience. Any success he may have been fortunate enough to gain was, he said, inseparable from his past failures. With a candour that brought tears to her eyes and seemed to touch the hearts of others around her, he spoke of how his foolish youthful errors had brought disgrace upon his family, and how he was transported in 1850 on the second ship to carry convicts to Fremantle, at a time when there were only some six thousand souls in the whole colony, a quarter of the present population. His deep remorse, he explained, led him to alter his name when he arrived here, from Alfred D. Letch to Alfred De Leech, so that the stigma of criminality would be less likely to taint his relatives by association. He went on to recount that, after receiving his ticket of leave two years later, he was initially employed by a harness-maker, just as he had been in Felsted ten years before when first leaving the family home – a salutary reminder, he said, that through his own stupidity he had wasted a decade of his life. He presented himself as a penitent sinner who had done his utmost to earn redemption through diligent effort. He expressed deep gratitude to those many citizens who had allowed and indeed assisted him to climb gradually into a respectable position in society; to his parents and siblings for their forgiveness, particularly to his late father who had left him an inheritance through which he was able to finance the early development of his business; and to his wife, Amelia, for her unflagging support.

'It was a fine generous speech for the occasion, right enough,' she told him as they climbed into their trap for the homeward journey. 'I'm sure everyone admired the fact that you spoke so frankly. But you were perhaps a little too hard on yourself. You said more about your youthful misdemeanour than about...'

'It was no mere misdemeanour, Amelia. I committed a serious felony, that's the simple shameful truth – and more than that, I betrayed the trust placed in me and jeopardised my family's good name.'

'But since then you've worked so hard and so honestly! Your family must be very gratified to know that.'

'My mother's letters said kind things, yes. I'm glad she lived long enough to know my fortunes took an upward turn. And my brothers continue to write in encouraging terms, especially George, the dear fellow. But there's sadness in the fact that my father passed away before I'd made my mark. Distressing to think that if it wasn't for his untimely death I might never have become successful. The inheritance came to hand soon after I got my ticket of leave – that's how I was able to set up my livery stables. And then it was only because of income from the stables, you see, that I could open the shop in St George's Terrace a couple of years later, and other things grew from that.'

Alfred fell silent. As their trap jolted along he sat with his hands together in his lap, fingers meshed and thumbs spinning around each other. From time to time he reversed the direction of the spinning. She was familiar with these despondent moods of his, when he convinced himself that his good fortune was undeserved.

'If you're drawing up a ledger in your mind again,' she said quietly, 'don't forget all the decent things you've done, m'dear. The dozens of ticket-of-leave men you've employed over the years as labourers and shopmen and bookkeepers. Carpenters, servants. You've handed them an opportunity to make amends, to make something of themselves, just as you've done. Then there's all the support, steadfast support, that you've given to the church for a long while now. And what you've contributed to the political life of the colony – through those petitions, for example.'

He looked down at his spinning thumbs but said nothing.

'Think of all you've done for me, too,' she added. 'Coming to this country with almost nothing in my purse, and in my mind no more than a vague hope of enough work to keep myself clothed and fed…Little knowledge or skill. But because you hired me, and soon became pleased with my services…well – one thing led to another, didn't it? Marriage within a year, making me the happiest woman in the whole town, I'm sure. You've taught me how to be more of a lady, to speak properly – most of the time! – and dress nicely and be, I hope, a credit to you. And we have our darling children. So you mustn't let your thoughts dwell so gloomily on what you owe to your father. You've been a generous man, too.'

He shook his head. 'Our marriage isn't something I've provided to you,' he said. 'You can say Providence brought us together, if you like. But you give me so many things. Including that soft smile of yours – there it is now!' And he smiled briefly in response.

Arriving home, they sat together in the snug little parlour to continue their conversation.

'We've never talked much about our parents, have we, you and I?' said Alfred. You know some things about my father but not really what kind of man he was, and why he still has…has a hand on my shoulder, so to speak.'

'Tell me more.'

'Nearly all his life he was such a dominant figure – a strong head of the family, a respected voice in the local church, in our whole district…Everyone looked up to him. I've been thinking lately about the cruel irony of the way he left this world. He became so…so pathetically diminished in his final weeks that he lost the power of speech.'

Alfred stood up abruptly, went to the escritoire, and drew out an envelope from one of the small compartments.

'This is my mother's letter that brought the news of his death years ago. Let me read part of it to you:

It was a disease of the lungs and throat that carried him off, and he was a sad shadow of himself towards the last. I'll never forget what he said to me as his voice began to fade. 'If I can't speak when I'm going,' says he in a hoarse whisper,

'I'll just wave my hand to you, and then you'll know.' And so it was. In his last hours he couldn't utter a word, and he went off so gently that I'd never have known the minute of his departure if I hadn't seen his hand moving to bid me a feeble farewell.

Alfred put the letter on his lap and pressed his fingertips to his eyes. Amelia knew to say nothing at a time like this. She watched their small ginger tomcat as it padded into the room, batting a thimble around the floor with a curled paw, and then, suddenly tired of its sport, yawned and left. After several minutes Alfred raised his head and looked at her. 'Nothing you've mentioned in the past has given me a picture of your own parents. What were they like?'

She tried to stop her hands from clenching. 'I don't remember very much,' she said as calmly as she could. 'I was quite young when they passed away.'

'How young?'

'Barely ten.'

'You lost them both together?'

She nodded. 'My uncle cared for me after that.'

He persisted. 'You must be able to recall at least a few things about your mother and father. Childhood memories? It's only…What is it? – fifteen years since they died, if you were ten at the time.'

Her lips tightened involuntarily. She forced herself to take a slow breath. 'Well, I can see them both in my mind, of course, though it's like a faded picture. They made a handsome couple, I think. His hair was thin and dark; she looked pale beside him. They were good to me. I felt cherished.'

'What caused their deaths?'

Although she had been anticipating the question, the answer seemed to have stuck in her throat. There was a long pause. 'I'm sorry, but talking about the way it happened would upset me too much. I can't bear to go into it. Can we change the subject, please?'

She would not even let herself think about it.

## 22

# Perth, September 1871

She was walking back from their flower garden with the watering can when Alfred emerged from the house, waving a letter excitedly.

'It seems at last they've resolved to come,' he called out. 'I'd begun to think it would never happen, but George says here the arrangements are all in hand. The whole family will sail from the London docks at the end of next month.'

'Excellent news, my dear. I know you've been encouraging them for a long while to emigrate.'

'It's quite definite now, apparently. Their passages are paid for, they've settled with a buyer on the price for their house, and they're in the process of sorting out which possessions they should bring.'

'I wonder what made them decide to take such a big step, after all that hesitation?'

'Mainly, I suppose, it's just that times are so much harder in Essex now. With all those mouths to feed and scant income, George has been getting more worried about making ends meet. He hopes to become a partner with me in the business here.'

'Oh! Does he have a head for commerce?'

'I doubt it, frankly. Always been an unworldly fellow, George has.'

'Won't that be awkward, if he's expecting to benefit from the fruits of your labour?'

'No need to be anxious about that, Amelia. I won't rush into anything that might jeopardise what I've built up over twenty years. Let's see whether George can roll up his sleeves and work hard. There'll be plenty for him to do, plenty to learn. He'll have to earn the right to any share in the business. Who knows? He may thrive in a new environment. Perhaps it will be the making of him. Meanwhile, I'm delighted I'll be seeing him and Caroline again after so long. And meeting their five children for the first time. The youngest one is just a baby but the eldest, Mary Ann – or Polly, they call her – was born not long after I came here, so she's older than you were when you emigrated.'

Picturing her earlier self made her smile. He smiled back. Arm in arm, heads inclining towards each other, they went slowly into their house. Within a few minutes he seated himself at the piano, she stood beside him with a hand on his shoulder, and their voices blended together in the duet he had taught her soon after they wed:

*Believe me, if all those endearing young charms*
*That I gaze on so fondly today*
*Were to fade by tomorrow and fleet in my arms...*

∞

175

Ordinary household things gave her immense pleasure, a sense of fullness, as if they nourished her. There was something sustaining even in the smallest rituals, such as gathering from the front garden some carefully tended crimson china roses for the table. Although her servant days were well behind her, she still drew satisfaction from any domestic routine, no matter how simple. Making sure the larder was kept well stocked. Supervising the cook's production of jams and preserves, or the maid's polishing of cruet and tureen, salver and teapot. Rearranging crisply starched garments in a chest of drawers. Responding to the faint vibration of a kettle coming to a boil on the hob. Watching her little boys as they played hopscotch in the sand in front of the house or peg-top on the verandah.

What would they think, those folk she'd known back in Ashton, if they could see her now? Although she wished she could tell Uncle Harold how well things had turned out for her, there was no point sending him a letter; he couldn't read. A daydream came to her of writing to the only gentleman who'd ever spoken with her in those days, the mill owner Hugh Mason – perhaps he'd remember their conversation, and be impressed that she'd risen so rapidly in the world since then...With a twinge of regret she brushed the notion aside as frivolous.

In the letters she still sent now and then to Lucy Smeddles, Amelia tried to express something of her deep contentment with domestic life, but it wasn't easy to get the tone right because Lucy had been less fortunate and the contrast between their situations was awkward. Having married a plausible young horse breaker who before long was convicted as a horse thief, Lucy was stuck on a farm out beyond York in a menial job, childless and lonely. Besides, Amelia was conscious of being able to write more fluently than her friend and found it difficult now to avoid casting her thoughts in phrases that Lucy would probably see as lofty and ladylike. So their correspondence had become less frequent with the passing years.

Marriage to a man twice her age could have turned out badly for Amelia, especially a man still troubled beneath an apparently self-assured surface by his felonious past. But she'd sensed from the start his thirst for love, his parched yearning to be forgiven. She knew intuitively what had made him anxious when he, the master, asked her, a mere servant, to marry him: it was not that she might refuse, but that the material advantages of becoming a prosperous man's wife might lead her to accept while yet harbouring a secret contempt for him. She understood that his proposal expressed, more than anything else, the hope of living with someone who would show him both tolerance and honesty. Of course he wanted a companion for physical solace and procreation, but there were others who could have provided such things. She was no great beauty, with her unfashionably heavy eyebrows and jutting chin. She had limited abilities, limited experience of the world. He, being a citizen of substance, was no doubt well aware that in order to take a place at his side she would have much to learn about manners and social niceties – how to speak well, how to conduct herself with reliable poise. What she could offer, and she assumed that he'd seen this and recognised its value, was that she knew how to be simultaneously candid and forbearing.

'If we're to be wed, mind you,' she'd told him, 'I shan't hesitate to tell you when I disagree with you or dislike something you do.'

He had beamed. 'I'd expect no less,' he said. 'You'll be my forthright instructor.'

'But you'll instruct me, too. I don't want to embarrass you by sounding like a bumpkin when I open my mouth. You'll need to put me right if I slip into the common talk of a girl from the Lancashire mills.'

'You shouldn't be bashful about the way you speak. I like listening to your words, you know that. Most young women make a thin piping sound, but your voice...well, it's what first made an impression on me: the way you were singing when I came to the depot in search of a servant. And then your laughter – it crinkles like...like dappled light dancing on a swatch of satin.'

His fanciful language had amused her but she'd guessed it probably wasn't so much the particular *sound* of her laughing that appealed to him. Rather it was the simple fact that she would laugh readily but not unkindly at some of the silly things he did – laughter of a gentle sort that showed she didn't take his little failings too seriously. That seemed to be a relief, as if her tender amusement helped to free him from an earnest straining compulsion to be, above all, socially respectable. She saw how the stiffness in him, the tension, gradually faded when she showed no surprise at anything he said. Not at his confession of youthful misdeeds, not at his proposal of marriage. She would listen quietly, head tipped sideways, and then give a light laugh or one of her soft smiles and a little nod as if to say reassuringly, 'That was only to be expected. Nothing out of the ordinary.'

And now, reflecting on their eight years together, she saw it as an almost wholly comfortable marriage. They made a placid couple. He had never excited her; being with him or thinking about him aroused none of the tremulous feelings that still made her quiver when she thought of her brief conversation with Hugh Mason in Ashton. But Alfred was a decent, worthy man. *A jannock fella*, she'd have said in earlier days. He had a conscience, he worked hard and he did his utmost to please her. It would be churlish of her to want more.

The relationship wasn't a cloudless one. Amelia couldn't always hide her concern that, despite his assurances, he risked overreaching himself in his commercial ventures. Sometimes an obsession to expand the business gripped him. He mentioned grand plans to purchase a large range of vehicles – carriages, phaetons, gigs, carts and omnibuses – and hire them out, with drivers provided. 'Now that the roads around Perth are improving, there'll be more and more people who are looking for transport but can't afford to buy their own.' Although she knew nothing of the practical details, she feared hasty decisions. A desire for greater wealth was not, apparently, what drove him. More likely, she thought, a determined ambition to gain the approval of free settlers. In any case, it troubled her.

Yet at other times the preoccupied man of business would suddenly vanish for a while, and instead her spouse would take an uxorious form as Alfred the ardent, squeezing her in a tight embrace while he murmured sweet words that made her smile contentedly. Or he would let music occupy his mind for an hour or more some evenings as he played hymn tunes on their piano, eyes closed, and she'd hear him humming to himself and occasionally voicing a few words – 'Time, like an ever-rolling stream…' Or he'd invent tales, preposterously tall, to entertain their young sons, and she would listen too, happy that the family was bound together within a comfortable circle of storytelling. Or he'd sparkle with enthusiasm for some new word or phrase encountered in his reading. 'Listen to this, Amelia! It says here that people in London's fashionable circles are using the French term "frou-frou" for the rustling sound of fabric, especially ladies' dresses. What a wonderful addition to the language! Frou-frou!' At such moments, when he seemed temporarily to have forgotten the world of commerce and public affairs, she felt almost serene.

There was one shared area of deep sorrow in their lives, and she had to be careful not to let Alfred see the extent of its lasting effect on her. If he knew how often the loss of their infant daughters continued to shadow her mood, his own might well become incurably melancholy. The boys were spared and still had each other for comfort. Amelia could only guess how consoling the presence of a sibling must be, having never experienced it herself. But to see three small girls torn away from them in the space of a month by a fiendish disease – it had been so heart-rending that she could not bear to let her thoughts dwell on it for long. And yet her attempt to keep the terrible bereavement tightly confined within a small locked room of her mind was futile. The image of their coffins came to her all too often during the night, mingling with other painful graveside memories from her own girlhood.

Only once had Amelia been anything other than placid and tender towards those children. It was an occasion when her sudden outburst, quite disproportionate to its trivial cause, shocked her as much as her daughters; and its timing made her later memory of it even more lacerating because it came just few days before illness would strike down all three of them fatally. There had been a birthday celebration. Emily, the eldest, was turning five, and the cook prepared a cake to mark the event. The recipe was one that Amelia had approved, the baking process was flawless and the icing gave the finished handiwork a perfect sheen. But one detail caught Amelia by surprise: mindful of the new fashion in birthday cakes, the cook had managed to procure thin candles to adorn it, and brought it to the children's table with its five pale stalks surmounted by tiny pennants of fluttering flame. The children, squealing with delight, clapped their hands – and then Emily, in a fit of giggling exhilaration, seized one of the little candles, plucked it from the cake and waved it around.

'No!' Amelia's cry was loud and shrill. She stumbled to her feet, knocked over her chair with a clatter, and snatched the candle from her daughter's hand. Snuffing out the flame, she glared at her bewildered infants. Emily looked as stricken as if she had been smacked on the cheek, and then began to wail. Amelia herself felt too distressed to think of any words that might explain why this frightening fury had erupted in her. She could only kneel beside Emily and embrace her in an ineffectual gesture of contrition. The birthday party dissolved into tears.

Within a week the measles had carried off all three girls.

Sometimes since then, lying awake at night, Amelia would remember a song the machinists had often sung in Ashton, but she no longer had the heart to give voice to its words. 'For the cloud that's hangin o'er us now is sure to blow away' – no, not now, not sure at all. Some skies would always be overcast.

Every Sunday afternoon she would be driven to Cemetery Hill, past the eastern end of the town, to visit her dead daughters. Alfred never went with her. 'That place is too melancholy for me,' he said, as if his own feelings were what mattered and hers were supposedly less troubling. 'But you go. Jones will take you in the trap.' Jem Jones, their manservant, was a wizened emancipist, slow-speaking and slow-witted, to whom Alfred had given employment when others wouldn't. Jem seemed to like the weekly ritual of donning his best clothes and driving 'milady', as he insisted on calling her in his solemnly deferential way, to the cemetery. But Amelia wished her husband would accompany her and stand with her in front of the white marble stone. She always read the girls' names aloud, summoning images of each of them in turn as she did so in a little rollcall of remembrance. Emily Letch: the curls around her temple, the mischievous grin. Lucy Letch: that lisping chatter of hers. Charlotte Letch: her quartet of tiny teeth. And then she would quietly recite the lines inscribed beneath their names:

*Like clouds that rake the mountain summits*
*Or waves that own no curbing hand*
*How fast has sister followed sister*
*From sunshine to the sunless land!*

Gloomy, and not at all in keeping with the sentimental orthodoxy that envisaged a brighter place of consolation beyond the grave – but she had deliberately chosen those words, adapted from a poem in Alfred's favourite anthology, because they were true to what she felt. Her three darlings were lost in utter darkness.

# Polly

# 23

# The *Ivy*,
# November 1871 to February 1872

Dazzling jags of light split the sky open. The dark ocean was bristling now with crested waves, and a sudden bluster filled the barque's broad sails. Within minutes a storm broke violently above them and began to toss their vessel about as if it were a flimsy piece of flotsam. There had been rough seas earlier in the voyage but nothing like this. As the family cowered in their cabin, every moveable thing went spinning from one side of it to the other and back again. Polly felt too sick to attend to her sisters and brother, though she could see they were all suffering, jolted and flung this way and that. One after another, with anguished groans, they brought up their roiling daily ration of brown-coloured lime juice.

A mighty billow struck the ship and it shuddered like a stricken animal. Until this moment the possibility that something as sturdy as the *Ivy* might founder had seemed too remote to contemplate. Now Polly was filled with terror at the thought of perishing in these terrible seas.

Above the bawling and shrieking of the gale they heard a loud rap-rap at their cabin door. Her father, trying to brace himself as he lurched to and fro, pulled it open. Captain Sanderson staggered in and the door slammed behind him. 'Pardon me for intruding, Mr Letch, Mrs Letch, young lad and ladies,' he shouted. 'I just want to say that although these squalls may alarm anyone who hasn't been in such wild weather at sea before, you really shouldn't fear. Ours is a strong vessel and the crew knows what to do. The mate's at the helm; he's been through worse than this in the past, and so have I. We'll probably be out of the tempest within two or three hours, I reckon. So hold tight and trust in the Lord, and all should soon be well. Goodnight.'

If she hadn't been so intent on calming her turbulent stomach, Polly could have flung her arms around the captain and kissed him. That he would take the time, amidst all the furious turmoil of the elements, to bring those kindly words of comfort – it made her feel deeply grateful. Besides, he cut a fine figure, with his big shoulders and black whiskers. There had been ample opportunities for her to observe him appreciatively and converse with him at length. Being the only passengers ('The most precious of all our cargo,' said Captain Sanderson with a gracious bow when they boarded the *Ivy* at Shadwell Basin), the Letch family had often dined at his table. He was always affable, with a deep tobacco-rich voice and a theatrical way of waggling his eyebrows and rolling his eyes at eight-year-old George to dispel the boy's shyness.

When at last the storm did subside, and the Letches had slowly restored their cabin to order, Polly made her unsteady way up to the poop deck and greeted the captain.

'I hope you won't think it presumptuous of me, sir, if I linger to talk with you for a while?' she asked coyly. 'There's nothing much to do in our cabin, you see, except crochet and sewing. Papa has been reading aloud to me from a novel about Australia called *Geoffrey Hamlyn* but I think it's a tiresome story. The fresh air up here is a pleasant change.'

Drumming his fingers on the rail, Sanderson gave her a guarded glance. 'I trust you've all recovered well from the effects of the storm,' he said with careful formality. She'd hoped for a warmer response, and tried again.

'Oh, yes,' she said, 'quite recovered. For my part, I began to feel better the moment you came down to reassure us. That was very considerate of you, Captain. It heartened me, just seeing how dauntless you were.'

'Well, I'm glad you felt encouraged – but at such times a captain is only as good as his crew. So I wanted you all to know that I had great confidence in my men.' He pointed up to the rigging. 'You can see they're agile and skilful.'

Polly watched as half a dozen of them scurried spider-like up and down the ropes. Two men sat astride the topmost yard on either side of the mainmast, as much as 150 feet above the deck, apparently as calm as if straddling a workshop bench.

Annoyingly, the captain seemed to be more attentive to his ship than to her. Polly tried to think of some little stratagem for attracting his interest, but her repertoire of wiles was limited and she couldn't change her shape even though a more slender woman might well be more to his taste. Perhaps she just needed to break down his reserve by appealing directly to his sense of gallantry.

'I suppose the life of a sea-captain must be lonely at times,' she ventured, 'but no doubt you meet some alluring young ladies on your travels.'

'Lonely? Not really, Miss Letch. I don't have much leisure to contemplate my own state of mind, at any rate.'

She put an experimental hand on his arm. 'I'd like to escape from my family now and then,' she said softly, 'and converse quietly with a stalwart man.'

He moved away from her hand and there was a long silence. 'I hope you don't mean to play the coquette, Miss Letch,' he said, not looking at her. 'My wife wouldn't be pleased if she knew; nor would your parents, I'm sure.'

She pouted and went downstairs with a swish of her skirts. He wasn't the only man on board.

A few days later she made her way to the galley and engaged the cook in flirty chatter.

'What special dishes and tidbits are you planning for me, Mr Mudge?' she asked. 'I heard that a flying fish landed providentially on the deck this morning.'

'It did indeed, Miss, and there tis on the bench. I'll be putting it into a hot pan later. Meanwhile I can give you them wings – not for eating, of course, but for keeping.' He took a large knife, removed the long gauzelike fins and handed them to her. 'If you soak em in water for a few minutes you'll be able to spread em out flat and then dry em and press em between the leaves of a book. They'll form a fine pair of pretty little toy fans.'

'That's very sweet of you, Mr Mudge. Every time I fan myself I'll be reminded of you.'

He simpered bashfully. 'You'll like the fish, I'll warrant, when it's served on the captain's table tonight. Tastes just like sole, you'll find.'

'I hope it doesn't make me more plump than I am already. All your good cooking will be the ruin of my figure.'

'No, no, Miss,' protested Mudge with an effort of gallantry. 'Anyhow, men like the look of a buxom woman,' he added as a bold afterthought.

'Now you'll make me blush, Mr Mudge,' said Polly as she left the galley. It was useful to practise her bantering, and pleasant to think she was being ogled.

She hoped she had caught the eye of the muscular first mate, Mr Gruchy. Even her father had observed what a brawny fellow he was, but nimble too. 'Full of manly energy, that Gruchy,' said George Letch admiringly. 'And spry as a squirrel.'

Gruchy could be teasing, and she liked that. Early in the voyage, when she and her mother stood at the ship's rail, a sudden twisting gust had blown her bonnet overboard, and immediately her mother's bonnet pursued it. At once the mate offered to dive in and fetch their capricious headgear. Thinking he meant it seriously, her mother expressed horror. He swallowed his smirk, gave Mrs Letch an apologetic smile, and then winked at Polly, who giggled.

Another time he brought a small caged bird out on the deck to show her. Its plumage was bright yellow and blue, with a dark line encircling its white cheeks. 'It's a blue tit,' Gruchy told her. 'A girl one, I reckon, the way she twitches er tail. Just hopped in through a window onto my bunk when we was near Tenerife. In a twink, I grasped the little wench and thrust er into this cage. We keep each other company of an evening. Whistle to each other.'

*Lucky birdie*, she thought.

∞

When at last their ship anchored in Fremantle's outer harbour they had to wait for a couple of hours before a small cutter was rowed out to take them ashore.

'You've grown too stout for that dress, Polly,' said her mother, as they stood waiting by the rail. 'Once we find a place to live you'll have to get working on your clothes with needle and thread, or before long there'll be nothing you can fit into.'

Polly was about to make a sulky retort when her father let out a loud cry beside her, and at the same instant a man sitting near the cutter's bow in front of the rowers waved and yelled.

'It's Alfred!' George exclaimed joyfully. 'He must have been waiting for news of our ship's arrival!'

Anyone who could arrange to be rowed out like this to greet passengers in person must surely be a man of substance in the town. She scrutinised her uncle as he clambered aboard and embraced her parents. Although he didn't look much like her father, she thought him a moderately handsome man except for his pocked skin. His nose and mouth were neatly sculpted, the close-set brown eyes suggested intensity, and the grey flecks in his thick waves of hair gave him a distinguished appearance.

'So this is your Polly!' he said, turning to her with the easy kind of smile that she had seen before on men who occupied an eminent social position. 'Quite the mature young lady. I trust you'll find much to amuse you in our little colony here, my dear Polly. It's rough around the edges, but a go-ahead place.'

The cutter that took them to the wharf made slow progress in the stiff wind, and then there was a tedious delay before their luggage was all stacked near them. Two of Uncle Alfred's own vehicles were waiting to take them to Perth, impressing Polly with their smart livery. George rode beside his brother in an elegant carriage drawn by greys, taking the largest bags and boxes and chests with them. Polly, her mother and the younger children followed in a wagonette with the lesser chattels, lurching through the summer heat along rough roads of sandy rubble on a meander towards the town that sprawled above a bend in the sinuous River Swan.

Alfred's house, they found, was in Perth's impressive main street, St George's Terrace, behind his large shop. But when their wagonette arrived in front of the two-storey building, they were startled to see an unfamiliar name emblazoned across it: 'A. de LEECH, GROCER & DRAPER'.

'Ah, yes,' he said later, in response to Polly's question about this. 'Ah, yes. It was injudicious of me, when I first arrived in the colony, to change my surname. I did it for family reasons, you see – so the convict stain wouldn't discolour the good name of my parents and siblings. But now that I've achieved a measure of respectability, and family members have joined me here, it's time to return to my real name. I plan to put a prominent notice in the newspaper announcing that from this date I'll once again sign myself A. D. Letch.'

'Good, good, if you think so,' George said, and then added fatuously, 'but don't bother on our account. After all, as the bard puts it, what's in a name?'

Polly saw her uncle wince. How could her father fail to understand that Alfred's gesture was his way of trying to rejoin the family from which he'd been pulled asunder? Names did matter. They proclaimed who you were. Or what you wanted to be. Or what others wanted you to be.

## 24

# Perth, February 1875

'Three years – almost to the day – since you stepped ashore, George!' Putting down his knife and fork, Alfred raised a glass in cheerful salute. 'And very successful years they've been for you, too. May you and your family continue to thrive here.' There were concordant murmurs from the other dinner guests.

Polly suppressed a sigh and a scowl. Thrive? She'd been languishing in this dismal little town, where there were so few options for a lively young woman. Social occasions were far from exciting, and most of the single men remained single for obvious reasons: they were ungainly, even uncouth, or simply penniless and lacking material prospects. All the same, it was galling that she had no suitors. Her face was surely pleasant enough and she wasn't quite as fleshy as her mother kept hinting. Glancing around the long oak table, it now occurred to her that the invitation list might reflect family concern at having a twenty-three-year-old spinster still on their hands. Perhaps her aunt and uncle had conspired with her parents to include the unsmiling and apparently unwed Mr Browne in the hope he would regard her as a potential spouse.

It was already clear to her from the drift of earlier conversation that both Thomas Browne and another guest, Henry Seeligson, were what people here called emancipists – pardoned ex-convicts like Uncle Alfred – and that both were beginning to establish themselves in business. No doubt they saw Alfred as an enviable exemplar, someone who'd managed to prosper despite the stigma of arriving as a convict. They were probably of similar age to him, but she guessed that he'd been in the colony a considerable while longer. Rather than sit in silence on the outer edge of the table talk, she asked them about that directly.

'I arrived over a decade ago, Miss Letch,' Seeligson replied. 'But it's barely four years since I started my jewellery business in Perth, soon after my wife sailed from London to join me.' He bestowed a little smile of acknowledgement on the woman beside him, who hadn't uttered a word during the meal but nodded meekly like a pecking pigeon at everything her husband said.

'It was just a few months before Mr Seeligson that I came here,' said Browne. 'Since then I've been busy with various pursuits, including a stint as a school teacher, and now I'm setting myself up as an architect and land agent in Fremantle. I acquired a good deal of experience in architectural and engineering work in England.'

He sounded somewhat pompous, Polly thought.

'Teaching, eh!' her father exclaimed jovially, rubbing his hands together like a child. 'Do tell us about that, Mr Browne. My wife and I – you may know this? – run the little

Commercial School along the Terrace here, so naturally we're always interested in what other teachers have been doing.'

'I taught in the Ferguson Valley,' Browne said, 'inland from Bunbury. First employment after my ticket of leave, and I was there for three years. Sole teacher, of course – a small school in a quiet district among farming families.'

'The local settlers made you welcome?' George asked him.

'Treated me cordially enough. But I felt out of place. They were free colonists with strong ties to each other – their farm work, their religion. I was better educated, but very conscious that I'd recently worn convict clothes. So an outsider, always, no matter how they behaved towards me.'

'What was it like for you in the classroom?'

'Far from satisfying. Everything was at such an elementary level – a world away from the ambitious educational ideals my father and uncle used to discuss so passionately. With some of those children, just getting them to the stage where they could read and write a few sentences was a tedious chore. There was one thing I did enjoy, and it used to keep them quiet. Every Friday afternoon I'd tell them stories about the astonishing feats of British engineering. The canals, the railways, the bridges, the great buildings.'

'I wonder what they made of your tales about things and places so removed from their own experience.'

'Isn't that what we all need from storytelling? To be taken away for a while from familiar everyday situations so we can see them in a different light when the story's over?'

'An interesting thought. What of the Ferguson district: an agreeable place?'

'Peaceful. Streams and rolling hills, thick forest except where it's been cleared for pasture. Beautiful vistas. I'd often walk up a hillside near the schoolhouse to a favourite spot where I'd sketch and paint when classes were over for the day.'

'You're an artist, Mr Browne?' George leant forward eagerly. Her father did look daft, thought Polly, with those large drooping side-whiskers. Like a lop-eared hound.

'I had a good training as a draughtsman,' Browne replied, 'so my forte is to draw houses, public buildings, things like that. I've done a number of watercolours of places around Fremantle and Bunbury.'

'I'd like to see what you've painted,' interjected Polly. Perhaps there was more to this Thomas Browne than she'd thought, although she was wondering whether anything ever made him smile.

'I've sold my pictures,' he said. 'Most of them were commissioned. But thank you for your interest, Miss Letch. When I find time to produce any more I'll gladly show you. At present I'm trying to establish the business I mentioned.'

'So the time you spent at the Ferguson school couldn't persuade you to remain in teaching, Mr Browne?' A gobbet of lamb and potato dropped from the corner of George's mouth as he spoke. Polly looked away, wishing her father wouldn't talk when his mouth was so full. 'A dull life out there in the bush, I suppose, but you didn't think of looking for a school in Perth or Fremantle?'

'I took the teaching position simply because that's what was on offer at the time for educated men of the bond class. But since receiving a pardon I've wanted to work in my own professional field. By the way, I wouldn't describe life in the Ferguson Valley as dull. In fact there was quite a commotion during my last month there when one of the Fenian prisoners,

O'Reilly, escaped from a road gang near Bunbury with the help of some Irish farmers from Ferguson and Dardanup. The local priest had a hand in it, too. Police searched our district thoroughly, knocking on doors, questioning the Catholic families.'

'I remember the public uproar here in Perth when O'Reilly got away,' said Alfred. 'This was two or three years before you arrived here, George. People were alarmed at the idea that a lot of the other Fenians would follow him – a mass escape. But it didn't happen. Anyway, he managed to get to America, and I heard he's become a person of influence in Boston, where there's a big Irish community. Quite a public figure, that John O'Reilly. Clever and energetic. Writing, lecturing, raising money for his political cause.'

Seeligson drummed his fingers on the table irritably. 'So an escaped convict, guilty of treason, can be lionised in Boston,' he said wryly, with an edge of bitterness, 'while those of us whose crimes were minor and who've earned a pardon and become industrious upright citizens won't ever be fully accepted here by free settlers. And for people like me, our religion also keeps us on the margins of society. The gentry come to me for fine rings and brooches and bracelets and necklaces, and some of my jewellery even adorns hands and necks in Government House – but respectability…?' He shook his head. 'Always out of reach for Jews in this town.'

'Certainly,' Alfred nodded, 'there should be more rec-ognition of how much the colony's prosperity depends on what's handled by jewellery importers such as you, Henry. Especially with the growth of the pearling trade. How many luggers operate along the north-west coast these days?'

'More than eighty of them working out of Shark Bay, King Sound, places like that. Yes, pearls provide the principal income of our town now.'

'I don't think you're right about religious prejudice, Henry,' said Alfred. 'Some men of high standing in Perth and Fremantle are Jewish. Lionel Samson on the Legislative Council, for one. But then he's a free settler, and we former prisoners do come up against limits, I agree, to social acceptance. Or to full participation in civic life – not being able to serve on juries, for instance.'

'All too true!' Thomas interjected vehemently. 'And here's another example: debarring emancipists from membership of mechanics' institutes. Bunbury, Fremantle, and the Swan River one here in Perth – they've all given me the cold shoulder, and I resent it. I remember, years ago in England, how enthusiastically my uncle spoke about mechanics' institutes as a new kind of opportunity for self-improvement. Not here! Refusing to let a well-qualified professional man become a member, merely because of a mistake made long ago – it's unforgiving and unjust.'

Seeligson nodded, frowning, and removed a stubborn piece of gristle from the side of his mouth.

'But changes are occurring,' George pointed out in his irrepressibly cheerful tone. 'Look at the way Reverend Johnston has managed to reform the Literary Institute in Fremantle – very clever of him, I think, setting up a rival organisation first with more open membership and then amalgamating it with the institute. Do you know him? A learned man, and good-hearted.'

'Haven't met Johnston, no,' Thomas replied, 'but the leading merchants and politicians seem to respect him, and

I take my hat off to anyone who uses his influence to soften prejudice.'

As the plates were cleared away and the evening lengthened, Thomas shook off his irritability and became the centre of conversation, at times almost animated in recounting more of his experiences since being transported. He told them about particular commissions he'd undertaken as an artist in Fremantle and further south. About his futile pursuit of gold during the short-lived rush to godforsaken Peterwangy. About the vagaries of land values in such an isolated colony as this. He spoke, too, of his schemes for improving Fremantle Harbour and building a railway all the way up to the agricultural region of the Avon Valley. Although Polly thought him an odd, stern-faced sort of fellow, determined to succeed yet devoid of youthful verve, she found herself warming to him. And his business prospects appeared to be good.

But then, just as she'd begun to contemplate the possibility that her matchmaking parents might have found her a tolerably interesting and even congenial person this time, Thomas Browne revealed something disagreeable. In explaining how he came to be arrested, he referred to a wife and to many children. The former Mrs Browne, he said, was reportedly dead and his children had broken off all contact with him, but in Polly's mind it was an unpleasant complication that he already had a family. And yet, on the other hand, it did at least show that he was not averse to intimacy with a woman – something she'd wondered about because of the way he'd addressed his comments almost exclusively to the men and avoided looking straight at her. Perhaps his sidelong glances just meant he was shy and needed encouragement.

Alfred

## 25

# Perth, October 1875

No one could claim that his niece was a great beauty, or deny that she was rather too plump to walk gracefully, but as he watched her standing outside the chapel doorway, arm in arm with her new husband, Alfred took considerable satisfaction in Polly's appearance. All his experience as a draper and tailor had produced a wedding costume that flattered her by drawing attention to itself rather than to her ample proportions. Although the dress of ivory-hued figured silk had been very expensive – not just because of the splendid fabric with its silver glints but also because it was so ingeniously shaped and stitched, making skilful use of whalebone, cording, hooks, lining and lace – it created a head-turning impression and he'd managed to subsidise the cost discreetly, knowing that George's budget was constrained. Her accessories, too, caught the eye, particularly the matching gloves and veil, delicately embroidered.

The groom, in contrast, looked far from modish. His frockcoat – a dull one at that – was not a happy choice. If only Thomas Browne had thought to ask Alfred for advice he'd have known that the right thing to wear for one's wedding these days was a morning coat with matching waistcoat. His conspicuously unfashionable attire emphasised how much older than his bride he was.

But the little ceremony at Fremantle's Congregational Church had proceeded cheerfully enough, with Reverend Johnston officiating in a smooth and blithe manner. The morning was benignly cool for October, and the bridal party all smiles. Polly's young sisters, Florence and Maud, discharged their bridesmaid duties with decorative charm. George and Caroline exuded a cordiality that seemed slightly hectic – no doubt flushed with relief, thought Alfred, that their eldest and occasionally difficult daughter was now someone else's responsibility. And he himself, her affectionate uncle, had played Mendelssohn's wedding march with gusto on the gasping harmonium as the bridal party, followed by the small congregation, made its way slowly out of the church.

That evening, when the genial light was fading away, Alfred expressed to Amelia, in the privacy of their parlour, some misgivings she'd heard him voice before.

'Today's ceremony was pleasant enough, but frankly I can't be wholly optimistic about their prospect of happiness. It does trouble me, you know, to think that there are such obvious differences between Polly and Thomas. They're not cut from the same cloth.'

'Oh, it's no bad thing, Alfred, for a husband and wife to differ markedly. You and I present quite a contrast in age and temperament, but it's been no barrier to happiness during our twelve years of marriage.'

'True, my dear, true. Yet I still think the age gap in their case is too great. Thomas is so much older than Polly! A third of a century stretching out between them! Not similar to our situation by any means. I'm hardly twenty years older than you.'

'Twenty-one, actually. But I admit you're a youthful man for your age.' She chuckled in that merry way of hers, eyebrows raised teasingly.

'Besides, Amelia, you're a much calmer person than Polly. At times her manner is almost…well, I was going to say frivolous but perhaps that's too harsh. My mother would have called her flighty. And there's something else: you and I share particular interests that hold us together, don't we? Things we both cherish, like our love for music. What do Thomas and Polly have in common, apart from wanting – for different reasons, probably – to be married? And married to almost *anyone*, I suspect, not necessarily to each other. It's hard to see how people of such different inclinations and backgrounds can form a harmonious couple.'

'Yet Thomas seems to be a decent man. He's hardworking and talented. That must count for something in Polly's eyes.'

'What about *his* eyes?'

'Strange colour, aren't they? A sort of hazel, but darker. They stand out against that pallid complexion of his.'

'But what I mean is that there's an odd way he often looks at people, or rather, doesn't quite look at some of them. Have you noticed that? With women, especially – when he's talking with women he stands or sits at an angle. An oblique angle. His eyes don't connect with the other person. As if he's uneasy.'

'The main thing that strikes me about his manner,' said Amelia, 'is that he can be so quick to take offence. Resentful. I wonder where that comes from.'

'I have the impression he feels aggrieved at encountering obstacles to his schemes. Not surprising, really, for someone so clever and capable. It frustrates him, I think, to be held back. He wants plenty of scope to show what he can do. I like him but he's an odd fellow at times.'

Amelia shook her head. 'It's more than just thwarted ambition that troubles him, I'd say. Do you remember that dinner party we gave – six months ago or more – and how he spoke of his first wife? It was clear he holds her responsible for his conviction.'

'I'd guess there's more than one side to that story,' said Alfred. 'And who knows what deep-seated tensions there may have been in Satan's family, anyway?'

'*Satan's* family?'

'Oh, that's Thomas's nickname – Satan. You hadn't heard? He doesn't like it, of course, but it's what most people have been calling him for years.'

'It sounds hideous. Does Polly know?'

'I can't say, but I'd be surprised if she wasn't aware of it by now. Mind you, the name didn't come from his character or behaviour. There's nothing satanic about Thomas! It's just a convict joke about his appearance – the dark hair and eyes, the thin sallow cheeks.'

∞

A few days later Alfred was walking back to his shop from the bank when, turning a corner, he found himself face to face with Henry Seeligson, accompanied by a short stocky man he didn't know.

Seeligson greeted him warmly and introduced his companion. 'I'd like you to meet Detective Sergeant Rowe.

Rowe – this is my friend Mr Alfred Letch, one of the most successful traders in our colony, as you probably know.'

Pleasantries and compliments were exchanged as they moved out of the wind into the shelter of an alley to talk for a few minutes.

'I've heard about your detective work, Sergeant Rowe,' Alfred told him. 'I remember particularly the reports of your swift action in apprehending the ruffians who took jewellery from Henry's store last year, and recovering the stolen stock.'

'That publicity caused me some embarrassment, I confess,' Runty replied, 'because of the generous reward Mr Seeligson insisted on presenting. It's not every day a man's given a gold ring for simply doing his duty. Newspapermen and town gossips, you may recall, suggested it could be a first step on the downward path to corruption! Fortunate that my superintendent publicly supported me. And of course I'm grateful to Mr Seeligson for the kind gesture.'

'But the primary gratitude was mine,' said Seeligson. 'Duty or not, you did me a great service.'

'And when you help one trader you help every trader,' Alfred added. 'We all value the work you do. It's a great boon for our colony to have a detective branch of the police service now, and a man with your background in charge of it.'

'The encouragement's welcome, certainly,' said Runty. 'But that's enough about me. Mr Letch, allow me to congratulate you on your recent election to the Central Ward. The Perth City Council will be the better for the service you can provide as a man with such wide business experience.'

Alfred inclined his head, as if to acknowledge graciously that such esteem was quite well founded.

'By the way, Mr Letch,' Runty added, 'I happen to be acquainted with your kinsman Mr Thomas Browne.'

'Oh! How so?'

'I bought a small parcel of land from him three or four years ago, and since then our paths have occasionally crossed. Both of us were well satisfied with our real estate transaction. I admire the conscientious way he works. He's a man of many talents, as no doubt you're well aware. I expect he'll make a valuable contribution to the future growth of this colony, if he's given a fair chance. The grim name that people foist on him – Satan – is one of the unfair things he has to cope with.'

They were taking leave of each other when another name was mentioned, one at which Alfred felt a sudden jolt as if a hand had stretched towards him from the past and clenched his conscience.

'Oh, I've just remembered something!' Seeligson turned back to Alfred. 'When I went up to the Toodyay district a few days ago I saw John Wroth in the main street of Newcastle there, and he asked after you. I promised to convey his greetings. But I must say he looks and sounds rather frail, though I suppose he's a little younger than we are. Not in good health or spirits, seemingly.'

'I'm sorry to hear it,' said Alfred, eyes lowered as he tried to disguise feelings of discomposure. 'Haven't seen John Wroth for a long while, but I knew he was struggling to make ends meet. I hope things will improve for him. Anyone would find it hard to combine the roles of trader and farmer in such a remote place, and he's never been robust.'

'I know Mr Wroth too,' interjected Runty. 'Well, just a slight acquaintance, really. Met him a few months ago when I was up Newcastle way to make inquiries about a horse-stealing problem. Wroth wasn't involved in that, but I needed to get information about property boundaries from him in his capacity as clerk of the Roads Board. A pleasant companionable sort of fellow, keen to talk about anything and everything. And intensely compassionate – I remember well his heartfelt sympathy for a neighbour in troubled circumstances.'

∞

That evening, over the supper table, Alfred sank quietly into a mood of remorse as he thought of Seeligson's gift of the ring to Rowe and, in contrast, his own mercenary meanness towards Wroth. Amelia asked whether anything was troubling him. He hesitated before answering.

'I happened to meet Henry Seeligson today and we had a chat. He introduced me to the man he was with, a detective called Rowe, who's acquainted with Thomas Browne, as it turns out. Anyway, Henry mentioned someone I used to know well. A fellow expiree called John Wroth. He's been living up in the Toodyay Valley and it's years since I last saw him, but we were close friends once.'

'Why does this bother you?'

There was another pause.

'Hearing Wroth's name unexpectedly was a sharp reminder that I haven't always been scrupulous. I treated him shabbily, that's the truth of it, and I feel ashamed to recall the circumstances.'

She rested a hand on his shoulder. 'You're probably making a mountain out of a molehill. I can't imagine you behaved so badly that an apology to Mr Wroth wouldn't set it right. Do you want to tell me what happened?'

Alfred pressed his fingertips against his forehead.

'Long ago, soon after being transported here, I befriended John Wroth warmly and we pledged fraternal fidelity, but then I turned against him in a capricious way.'

'How did you become friends?'

'We met soon after he arrived in Fremantle. Mine was the second of the convict transports to this colony and his was the third, so I'd already been here for some months before he came, and good behaviour had earned me a few privileges. Instead of being locked up in the barracks with the others, I was placed in the dispensary of the surgery. They also gave me tailoring work to do, and didn't require me to wear prison garb myself. I suppose young Wroth, not yet twenty years old and easily impressed, saw me as a cut above the rest of the convicts. We talked often. He was well educated. Lively in conversation. We found we'd both come from good families – quite genteel in his case – and from much the same part of England, and our crimes were of a similar kind, more foolish than vicious.'

Pushing his plate away, Alfred picked up a silver saltcellar and stared into it as if the ghost-white grains it held were the sands of time.

'So…?' Amelia prompted.

'Oh, yes – well, the experiences we had in common were a natural basis for sociable companionship. Because I was in a position of influence, and Wroth was several years my junior, he looked up to me. Sought my advice about this and that. I was able to do a few things for him, such as making him a waistcoat and a good cloth cap, and offering practical suggestions for enhancing his comfort. I remember writing a letter at his request to his father – the superintendent had given me permission to send correspondence, unlike most prisoners – with assurances that young John was in good fettle and that I'd be a reliable friend to him, like an elder brother. Which I was, at first. When he was sent on probation up to York to work as a clerk at the Convict Hiring Depot, I lent him money and wrote encouraging letters. He was full of affection and gratitude. Then we both received our ticket of leave, and in my case there was an inheritance from my father soon afterwards, so I set up livery stables on the banks of the Swan, and Wroth was one of the men I hired.'

Alfred fell silent. Amelia quietly fetched a glass and poured him a whisky. After a few sips he resumed his story.

'Wroth started to run up debts over one thing and another. Medical treatment when he had a persistent fever. A weakness for fine clothes. He borrowed money from a Jewish lender, Elias Lapidus, with me as guarantor for the loan. The agreement had to be drawn up formally, specifying a security – which was a splendid gold signet ring, a Wroth family heirloom. As a friendly gesture I let him retain possession of the ring. Lapidus was to get regular repayment from Wroth's wages, but before long those payments stopped and so I was obliged to make good the default with my own cash. I sent letters to Wroth – he was back in York by this time – demanding prompt reimbursement, or surrender of the gold ring. He tried to fob me off with apologetic offers to send small instalments. The more he pleaded, the more impatient and peremptory I became. He wouldn't give me the ring, he wasn't able to pay, and I wasn't able to forgive. So what had been a brotherly friendship dissolved acrimoniously.

I should have waived the debt and shown some generosity, but I didn't. The way I insisted on legal obligations was mean-spirited. Wroth must have felt betrayed.'

Amelia bent over him and kissed his forehead. 'You shouldn't judge yourself too harshly, my dear. You were young and impulsive. Perhaps there's some way you could try now to make amends to Mr Wroth? Render some practical assistance?'

'I doubt it. Too late to repair that broken loyalty. Regrettably, some things just can't be set right.'

Hands clasped, he looked down at his thumbs as they began to move slowly around each other.

'Well, moping won't fix anything,' said Amelia. 'Come to bed now.' He sensed that she was feeling twinges of impatience with his mood.

'You go ahead, m'dear,' he said with a sigh. 'I'll follow soon.'

A few minutes after she left the room he walked slowly over to the window and looked out into their moonlit garden. The bushes were garbed in tints of silver and ivory, as if imitating his niece's wedding dress, though with dark folds and plackets. Somewhere nearby a magpie began to rehearse its warbling nocturne, but irresolutely, disconsolately, and soon fell silent again.

No, moping wouldn't fix anything, of course. She was quite right about that. But surely it wasn't possible for anyone to be always free of moping – anyone except a simpleton. Even Amelia herself, though usually buoyant in her manner, would sometimes withdraw quietly for a while into a remote corner of her mind where he couldn't reach her.

# Runty

# 26

# Fremantle and Perth,
# April to August 1876

Until the telegraph message startled them just after ten o'clock, it had been a quiet morning at police headquarters in Perth, with Monday's usual lethargy deepened by a drowsy residue from the Easter weekend. But it soon became a day Runty would long remember – not only because it tested sharply his mettle as an officer of the law but also because it left him doubting whether the law should always be paramount.

The message came from Sergeant Campbell at the Fremantle station: six men, all Fenians, had escaped simultaneously from various prison working parties. Campbell requested instructions.

Runty replied at once. 'Send a mounted man to Rockingham and another to South Beach.'

Hours passed without further information. Waiting, waiting, he recalled O'Reilly's audacious escape some seven years earlier, and the news that had reached Perth months afterwards about an enthusiastic welcome given to that eloquent rebel by the many Irish sympathisers in Boston. O'Reilly himself, Runty surmised, might well be behind the planning of this latest escape. Liberating his mates with the help of American money – it was just the kind of scheme he'd have hatched, the rascal. Local Irish supporters would have conveyed messages, probably through priests. There must be a ship standing nearby, because the shore was a bolter's only possible gateway to freedom.

At a quarter past one a report came from Rockingham. A resident had seen a whaleboat arrive early that morning near the timber company's jetty. In charge of it was 'a man of Yankee appearance with a crew of coloured men'. Later someone on horseback and a group in traps, all armed, arrived at the beach, joined the crew and put to sea.

An exchange of telegraph messages with Sergeant Campbell made it clear that the water police and reinforcements from Perth were in pursuit of the boat but had little chance of catching it. On Runty's advice the superintendent instructed a police party to set out with rifles and ammunition in the coastal steamer *Georgette*. Runty himself went to the Fremantle station in a mail coach to coordinate the operation.

The process of what his formal reports called 'gathering intelligence' meant simply, to begin with, asking around in the local hotels for any recent gossip they'd heard about unusual behaviour, any strangers they'd noticed in town, Irish or American particularly.

'American? Well, yes – there's been a Yankee businessman of some sort staying at Maloney's of late, goes by the name of Collits or Collins if I recall rightly.' The barman wiped the counter with a grimy rag as he looked round the room. 'Old Hogg over there in the corner, he can probably tell you more. Knows everything that's going on around these parts, and

I heard him chatting a few days ago to his drinking mates about this Yankee fellow.'

After Runty had bought him a pint of porter, Hogg was happy to talk about the suspect American. 'We reckoned he was up ter no good, that Collins,' declared the bleary-eyed drunk. 'Wouldn't let on what kind of business he was in, y'see. Kept his lips buttoned. Made some visits to country districts, don't know why, and then Billy Burke spotted him down on the wharf havin a quiet gab with another Yankee, captain of the *Catalpa*...'

Pursuing his inquiries at the harbourside, Runty soon established that the barque *Catalpa* had left Bunbury a couple of days earlier, purportedly for whaling grounds. A description of its captain matched the person in charge of the boat that had picked up the Fenians – probably the same man, George Anthony, who had spirited O'Reilly away years before. Runty sent his findings to Superintendent Smith that evening, and a flurry of further telegraphing began early the next morning. There were now several people to keep rapidly informed: not only the superintendent in Perth and officers in Rockingham but also the comptroller-general of convicts and even the Governor. And there was much to check and organise and report as the day went on. The *Georgette* had sighted the whaleboat and then, unable to draw close to it and being low in fuel, returned to Fremantle for more coal and for a cannon to be mounted on her deck. She sailed again with a larger complement of police and pensioner guards on board. Meanwhile, two constables, having ascertained that Collins hired 'for a picnic outing' the traps and horses used in the escape, were now restoring them to their presumably innocent owners.

Yet all attempts to find out how the escape had been coordinated and who had provided local assistance were getting nowhere. To be so short of men and resources! It was acutely frustrating in an emergency such as this. Runty worked himself to a frazzle checking lines of inquiry, responding to telegrams, making frequent entries in the occurrence book, and drafting a formal summary report requested by his superintendent. Then, on the Wednesday, the police party from the *Georgette* returned shamefaced to Fremantle. Their eventual encounter with the *Catalpa*, they told Runty, had been mortifying. When their steamer had at last approached the American vessel the Fenians and the whaleboat crew had already gone aboard. John Stone, superintendent of the Water Police, had used a loud hailer to demand that the prisoners be released, but this was met with defiance. 'We have no prisoners with us,' replied the captain. 'Only free men.' The *Georgette* then fired a shot across the whaler's bows, and Stone bellowed an ultimatum: unless the Irishmen were handed over within fifteen minutes, the ship would be 'blown out of the water'. In derisive response, Captain Anthony pointed to the American flag at his masthead. 'We are on the high seas,' he claimed, 'and therefore protected by international law.' There was muttering among those on the *Georgette*; none of them could be sure whether they were in fact outside the three-mile limit. While they dithered, the *Catalpa* sailed away from them further out to sea.

Chagrin was palpable among the senior police and prison officers, despite the fact that the newspapers were not levelling blame at them. The colony's guardians of law and order had done their best in difficult circumstances, declared the journalists, and the British Government was at fault for failing to provide adequate naval protection. There should be a warship stationed at Fremantle, they said, 'to avoid a repetition of this unparalleled piece of Yankee impudence'. For a short while Runty took the humiliation to heart. But as he thought more about what had happened, he came to recognise in himself another emotion, an incipient one he couldn't share openly with his fellow officers: it was sneaking admiration for the Fenians – for the boldness of the rescue itself, yes, but also for the ardour of their beliefs and the loyalty that bound them together wherever they might be, as if Ireland were a place in the mind as well as on the map. They desired freedom passionately, but not as an end in itself; it was a means to the achievement of political goals. There was something enviable in men like O'Reilly, in the fervent way they remained true to their cause, true to each other. A brotherhood of republicans. Not having a brother himself, or a sister, Runty could only imagine what it might feel like.

He couldn't express these thoughts without seeming disloyal to his fellow officers. The need to show solidarity with other upholders of law and order became especially pressing as the weeks went by and whispered innuendo grew louder. Around the town it was being suggested that the Fenians couldn't have got away from their work gangs and travelled to Rockingham so easily without connivance from inside the prison, or at least carelessly preferential treatment. A particular target for the gossip was the Fremantle Prison's assistant superintendent, Joseph Doonan. Well, he was Irish, wasn't he? And therefore sympathetic to the political prisoners, no doubt. Runty knew Doonan to be a conscientious man who had no good reason to feel culpable, and it was painful to see how the calumny made him suffer.

One morning in mid-July Runty was returning to his Perth office after investigating a robbery when his young assistant, Detective Constable Hansford, stopped him in the street, looking agitated.

'Some bad news has just come through from Fremantle, sir,' he said, 'from the Convict Establishment. It's Mr Doonan, sir. He's gone and cut his throat!'

As soon as he got back to his office, Runty learned that Doonan had been sitting quietly at breakfast when he snatched a knife from the table and slashed at his neck, nearly severing the windpipe. He was 'hovering between life and death', according to the prison's medical officer. Doonan's colleagues thought the balance of his mind had been affected by a recent formal inquiry into the circumstances of the Fenians' escape, even though he'd been exonerated.

By the time Doonan recovered more than a month later, news had reached Perth of the arrival of the Fenians in New York. Runty kept to himself his respect for their audacity; and besides, on the day he read in *The Inquirer* about those successful escapees, something else was uppermost in his mind. It was the anniversary of his mother's death, and the intervening years had done little to lessen his pain. Toxic lead had been the cause of her fatal illness; adding lead to a glaze made it more likely to fire well, but the practice was gradually poisoning the pottery decorators in Tunstall and other Staffordshire towns. When she succumbed, Runty had felt a grey nimbus of lonely grief descend on him – not for the first time, nor the last. The previous loss of his father had taught him that anyone could be swept cruelly away at any time. Much more recently, less than two years ago and barely a year after following him to the colony, Runty's own wife Sarah had died in childbirth, and their four children were now in the care of a housemaid. Death could suddenly snatch young or old. But being desperate enough to want, like Doonan, to take one's own life and leave a family bereft – that was something frighteningly different, and to Runty almost incomprehensible.

The Fenians lingered in his thoughts long after their successful escape and its aftermath. The train of events had revived his doubts that lawfulness should always be society's supreme principle. He remembered the persuasive things O'Reilly used to say during that brief period when they worked together in the prison library – about the injustice of repressive laws imposed on the Irish, about the exploitation of convict labour by English colonists. And his own earlier conversations with Father Delaney on the *Hougoumont* came back to mind – earnest exchanges of opinion about distinguishing between the illegal and the immoral. There were occasions, Runty acknowledged, when those on the wrong side of the law could plausibly claim, by appealing to a higher principle, to be in the right. Where did that leave him, as an officer of the law?

It was the kind of question that made him feel sorely lacking in wisdom, and he wished he could mull it over with his parents. Their long absence from his life weighed heavily on his heart at times like this. He had no close companions, and no relatives apart from his young children. Envy was a useless emotion to indulge, but he couldn't rid himself of a wistful sense of having been deprived of the familial bonds that many adults apparently took for granted.

And it was the kind of question Runty often found himself contemplating now, particularly in the late evening after his children had been put to bed and Connie the housemaid had retired to hers. Even when his wife was still alive it had been his habit to sit quietly alone in the parlour for a while, interrogating the day's events, before he felt ready for sleep. 'Come to bed!' Sarah would sometimes plead. 'It's late. You need your rest.' But he needed this meditative interval as much as he needed rest. And in the workplace, too, no matter what claimed his attention or required him to act decisively, part of his mind was already reflecting on it all in a detached way. It wasn't that he withdrew perceptibly from the people around him; things he'd overheard or been told had made it clear that his colleagues and others saw him as good company, a gregarious fellow, easy to talk to. Yes, he'd learnt the art of sociability. But all the important action was going on, as it always had, in the cranny behind his eyes, in the mind's interior life.

So tonight, as his children's sleepy whispering gradually ceased and silence spread through the house, Runty sat in an armchair and let his thoughts wander. Poor Doonan came to mind again, slashing at his own throat in a fit of despair. Which was the more wretched act – inflicting such a wound on oneself, or on someone else? Runty saw every day the disfigured face of his servant Connie O'Sullivan, victim of her former husband's drunken brutality. Livid scars that stretched from her eyebrow to her neck, crimping the cheek and lips, were visible signs of her suffering, but Runty knew that her spirit was even more lacerated than her skin. Employing her to look after his household and children was his way of helping her to heal.

He'd heard about Connie when he went to Newcastle to investigate the trapping and theft of horses, and met in the course of his inquiries the clerk of the Toodyay Roads Board, John Wroth. Runty had taken a liking to Wroth, a good-hearted if somewhat ingenuous chatterer, who mentioned during their tangential conversation the plight of a young woman in the town, savagely beaten and gashed some months earlier by the degenerate emancipist she'd married. O'Sullivan was back in prison, but she was penurious now and inconsolable because of her ugly injuries. 'The pity of it,' said Wroth, 'is that she's been such a sweet-natured person, mild-mannered and kindly. There's a lot of sympathy for her around here but times are very hard after the long drought and nobody can afford to give her any steady work. Mrs Brogden has let her live in a room at the back of her place, just a flimsy little lean-to, and Connie hides herself away there, quite alone with her affliction.'

Wroth's words stirred Runty's compassion so powerfully that he went at once to see the hapless Connie. She stood cautiously in her doorway, a shawl held across part of her face, as Runty introduced herself.

'Pardon me for intruding on your privacy, Mrs O'Sullivan,' he said, hat in hand. 'Mr Wroth has told me about your situation, and your good character. It happens I'm in need of someone reliable to look after my house and young children in Perth. I'm recently widowed, and my job sometimes takes me away from home. I can't pay you much but there'd be a roof over your head and regular meals, of course.'

Sidelong, she squinted at him and then gave a sceptical shake of her head. 'My face would alarm your children,' she said despondently.

'Oh, you needn't worry about that,' he assured her, thinking, *I'll have a word with them beforehand, prepare them carefully to accept her.* 'I'd be grateful for your help,' he added. 'It's been difficult for my little ones since their mother died, and I'm not much of a housekeeper myself.'

It took more coaxing, but by the time he turned to leave, having arranged for her to travel to Perth later that week, Runty had seen the hint of something like a smile flickering at the corner of Connie's misshapen mouth.

Now, as he sat quietly in his armchair and recalled that impulsive hiring nearly two years ago, it was hard for him to imagine how he could have managed without her. She'd become a fixture in the Rowe household, dependable, deferential, loyal to him and devoted to the children, who'd responded affectionately to her ministrations. His own sense of isolation remained unassuaged; Connie was not the sort of person who could ever provide him with intimate companionship – or would want to do so. Yet it was gratifying to know that he'd given her a place where she was able to feel she belonged. Many people in this colony apparently lacked that feeling.

Alfred

# 27

# Fremantle and Guildford,
# July to August 1876

For months it had been plucking at his conscience. High time now to do something about it: he would try to put things right with John Wroth.

Hearing about the hardship John was facing had thrown a shadow across Alfred's memories of the brief period, a quarter of a century ago, when they'd seemed like brothers. Back then, though chastened by their fall from grace, they were daring to imagine a redemptive future for themselves. He could still recall one of their earliest conversations in particular: John had been momentarily down in the mouth, expressing dismay at the coarse behaviour of the ruffians around him – 'depraved and low,' he'd called them – but Alfred restored the younger man's habitual good spirits by suggesting they'd both soon be able to shrug off such uncongenial company. They had much better prospects than most of the convicts, he pointed out, because their upbringing had given them ample inner resources to draw on.

'Half of those lags can't even read or write,' he'd reminded John. 'They've no understanding of commerce, let alone any social graces. With only a few exceptions they lack character and won't ever amount to anything. We're different from the rest, you and I. We've arrived here with talents that the colony needs. We know how to conduct ourselves decently. It won't take us long to get our ticket of leave; after that, if we work hard we're sure to earn respect and find a place in the sun. So perk up!'

John's eyes had brightened with responsive hope at those words, and a buoyant note returned to his voice. 'You're right, of course, Alfred. Yes, we'll surely do well for ourselves.'

It was easy for them, in those days, to assume cheerfully that they deserved to be lucky and had equal shares in a prosperous future. But as it turned out, fortune hadn't treated them even-handedly. By all accounts, John was neither robust nor well-to-do these days. Alfred could no longer avoid the disconcerting thought that his own past disloyalty at a stressful time may well have contributed to John's inability to thrive.

So having brooded for a few months over the news of his former friend's setbacks, he resolved now to do whatever he could to make reparation. He spoke to Amelia about it as they sat near the fireplace one evening.

'I've thought over a comment you made some while ago,' he said, staring into the embers, 'when I confessed to being a poor friend to John Wroth. You said it shouldn't be difficult to repair the breach. I felt I couldn't do it – too much water under the bridge – but the matter's been weighing on my mind since then. It was mean-spirited of me to treat him as I did, and the fact that I behaved impulsively doesn't lessen the blame. What's stopped me, I think, from holding myself to account is that I'd never really faced a simple question: why I was so harsh towards him.'

'Can you answer it now?'

'I've been pondering that. In part, it was probably that John Wroth reminded me too much of the person I'd been.'

'Resembled a younger version of yourself?'

'Yes, and more innocent. Although that was attractive at first, it soon came to seem…almost repugnant. For one thing, he was too fond of well-cut garments, and even before getting his ticket of leave he began borrowing money so he could place orders with a tailor. To see him flaunting elegant white shirts and other finery within a few months of reaching Fremantle…It was a self-indulgence he could ill afford.'

Nodding, Amelia drew her chair closer and patted her husband's forearm. 'And it must have seemed to repeat the pattern that led to your own downfall.'

'Just so. That was one reason I became impatient with him, no doubt. But there was probably more to it. The families we'd each left behind…well, I was missing my own brothers, and I suppose young Wroth seemed a sort of substitute for them. The letter I wrote on his behalf to his father, too – well, it was as if I could somehow please or appease my own father by doing it. So I began to see John as – in one way and another – an uncomfortable counterpart of myself. That's why I needed to push him away.'

'But you're older and wiser now. Can't you become friends again?'

'I want to, Amelia. I want to. I'm just not sure how to do it. He's in straitened circumstances and I have the wherewithal to help him, but money can't rectify the problem. I'm sure

John would be too proud to accept charity, even a loan, and besides, it's not really a financial matter – it's about healing the wound I inflicted. That's the long and short of it. So I ought to go to him, look him in the eye, and ask to be forgiven.'

'Then go!'

'Well, it's not quite so simple. After so long…To be frank, I fear a rebuff, though it may be no more than I deserve. Perhaps it would be more tactful to make indirect inquiries first.'

'How would you do that?'

'I've been mulling it over, and I've thought of something. The man I employ as a driver for the omnibus service between Perth and Guildford has told me that one of John Wroth's sons brings a mail-coach twice a week from Newcastle, where John lives, down to Guildford. It's timely for me to call in at my own shop there – I want to see how its stock compares now with what Padbury and Loton are offering at their big store. So it would be a simple matter to travel to Guildford by omnibus in time to be at the inn beside the coach depot when the Wroth lad next arrives, and strike up a casual conversation with him – ask after his father, and so on – try to gauge whether John might be receptive to a visit from me. What do you think?'

'It's worth trying.'

∞

During the lurching journey to Guildford on roads roughened by recent stormwater, he reminisced about those early months in Fremantle when he'd been glad of the company of young Wroth, whose affectionate nature marked him out as unlike other convicts. John seemed hardly out of boyhood – twenty years old but looking and sounding younger, his excitable head full of tales of adventure and romance drawn from Walter Scott's novels. Then he'd been sent off to York as a probationary prisoner assigned to clerical work, and before long there was that sudden falling-out over the loan guarantee. In the many years since their quarrel, contact between them had been infrequent and guarded. From time to time bits of information came to Alfred about John's vicissitudes – as an underpaid clerk for Toodyay's resident magistrate, later as a hard-pressed storekeeper and then competing for contracts as a supplier of provisions to the Government Commissariat. With a large family to support, it must have been an anxious struggle for him.

Yet perhaps living in a rural landscape had brought John some pleasant compensations. Only once had Alfred travelled up into the hills along the Toodyay road. It was springtime, and with its peaceful river, thickly forested hills, granite outcrops and rolling fertile farmland, the district had struck him as the most attractive he'd seen anywhere in the colony. Although its particular features had little in common with the scenery he'd cherished during his own youthful days in Essex, Alfred could imagine finding in it some comparable satisfactions. If he could persuade Amelia to make such a bold change, they might eventually move away from Perth, up into that river valley, establish a new homestead there and breed horses. And if in the meantime he could repair his relationship with John Wroth, there would be neighbourly goodwill to enjoy.

Interrupting his daydream, the omnibus suddenly stopped on a bend and a shrill whinny came from one of the horses.

He pulled out his pocket watch: still half an hour from their destination. Leaning from a window to look ahead, he saw an enormous Hereford bull blocking the road, staring at their vehicle with an impassive mien. It looked them slowly up and down, snorted, turned its head away, but didn't move its legs. During the five minutes that went by before the massive beast lumbered off towards the loamy river flats, two of Alfred's fellow travellers – farmers, he guessed by the cut of their clothes – became excitedly lyrical in estimating the prodigious capacity of its bottle-shaped scrotum. He chuckled at this reminder that the colony's growth depended as much on fecund animals and fecund soil as on any human activity.

∞

He'd allowed himself plenty of time in Guildford. After checking inventory details at his store and comparing its prices carefully with those of rival traders along the street, he walked over to the Rose and Crown, bought a jug of ale and waited. The mail-coach from Newcastle was due soon. His own driver had told him that Will Wroth always had a drink or two at this inn before setting out on the return trip.

When a slight young man came into the bar room, Alfred knew without hesitation who he was: he looked exactly as John had at the same age. Introducing himself, Alfred was unsurprised that the lad nodded in quick recognition: the name of Letch was prominent in the colony's business affairs, especially since the Perth City Council had licensed him to hire out carriages, phaetons and other vehicles.

Alfred invited Will to sit with him, poured him a drink and soon put him at ease by keeping their conversation to familiar topics – mail services, horses, roads, the growth of townships. The young fellow was well spoken, his manner respectful but composed – no false humility. *A credit to his parents*, Alfred thought.

'Your father and I used to know one another well in years gone by,' Alfred told him. 'I hope he's in good health.'

Blenching, Will lowered his eyes and spread a hand across his forehead. 'Far from it, Mr Letch. Gravely ill, I'm sorry to say. Delirious. Doctor says it's the typhoid fever,' he faltered, 'so we expect the worst.' He moved his fingertips to his closed eyes, as if to hold in the tears. 'It's painful for me to be away from home at such a terrible time. Mother insists I keep working – the family can't afford any pause in my wages, that's the simple truth. My father has been the gentlest of men, and we all love him dearly, but...'

∞

News of John Wroth's death reached Alfred three days later, bringing a twofold sense of bereavement: he mourned not only the loss of a man whose friendship he should have retained but also the lost chance to expiate his wrongdoing. The intended meeting could surely have restored with just a few candid words and a handclasp the mutual trust they once enjoyed. Death had torn away that hope of reconciliation. And his hope, he now began to see, had extended beyond the pair of them. By making amends with John he'd desired somehow to make amends more largely with those who'd suffered because of his youthful crimes. The folk he'd deceived in Great Baddow. The family he'd shamed in Finchingfield. But that possibility of finding a general release from blame had evaporated.

He remembered asking the prison chaplain in Chelmsford what to do about his burden of guiltiness, and being told he must learn to live with it. What did it really mean – to go on living with guilt? He wasn't quite sure, but supposed it meant accepting that transgressions couldn't be erased and their consequences were permanent. Nothing would alter what he'd done and who he'd been. Good deeds in the present would never dislodge past wrongs from their central place in his mind.

Only through his children was there any prospect of a fresh start, free of taint. No doubt John Wroth would have found some consolation in his own family, and Alfred tried to. His own sons were much younger than Will Wroth – Edward just nine, Hugh eight – and had yet to show any sign of self-reliance. *They cling too much to their mother*, he thought, *and she doesn't discourage their dependency* – but he couldn't bring himself to voice his concern that she held them too close. Ever since the death of their daughters she'd watched the boys with an anxious vigilance, as if they too might suddenly disappear.

# Polly

# 28

# Fremantle,
# October to December 1876

Whatever she'd imagined marriage would be – and after a year of it she couldn't exactly remember her prenuptial expectations – it wasn't this.

She'd looked forward to some kind of companionship, at least. Not that she could have supposed her life with Thomas would be as mildly affable as the relationship between her parents; Thomas was so different in temperament from George Letch, and she herself so unlike Caroline, that Polly had known without thinking much about it that her own experience of the wedded state wouldn't replicate her mother's. But although Thomas remained somewhat formal towards her in the weeks leading up to their union, it seemed reasonable to anticipate that before long they would become comfortably accustomed to each other's ways, relaxing into friendship and enjoying simple things as a couple.

That hadn't come to pass. Companionable feelings were hardly possible between two people who lived hundreds of miles apart. The first anniversary of their wedding was now approaching, and for most of the year since that ceremony made them man and wife, Thomas had been working far away in Geraldton. Left alone in their rented Fremantle cottage for so long with so little to do, Polly was beginning to languish. And now temptation beckoned.

She knew it wasn't really her husband's fault that he was still a stranger to her. 'It's not that I *want* to go up north while you're having to stay behind here,' he'd said. 'Of course I don't, especially so soon after getting married. It's regrettable, but we do need the income, and at present there's no other well-paid employment available where I can use my professional skills. We can't afford to miss an opportunity like this.'

'But why not find lodgings for ourselves in Geraldton?'

'I did make inquiries about that. Unfortunately they just have nothing suitable up there for married couples. It's a small rough town, Polly. All of us who are working on the railway line will be housed in a men's camp. Primitive conditions, no doubt. So you and I have to be separated for several months.'

It was a situation she had to accept – if not graciously, then with a resigned shrug. But it meant being cut off from sociability, the thing that had made the idea of marriage most attractive. Although there were regular letters from Thomas, their main topic was his work as supervisor of a plate-laying gang on the Geraldton-to-Northampton railway. Questions about her welfare seemed perfunctory. It was if his correspondence addressed a general readership rather than his wife, making her feel even more peripheral to his preoccupations. Her days were long, with few reasons for stepping outside the house except to walk down to the store now and then for household supplies or do some desultory scratching in the little 'garden' – a dry sandy patch at the back of the house. Sunday worship at the local chapel where they'd been married had no great appeal, but it did occupy a couple of hours each week and brought her a modicum of human contact. Indoors she found few activities to keep her mind from the sluggish passage of time and the drooping of her vacant life.

For much of the day Polly's part of the street was quiet and still, unless dogs or birds happened sporadically to clear their throats. The neighbour on one side, according to their landlord, was a reclusive elderly widow – 'Her name's Mrs Bunt, but she's so deaf you can't have a conversation even if you spot her, which you probably won't because she keeps so much to herself.' In the cottage on the other side, the same informant told them, lived Jock Merrilees – 'Gets up long before dawn to start work at the High Street bakery, so until he returns late in the day you won't see hide nor hair of him either.'

Near the end of an afternoon some weeks after Thomas had departed for Geraldton, Polly was sweeping her front step when a big paunchy fellow, jacketless, came ambling along the street and stopped in front of the entrance next door, taking a key from his pocket. So this was Merrilees. As she glanced at him, he raised his hat with a flourish and called out a cheerful greeting. She half lifted her hand from the broom and gave a demure nod of acknowledgement. He looked to be somewhat older than she, but probably not much, and his smile was broad and handsome – that was all she noticed before he went inside. The following afternoon at the same time, without quite intending to do so, she kept an eye on the street and emerged from her front door just as he was approaching his. This time, catching sight of her, he waved, walked around to her entrance and introduced himself. They stood there for a few minutes, exchanging bland remarks about nothing in particular until he managed to get her talking about where she'd come from.

'Now pardon me for asking this, Mrs Browne – I've been listening to thy manner of speech and trying to guess what region of t'home country tha might hail from, but I can't tell, though I'm sure it ain't Yorkshire, which is my part. So if t'question don't seem too nosey...?'

'My family's from Essex, Mr Merrilees.' Then, as a shield against undue familiarity, she thought she should mention Thomas. 'And my husband's from London.'

'Ah, so there's a Mr Browne. I don't believe I've seen him.'

'Thomas' – as if naming him would substantiate his existence – 'has been working up north for a while. On the Geraldton railway.'

'Thomas Browne? Wouldn't be t'one they call Satan, I spose? Ah. So – London and Essex, eh? Well, Rotherham is where I used to live, near Sheffield. I sometimes think about t'old home town, but I wouldn't go back there now, not if tha paid me. Nah, I wouldn't, and that's truth. Nowt to enjoy back there. Rotherham's a place of misery, befouled by t'ironworks. I was a puddler at Masbrough forge, and hot filthy work it was. I hated t'weather, too – most days dowly and cold, with soaking rains that used to flood River Don and make t'soil claggy. Getting on t'wrong side of t'law and being transported to this colony was t'best thing ever happened to me.' He grinned broadly. 'New world, new life, eh? Plenty of opportunities for a man who works hard. Plenty of food and sunshine and fresh air. A fine seashore

to walk along of a Sunday morning. Talk about fortunate!'
Chuckling, he folded his sturdy arms across his thick chest as
if to hug the good luck and keep it safe.

Over the next couple of weeks they had further conversations. He talked openly about the 'gormless' misdeeds of his
youth, the clumsy poaching escapades in particular, and the
night of eventual reckoning when he and a pair of friends,
carrying nets and guns, were apprehended in the woods by
police who'd been watching from behind a hedge. Because
there were more than two miscreants and they'd armed
themselves, a long sentence was inevitable. But for Merrilees,
looking back on it now, there was 'nowt to regret', he told
her. He laughed loudly at the happy irony that crime and
punishment had providentially rescued him from his loathsome little industrial town.

All sorts of things amused him. Hilarity was his regular
companion. It would well up suddenly and bubble from his
throat, and he'd throw back his head, hands on hips, elbows
out, belly shaking. It made Polly laugh too, just hearing and
seeing what genial pleasure he took in observing or recounting the simplest aspects of life around him – little workaday
incidents like a foolish argument between two of his customers about precedence at the bakery counter, and how it came
to a climax when one woman gave the other a parting smack
on her shoulder with the loaf she'd just bought; or the time
he'd tried to chase away a cat that had strayed boldly into the
kitchen, but succeeded only in tripping and knocking a bowl
of flour over himself as he fell.

His laughter was full of masculine vigour, rippling
through his flesh like powerful muscle. But how, she found
herself wondering, could such a virile man enjoy life so

much when he continued to live alone? Emboldened by his candour about other things, she tossed the question into his lap. 'You're content to be single, Mr Merrilees?'

'I wouldn't say *content*,' he replied, 'for I know what it is to be a husband, and truly I miss its pleasures, I don't mind tellin thee. My wife Meg died soon after I went into prison. Died in childbirth along with our first baby, God rest their souls. Getting wed a second time is something I'd be open to, but only if I found a suitable person and had t'means to keep her. I don't take marriage lightly. There are young women around this town, right enough, but any I'd fancy are either married already or above my station. Meanwhile, I need to work hard and save some money. It's only two years since I got my ticket of leave.'

Apart from that solemn little speech, Jock Merrilees seemed to radiate joviality. *Hearty* was the word that came to her one evening as, brushing her hair with slow strokes, she ruminated on what they'd talked about – and how they'd talked, too: the tone of it, the easy way his words and hers came together in a smooth fit. Yes, *hearty* – it described his manner perfectly, his particular kind of bluff cheerful demeanour. He wasn't chirpy like her father George, whose blithe attitude to life always seemed to verge on the inane. No, Jock was a shrewd and amused observer of human foibles, including his own. He also had a simple gift for embracing any chance to widen his outlook. He'd done foolish things in the past but wouldn't let himself dwell on them remorsefully. He had an appetite for whatever new experiences lay ahead. Liberated from the drudgery of labouring in a forge and the fear of ending up like his sister in the pinched dismal confines of a workhouse, he could now relish the prospect of making his way in the world through his own merits and hard work.

Conscious that their talks outside her front door were continuing with a frequency noticeable from the street – she had seen a curtain flick aside more than once in the window of the house opposite – Polly invited Jock into her kitchen for a cup of tea one afternoon. Soon it was a regular arrangement. He would go straight to her back door on returning from his day's work in the bakery, often with a trace of flour still dusting the hair that curled on his thick forearms. Coming through the doorway, he'd grin as if they shared an unspoken joke, and in response her mouth would lift happily at the corners as she put the kettle on.

After a couple of weeks of this, he turned up one day with a hand behind his back. 'No tea for me this time, thanks,' he said. 'Matter of fact, I've had enough of t'taste of tea. What about this instead?' He produced a bottle of brandy and, when she nodded, took a couple of tumblers from her shelf. 'Brandy's t'drink for me,' he declared. 'A man's gotta keep his pecker up, eh?'

Polly began to titter, and then checked herself with the thought that she didn't know whether the expression meant something rude. But as the viscous liquid warmed her throat and stroked her tongue, she talked on comfortably with Merrilees until darkness fell.

This simple ritual of drinking and conversing together became for her the cherished pivot of each day. While she awaited the time for him to arrive she would find herself getting physically restless, and beginning to imagine the intimacies that more and more often seemed about to occur, yet hadn't. A memory of Arthur Ridgen's hands on her in the barn at Finchingfield kept straying disconcertingly into her mind and she had to shove it aside. She didn't want to think about *him* any more – or that trollop of his, Moll Seccombe.

The damp gusty days of spring had given way to unremitting summer heat, which by midafternoon would seep through the cottage walls. As she stood by the window and watched for Jock she could feel a prickling of sweat between her large breasts and around her belly. Her hands wouldn't keep still.

∞

There he was now, with that gait of his, looking both relaxed and vigorous at the same time, shirtsleeves rolled up to the elbows and sunlight playing on his muscular arms. She patted her hair into place and opened the back door. *I won't wait any longer for him to make a move. Can't bear this daily tension. As soon as we've wet our whistles from his brandy bottle I'll put my arms around his neck and draw him into the bedroom.*

But as he came into the kitchen he didn't have his usual lighthearted expression, and this time there was no bottle in his hand.

'I've something to mention,' said Jock as he removed his hat and began to turn it around in his hands. He took a deep breath.

Polly sat down at the kitchen table. He remained standing. She had an impulse to tell him he didn't need to make a declaration – they should just lie down together immediately and let their bodies do the talking. She started to speak: 'Please don't —' But he held up his hand and his own words cut in quickly.

'We've become close friends, haven't we? Our conversations – well, I look forward to them keenly, and I know it's t'same for thee. More than that, to speak straight, I'm sure tha must feel, as I do, t'call of flesh to flesh. It's been troubling me of late, to t'point where I'll have to stop coming in here. Tha's a married woman, that's t'long and short of it, and things wouldn't have got to this if Satan – Mr Browne – hadn't been summoned away by his work. I won't let myself take advantage of him, or of thee. I hope tha'll see it's necessary to give up our drinking and talking, and stay apart.'

Flabbergasted, hand to her mouth, she sat in silence as he walked to the door with his head down and let himself out.

∞

That was not the end of the matter. Jock continued to loom in her mind, and not only during the daytime. She kept imagining the embrace that had not quite occurred. She pictured him in bed with the wife he'd once had, or with whores, or with herself.

Then Thomas returned suddenly from Geraldton, having lost his job there, and she was so glad just to have someone with her in the house, dispelling silence and loneliness, that for a while she overlooked the self-absorbed moods he'd brought back with him. She tried to be attentive to her unsmiling husband and forget about the man next door with his strong forearms, his big frame, his ringing laugh, and the rich brandy tang of his voice.

But some busybody must have said something about Polly's conversations with Jock. One day when Thomas came in from a walk she looked up and saw that he was scowling. 'Something wrong?' she asked.

'I've heard you didn't waste any time getting very friendly with our neighbour Merrilees in my absence.' His tone was cold.

Startled, she tried to maintain her composure. 'We chatted pleasantly from time to time,' she said. 'Nothing out of the ordinary.'

'But he was seen bringing bottles here. Frequently. And spending a lot of time in this house.'

'I assure you, Thomas, he – we – never behaved improperly.'

'It's improper of him to be drinking and talking with you in this house. And improper of you to invite him in. Later I'll go next door to speak to him strongly about this lewdness.'

'Don't do that. There's no reason. You'll embarrass yourself.'

'It's you, Polly, who've caused us embarrassment. And shame.'

He would not discuss it with her any further. Resentment smouldered between them. That evening he went to see Merrilees, who moved out of his house within a fortnight.

29

# Point Belches and Fremantle, November 1877

'There, you see! I promised this place would charm you.' Uncle Alfred's sweeping gesture offered the whole of the little inlet for their grateful admiration. And indeed it did appear to be a perfect picnic spot for the extended family.

Cradling her daughter Bella in one arm, shielding the tiny hands and face from the bright sunlight with her other arm, Polly looked slowly around the sandy crescent of the small sheltered bay – 'It's known as Miller's Pool,' Amelia told them – and then back northward over the expanse of water they had just crossed. There was a clear view towards Mount Eliza, rearing up to their left a short distance away on the opposite side of the river. At the foot of its eastern slope she could recognise the distinctive shape of the Pensioner Barracks, and further around to her right stood another pair of handsome brick edifices, even more imposing: Government House and the Town Hall, both the work of convict labourers. Alfred's shop was not visible from this angle, nor her parents' school, but she could see where their positions must be, nestling among the cluster of buildings that lined Perth's main streets.

Now the men were unfolding blankets and scattering cushions while Amelia and Caroline began to unpack items from the baskets. Polly sat a few yards away on a tree stump and put the baby to her breast, draping a shawl over it for modesty's sake. All the children were paddling in the shallows and squeaking with excitement.

Except for Alfred and Amelia, who had arranged the excursion, it was the first time any of them had been to Point Belches, though from time to time they had all gazed across the Swan at this low narrow promontory on the southern side, with its forlorn-looking old mill and only a scatter of other buildings. It had taken no more than twenty minutes for the chartered boat to bring them here over Perth Water from the pier, using the newly dredged channel, but that short journey was time enough for Polly to feel as if an oppressive load had slipped from her shoulders. The prospect of spending a few relaxed hours with her parents, siblings and cousins was a pleasant one. Perhaps even Thomas would become less tense. These days he always seemed anxiously preoccupied with his grand schemes, and often had a frown on his face. For her own part she was weary more than anything else. Most nights little Bella woke her often, fretful and demanding. Housekeeping money being meagre now, Polly had to spend long hours not only cleaning, cooking and washing but also tending to the vegetable garden so that she could put enough fresh food on their table. Thomas insisted on thrift, watching every penny – understandably, because of what he'd told her about his first wife's extravagance – yet he seemed not to recognise how much of a strain it was for Polly to make ends meet.

But today there was plenty to go around, each of the three couples having brought a variety of dishes with them. The group shared lunch tasks in the customary way: women did all the serving while men did most of the talking and eating.

Before long, George and Alfred were full of sentimental reminiscences about their early days in Essex.

'I remember,' said George, gesticulating with a half-chewed potato in one hand and a hardboiled egg in the other, 'when you were working on our family farm, before you went off to Felsted, that you'd take more care with how the horses looked than with the chores of ploughing and carting or cleaning out the stables. You used to spend as much time as you could plaiting their tails and tying coloured braid on their manes, and feeding them extra linseed cakes to make their coats glossy. You turned them into equine dandies! No wonder you did so well later when you set up your livery stables here – I'll bet yours have been the smartest-looking beasts in Perth!'

'You're right, George,' Alfred sighed. 'I always loved pampering and primping our horses when I was a young lad. But even happier times for me, back then, were indoors – when the family used to sing together and play our instruments in the living room. I can still hear the harmonies. For a long while after I was shipped out here I couldn't stop thinking fondly about our home in Finchingfield. I'd remember especially the smell of fruit stewing in the kitchen pots. Other things, too – the fireside warmth on winter nights, and then the frosty mornings with moisture frozen on the inside of windowpanes.' He paused and lifted the back of his hand to his forehead, as if to fend off regretful melancholy, before continuing. 'In prison and on the transport ship, I used to while away the time by recalling all the parts of our village as well. During the lonely hours I tried to picture each detail of each building. I'd linger especially over our chapel, not only the outside shape with its pattern of red and grey-blue bricks but the cool interior, too.'

George nodded. 'That horseshoe gallery,' he said.

'Yes, resting on its sturdy cast-iron stanchions. I could see the whole structure so clearly. The surrounding streets, too. In my mind I'd move along every one of them, recollecting the exact sequence of cottages, shops, churches. And all the other things that made Finchingfield slightly different from anywhere else in the county, and quite different from where we live now. The way the old main street curved down to the big pond at the bottom of the hill. The village green overlooking it, where we used to have fireworks on Guy Fawkes night. And I'd conjure up all the local people by name. Our neighbours. The whole little world that I'd lost.'

'But it's disappearing anyway,' said George, 'even for those who still live there. The whole countryside back home has been through great changes since you saw it last. Not so many farm workers now, nor village craftsmen neither. The young folk have been moving to the cities.'

'That old mill over there,' interjected Polly, pointing, 'on the other side of the inlet – it reminds me of the one Grandpa owned just north of Finchingfield, but this one has lost its arms.'

'Looks woebegone, doesn't it, partly dismantled,' said Alfred. 'Hasn't operated as a mill for many years, so I'm told. William Shenton built it – his brother George is on the Perth City Council with me. They were among the colony's earliest settlers, you know. William drowned somewhere off the coast a while back, and since then it's fallen into disuse. The cottage next to it was let to tenants but they've gone now.'

'Hmmm. It has potential,' said Thomas, as if to himself. He'd hardly spoken for the last half-hour, and seemed to be in a reverie, staring at the mill. Polly gave him an inquiring glance.

'What kind of potential?'

'I'm not sure yet, Polly, but it catches the eye. Such a fine location, the way it sits near the tip of this little jutting peninsula, directly across from the town. I'd like to have a closer look. It's a short easy walk from here.'

'Excellent meal!' said George, beaming appreciatively. As the women cleared away the leftovers, the three men lit cigars and ambled off to inspect the mill.

'Thomas is dreaming up some new scheme, I can tell,' Polly said, her mouth twisted with distrust.

Her mother raised an eyebrow. 'You sound sceptical, my dear, but he's a very clever man, you must admit that. Whatever ideas he may be brewing now, I'm sure he knows how to test whether they'd work.'

'Oh, he's not short of bright ideas or technical knowledge, that's true. And he works conscientiously, but…'

Biting her tongue, Polly shook her head. She shouldn't let her feelings show. But if only Thomas would think more about persuading other people to see things his way, or let himself be persuaded to change his mind when he couldn't win support. He kept running into conflict, and always reckoned it was someone else's fault. Something stubborn in his manner often raised other people's hackles. It was probably why he'd lost his railway supervision job last year, up Geraldton way. He hadn't said much about it, except to blame the Public Works Office for the cost problems and delays. Withdrew into a gloomy mood for weeks, buried himself in books from the Literary Institute in Fremantle, and then suddenly turned his energies to the next dispute. Couldn't resist getting involved in public altercations about railway lines and other construction projects. Just wouldn't compromise.

She wished she could tell her mother and Amelia, 'You may think it's admirable he sticks so firmly to his principles, but when that attitude gets in the way of a steady income for us, his own family, it's irresponsible. Maddening!' It would be indiscreet to say anything, even quietly, even to these women, about her domestic troubles – indiscreet and disloyal – but it was hard to stifle her exasperation.

Perhaps – though she had little faith in this possibility – there'd be a change of fortune around the corner. Thomas had been consumed lately with ambitious plans to develop a railway line up to the Avon Valley. He was certain, he'd told her, that it would be a great thing for the colony, and that he'd do very well out of it if he could become the supervising engineer for such a big project.

*If!* thought Polly. *If!* She looked away, conscious that her despondent mood was visible and not wanting to respond to the compassion she glimpsed in Amelia's watchful eyes.

Conversation lapsed. After a few minutes, Caroline suggested a stroll along the sand to stretch their legs and keep an eye on the children, who were frolicking at the edge of the little bay.

Polly shook her head. 'You two go,' she said. 'I'll rest here with my little Bella.'

When Caroline and Amelia had wandered off, Polly furtively drew a small silver brandy flask from her pocket and swallowed a large mouthful, then another. The drinking had become a solace in itself, and also a reminder of Jock Merrilees. As much as anything, it was his laughter she missed. He'd known how to enjoy life heartily. Her days now were devoid of enjoyment.

The afternoon had become uncomfortably warm and so she moved into the shade of a tree, placing her infant daughter beside her on the blanket. Feeling drowsy, she closed her eyes and sank into a dreamless sleep.

∞

'Polly! Wake up! Look at the baby, for God's sake!'

The men had returned; Thomas was standing there, anger darkening his face. He held Bella in his arms. 'You left her lying in the sun! Look how limp she is! Couldn't you hear her grizzling? She must be completely parched.' He turned to the other men. 'Can you find any drinking water?'

Alfred rummaged hastily in one of the baskets and brought a bottle. 'But I'm afraid it's not cool enough for her to drink,' he said.

'Better than nothing,' said Thomas tersely, and trickled some of it between the dry little lips. The baby spluttered, vomited and turned pale.

'How could you leave her exposed to the heat like that?' shouted Thomas.

'I didn't.' Tears ran down Polly's cheeks. 'We were both in the shade, but I fell asleep and the sun's angle has shifted.'

'You should have anticipated that.'

'I was so tired. I'm sorry, I'm sorry.' Her shoulders shook with heavy sobs.

Amelia intervened. 'I think we should get the poor little mite to a doctor, Polly. Her colour isn't good.'

Thomas took out his pocket watch. 'But it's more than half an hour until the boat returns for us.' Again he tried to give the baby some water but again this caused a spasm of retching.

Miserable, anxious, the group could do nothing but wait. Hardly another word was spoken.

∞

The following afternoon, when Amelia arrived unannounced at the Brownes' house in Fremantle hoping to hear that their baby had recovered, Polly came to the door swollen-eyed and dishevelled. Bella, she whispered, had died just before noon and the doctor confirmed that it was sunstroke. Thomas, distraught and bitter, was out making funeral arrangements.

As Amelia embraced her tightly, Polly knew that her own breath would reek of alcohol, but she was beyond caring whether the older woman would blame her for that. What could Amelia know of real hardship and sorrow? Although her daughters had been taken from her, that loss was the kind of misfortune suffered by many families and nobody could hold Amelia responsible. Bella's death was different: everyone would attribute it to Polly's negligence. And besides, Amelia still had her sons, and a comfortable life with servants and carriages and a husband who doted on her.

'It's a terrible loss you've suffered, Polly,' said Amelia, 'and there are no words of mine that could lessen it. Bella was such a sweet little mite. Part of the family snatched away like that in an instant – so cruel! But perhaps your shared grief may bring you and Thomas closer together.'

Polly clenched her teeth and felt her face reddening as she tried in vain to hold back an upsurge of despair. 'More likely the opposite!' she cried out. 'He's so dreadfully...so *furious* with me!' An involuntary moaning sound rose in her throat. 'It was already difficult enough between us before this happened. Thomas...he's...I don't know what it is. There's something strange in his manner towards me, Amelia. I've never really felt cherished. As a woman. As a wife.'

Until this moment Polly hadn't thought she'd be able to talk about her anguish to anyone, but now it seemed to pour out of her. 'To have and to hold – that vow – he doesn't seem to *want* to have and hold me!'

Amelia was looking away, probably embarrassed by this outburst, but Polly couldn't stop herself. 'I just long to be clasped passionately, and I don't know why he hardly ever touches me. Is there something about my body that repels him? I'm far from slender, but I didn't think...' She put her face in her hands.

# Runty

# 30

# Perth, April 1878

Arriving a few minutes before the appointed time, Runty saw that Alfred was already sitting there on a park bench in the shade, plump and nattily dressed, the embodiment of stylish prosperity. Satan's message had asked them to meet him in the botanical gardens near the courthouse – 'as near to eleven as I can make it'. He would be travelling from Fremantle for this rendezvous, but for both Alfred and Runty it was just a short stroll from their respective places of work, one in St George's Terrace and the other in Barrack Street.

'Morning, Mr Letch. You've found an agreeable spot.'

'Sergeant Rowe! Good to see you again.' They shook hands and sat together to wait. 'Yes, the trees are growing quickly. This is the first time I've lingered here long enough to contemplate the gardens.'

After an exchange of pleasantries Runty asked, 'Do you happen to know what exactly Mr Browne wants to discuss? His note to me said only that he'd value our counsel on a business matter.'

'Mmm,' Alfred nodded. 'Same general phrasing in what he wrote to me. My first thought was that he probably intends to ask me for a loan, on the basis of our family connection – his wife's my niece, you know – and our shared background as former convicts, I suppose. But if that were the case, it's unlikely he'd have asked you to be part of the meeting.'

'True. He knows I'm not a wealthy man, and we don't have a close connection. I bought a little parcel of real estate from him some while back – must be three years – but I've encountered him only occasionally since. Of course, it's part of my job to keep an ear to the ground, and from time to time his name comes up in conversations around the town, so I'm aware he's had some difficulties recently.'

'Perhaps you heard about the death of his infant daughter a few months ago? And the circumstances?'

'I did. Very sad.'

'Yes, though his behaviour – well, you know what he's like, and he's been quite erratic since that happened. Withdraws moodily into himself for a while but then there's a burst of hectic activity when some ambitious project engages him. He's thrown himself into public debates again about where this or that railway should go, and about the best kind of design for one bridge or another.'

'From his letters to the newspaper, I know he's never let go of an idea that he talked about passionately when I first met him – developing rail transport up to Northam and beyond.'

'I admire his ability to devise unorthodox schemes,' Alfred said. 'He's a clever fellow, no doubt of that. Problem is, when obstacles appear he's quick to feel frustrated, to think that others are deliberately thwarting him. Perhaps they are, sometimes, but the way he reacts doesn't help – dashing off letters of protest, talking to journalists, speaking imprudently at public meetings. He's always apt to bristle at perceived snubs and slights. Can be difficult at home, too – Polly has told us about it. His temper gets the better of him, and he accuses her of all sorts of things that I'm sure aren't justified. So she appeals to her parents, which only makes Satan even angrier.'

'Hush. Here he comes now.'

Thomas was hurrying along the path towards them, wiping his brow and hands with a kerchief. 'My apologies, gentlemen,' he said as he greeted them. 'An annoying delay with the coach. Not your fault, of course, Alfred. The roads are in such poor condition.'

'I'm sorry it wasn't a smooth journey, Thomas. The drivers do their best but – this is between ourselves – I plan to sell the coaching business before long. I'm already on the point of handing over my Perth-to-Guildford mail contract to Horton, and I expect to do the same later with the Fremantle contract. Within a few years, I'm sure, rail will carry mail and passengers to and from the port.'

'Not before time,' said Thomas, sitting down beside them on the bench. 'Half a century since the first settlers arrived, there's still no reliable public transport between Fremantle and Perth. Forgive my bluntness, Alfred.'

Alfred dismissed the matter with a smile and a shrug.

Thomas drew in a deep breath. 'Well now,' he said, 'let me explain why I asked you both to make time for this conversation. You're busy men, I appreciate that, but I need your advice. You've listened to me considerably in the past, and I'm turning to you now because there are very few people I can trust. The nub of the matter is this: I've devised plans for some public works that could contribute significantly to the development of our colony, but I just can't get a fair hearing for what I propose. There are powerful figures blocking my way – one person especially, whose behaviour is certainly immoral and probably illegal. I'm hoping, Alfred, that you may be able to exert some influence on my behalf through your connections in commerce and local government, and that you, Sergeant Rowe, can put in a favourable word for me through your access to guardians of the law.'

There was an awkward pause. Alfred responded gently. 'You'll need to give us more specific details, Thomas.'

'Of course, of course.' He took an envelope from his coat pocket. 'So I'd like to read aloud to you both, if I may, a copy of a letter I wrote some weeks ago to the secretary of state for the colonies. It didn't reach him, because I sent it in the care of my legal adviser in London for dispatch, you see, and instead of forwarding it he advised me to recall the letter and instead seek an audience here with the Governor to discuss my grievance – his point being that to go over the vice-regal head could be seen as disrespectful. I tried then to speak with His Excellency, whose response was to ask for all correspondence relating to the case, the whole file, which will include slanderous material about me written by the director of Public Works. So I fear this will sink into a slough of untruths and misrepresentations, and my rights won't be upheld. If you let me read at length now from what I intended to say to the colonial secretary, you'll know the particulars of my complaint. Then you can advise me how to proceed.'

He raised his eyebrows at them in a mute appeal for permission. *As if we could withhold it*, thought Runty. They nodded, and settled their buttocks. After glancing over each shoulder to make sure no one else was within earshot, Satan began intoning earnestly.

It is with great reluctance and regret that I have to bring under your notice a line of conduct adopted towards me by Mr J. H. Thomas who not quite two years ago was appointed to the office of Director of Public Works in this Colony.

I am a Civil Engineer and Architect having been duly articled to both branches of the profession. The term of my novitiate as an Engineer was passed chiefly on the works of the London and Birmingham Railway under the late Sir Charles (then Mr) Fox...

Runty couldn't take in every detail that followed, but the momentum of Satan's story was strong and clear despite its ornate phrasing. It recounted the particulars of his professional experience in England, his conviction for forgery – 'It was well known that I suffered to shield my (then) wife, long since dead' – his time as a convict, eventual discharge, and establishment of a respected practice as architect and engineer. The letter referred proudly to projects he'd carried out 'in various parts of the Colony, among them a system of light railways and a scheme of harbour works', to the satisfaction of many 'gentlemen well known in the Engineering World' and of 'the Merchants of Fremantle' – all of this 'long prior to Mr Thomas's arrival in the Colony'.

Runty saw the sweat running down Satan's face, which had become as florid as his writing style.

When Mr Thomas arrived here in June 1876 I was Inspector of Works on the Geraldton and Northampton Railway,
from which appointment Mr Thomas soon caused me to
be removed with a display of much acrimonious feeling.
I was thus at liberty to follow up my project for a system
of light railways, and I did so with very general support.
My scheme of harbour works remained in abeyance under
reference to Sir John Coode.

In the course of last year 1877 it came to my
knowledge that Mr Thomas was writing defamatory letters
and statements to Sir John Coode and other gentlemen
including my friends and correspondents in England with
the evident object of doing me injury...

His voice rose, and Runty could see that he was trembling
with indignation.

I have been made aware that Mr Thomas told Sir John
Coode that 'since the plans in question had been prepared
by Mr T. H. J. Browne, no reliance could be placed on
them, his estimates and prices of material being utterly
worthless'. The plans in question Mr Thomas had never
seen! They were made by me to order for the Government,
they had merited the approval of the then Commissioner
of Works the Hon. M. Fraser, and I hold a memo from
the then Acting Colonial Secretary A. O'G. Lefroy Esq.
expressing Governor Robinson's approval of the work I
had done – the very work condemned by Mr Thomas...

On he went, impassioned, piling up yet more details of
his antagonist's libellous correspondence. *This invective won't*

*bring him the recognition and remedy he craves*, thought Runty. He glanced at Alfred and saw him purse his lips – whether impatiently or sympathetically he couldn't tell. At last Satan came to his peroration, which asked the secretary of state 'whether what Mr Thomas has done is consistent with the duties of his position, and has the sanction of Her Majesty's Government at home'.

Satan folded the sheets of paper slowly and tucked them back into his coat. Over the top of his spectacles he looked imploringly at his two companions. 'I need your help,' he said, and there was desperation in his tone. 'It's not forthcoming from the new Governor. He doesn't have the courage of his predecessor. Robinson saw the justice of my claims, but Ord has rebuffed me – says he can't afford me any redress. Wherever I turn I'm blocked. I want work. I want a fair field. What can I do? My energies are as futile as those of a caged bird.' He put his hand across his mouth and lowered his eyes. Runty could see that the poor devil was on the verge of tears.

They sat in tense silence for a minute or two. A pair of well-dressed men walked past, doffing their hats to Alfred as they murmured a deferential greeting. Runty saw Satan watching the interaction, no doubt envious – and who could blame him? – of Alfred's status in the community as city councillor as well as prosperous man of business. Both men had been sent against their will to a place almost as far from home as they could go; one of them was thriving here while the other struggled. Runty tried to imagine what it must feel like to be in Satan's shoes, knowing it was possible for an emancipist to gain respect and advancement if he put his mind to it, but failing to achieve these things himself despite all his professional capabilities. Was it sheer misfortune in his case? What made him an object of spite among such people as the director of Public Works? Was there something in his character that created impediments? And whatever the causes, were there any remedies? It wasn't enough to feel compassion for him. He wanted practical help. But how should one respond to his appeal for advice?

Alfred, deliberating, cleared his throat. 'It seems to me, Thomas,' he said, 'that you've done everything you can to try to force the door open. The door to employment on civil service projects, I mean. That door has been slammed shut, and though you've been treated unjustly I don't think it's possible – sad to say – to overturn the resistance you continue to encounter from those with government authority. Not in the near future, anyway.'

'But I refuse to yield to their villainy!' Satan expostulated.

Alfred held up his hand. 'Hear me out, Thomas. If you persist in beating on a closed door you'll only exhaust yourself. And I must speak frankly: your idea that either Sergeant Rowe or I could somehow prevail on the authorities to change their minds is quite unrealistic. So I suggest you consider going about things in a different way. Relinquish those public construction projects, at least for a while, and try instead to make your name and fortune through some private commercial opportunity. Then perhaps eventually, when you've shown your mettle and made a triumphant success of a scheme that's under your own control, you'll be an irresistible contender for work with the civil service, if you still want it.'

Satan was quiet for a moment, stroking his chin. Runty could see immediately the good sense in Alfred's advice, and nodded vigorously to show his endorsement. It would steer

Satan away from conflict and encourage him to take matters into his own hands. If he could devise something with scope for his creative talents, and demonstrate an ability to manage it well, his luck might finally change.

'I'll give it some thought,' Satan promised. 'You may well be right,' he added, as the three shook hands, 'and I'm grateful, truly, to have had an attentive hearing. I don't get that from many people.'

*What a strange fellow he is*, thought Runty, turning away towards his Barrack Street office. *So intense! Hell-bent on gaining recognition, on proving himself right. He acts as if most of the world is against him. You'd think he'd been starved of any affectionate support, yet the impression I get from Letch is that Satan keeps finding fault with his wife, keeping her at a distance. It's as if he's just unable to put himself in another person's shoes. I doubt he could imagine what it's like for others of us who've had to struggle so much on our own. Three and a half years now since my Sarah died, and for me they've been years of worry about our children's welfare, with no intimate companion to share the responsibility. It's obvious Satan feels extremely alone, and if I could do anything about alleviating that I would, but although we've had several conversations it's probably never occurred to him that in some ways he'd be less alone than I am if only he stopped pushing his wife and her relatives away.*

# Thomas

# 31

# South Perth, July 1879

Emerging into a wet street, stepping around puddles and holding his hat brim with one hand and umbrella with the other as he leant into the wind, Thomas almost collided with someone.

'Pardon me, sir – ah! Sergeant Rowe! Good afternoon. How are you?'

'Very well, Mr Browne, very well. What brings you to this part of town in such dismal weather?'

Thomas gestured to the Land Titles Office. 'I've just been checking the documents for a property. I plan to take a lease on it. If you can spare a few minutes I'd like to talk the matter over with you.'

Over tea and cakes in a shop nearby, Thomas spoke at length about his new project.

'You'll remember our conversation with Alfred Letch more than a year ago in the gardens near here, when I was feeling so dejected because of obstruction in the civil service.'

Runty nodded.

'You both thought I should shelve my schemes for public works and devote myself instead to some private commercial enterprise. It was sound advice. I've been casting around and now I've decided quite definitely what I want to do. I haven't felt so enthusiastic for a long while.' Beaming, he sipped his tea.

'I'm keen to hear about it,' Runty assured him.

'Well, I have something quite grand in mind, with – I believe – considerable potential for profit. You know the old mill on the peninsula at Point Belches?'

'I've looked across at it from here, that's all. Abandoned, isn't it?'

'Yes, becoming dilapidated, in fact. I've been looking today at the land title documents and they tell an interesting story. The property has changed hands a few times. It's forty-five years since William Shenton had the first mill erected on that site in order to grind corn brought down the Swan from Guildford and upriver from Fremantle, and soon afterwards the present structure replaced it, very solid, made of large limestone blocks. Then he built the cottage beside it a year or two later. There's a small warehouse adjacent to it, too. When Shenton met an untimely end – drowned in a shipwreck – the mill and its cottage went to his young wife, who sold the freehold to a man called Hamersley. The amount of grain being brought in for grinding seems to have declined bit by bit, and eventually the mill stopped operating, with the cottage being let out as a residence. Then on Hamersley's death about four years ago the property was bequeathed to his daughter. She's the one who recently married Forrest the explorer. But the buildings have got into a poor state, and they're now sitting empty.'

'Your tea's getting cold, Mr Browne.'

'I've had all the tea I want. Anyway, I'm sure you can guess what my scheme is. I'm intending to sign a lease agreement – six pounds a year for three years – and convert the buildings into a hotel. Much more than a hotel, in fact – I envisage there'll be a balcony for patrons to watch events on the river, a garden and picnic park in the grounds, a residential arrangement using the renovated cottage, and so on. My plans are ambitious, but I won't explain other details now. The first challenge, as I don't have much capital, is that I'll need to borrow money to carry out extensive repairs and alterations.'

'It's a bold idea. Are you confident you can attract enough customers to cross the river regularly?'

'Well, Sergeant, if I can persuade just a hundred people each week to visit this place of mine, I shouldn't have any trouble paying off my debts and then beginning to make a profit. With almost thirty thousand people in the colony now, a mere hundred visitors per week seems a modest target, don't you think? I'll need to advertise vigorously, of course.' Thomas could feel his pulse thumping with exhilaration at the prospect.

'When would you expect to open this place to the public?'

'Oh, it'll be many months before that can happen. For one thing, raising a loan may be a slow process. All the architectural calculations and building specifications I'll handle myself, of course, so I should be able to complete them efficiently, but then materials will need to be ferried up the river from Fremantle or across from Perth, and that'll affect the construction schedule. So even if things go smoothly I don't anticipate being ready to announce an opening before the early months of next year. But in the meantime I'll continue to operate as a land agent.'

'And that's a role you're very good in. As you know, I was pleased with the land purchase you arranged so efficiently for me a few years ago. Tell me, when did you get this idea of turning the old mill into a social attraction?'

'It was during a family picnic outing to Point Belches, summer before last, that I first began to think about the possibilities of the site. But that day had a dreadful outcome – the death of my baby daughter —'

'I heard about it. Terrible tragedy.'

'Terrible, yes. It drove any thought of enterprising projects out of my head for quite some while. But then after that conversation with you and Alfred in the courthouse gardens last year, when you urged me to turn from public works to private business schemes, the idea of converting the mill for new purposes returned. Recently I've been developing sketches, estimating costs…'

'I wish you well. You deserve to prosper, and they say fortune favours the brave.'

'Let's hope so.'

'Well, I suppose I should be on my way soon, but it's been pleasant to linger here.'

'I think I'll order myself another pot of tea and just read quietly until the rain eases.' Thomas drew out a book from an inside pocket of his coat.

'What's that you're reading?'

'*Culture and Anarchy* – an essay by Matthew Arnold. I've borrowed it from the Literary Institute. Polemical, and there's much in it to stimulate the mind. A nicely ironic prose style, too. He looks at recent changes in England and asks what values are shaping the nation. The bustle of commerce and industry, political upheavals, educational reforms – they're all putting pressure on every social class, and so Mr Arnold urges us to think carefully about guiding principles. He gives examples of what he sees as a lax self-indulgent notion that individuals should be free to do whatever they like. With your background, Sergeant, you'd be interested in his remarks about the Fenians and the Hyde Park rioters. Wait a moment – unless you need to rush off? No? I can find the passage quickly.' Thomas flicked through the pages. 'It'll be in the second chapter, where he mentions someone who was a fellow apprentice when I was young. Ah yes, here it is – listen to this:

There are many things to be said on behalf of this exclusive attention of ours to liberty, and of the relaxed habits of government which it has engendered. It is very easy to mistake or to exaggerate the sort of anarchy from which we are in danger through them. We are not in danger from Fenianism, fierce and turbulent as it may show itself; for against this our conscience is free enough to let us act resolutely and put forward our overwhelming strength the moment there is any real need for it. In the first place, it never was part of our creed that the great right and blessedness of an Irishman, or, indeed, of anybody on earth except an Englishman, is to do as he likes; and we can have no scruple at all about abridging, if necessary, a non-Englishman's assertion of personal liberty...

Thomas looked up from the page. 'Very droll parody of complacent English attitudes, don't you think?' he said.

'Here's how it goes on, tongue in cheek: he describes Irish Fenians as "desperate and dangerous" dupes of "an alien religion", unable to appreciate English institutions or values. And then' – Thomas was relishing the role of lecturer, and wished Runty would show more appreciation in the role of listener instead of fiddling with that teaspoon – 'he turns his sarcasm on English labourers who mask their greed for material advancement with a show of political unrest. And this is where a man I used to know well – now a famous public figure – becomes an object of ridicule:

> With the Hyde Park rioter how different! He is our own flesh and blood; he is a Protestant; he is framed by nature to do as we do, hate what we hate, love what we love… the question of questions, for him, is a wages question. That beautiful sentence Sir Daniel Gooch quoted to the Swindon workmen, and which I treasure as Mrs Gooch's Golden Rule, or the Divine Injunction 'Be Ye Perfect' done into British – the sentence Sir Daniel Gooch's mother repeated to him every morning when he was a boy going to work: 'Ever remember, my dear Dan, that you should look forward to being some day manager of that concern!' – this fruitful maxim is perfectly fitted to shine forth in the heart of the Hyde Park rough also, and to be his guiding-star through life.

'So sardonic!' Thomas put the book down with a wry smile. 'Such mockery of people who rely on platitudes! I'm sure Daniel Gooch isn't happy to be taken down a peg or two so publicly by one of the leading writers of our time. He and I used to be friends many years ago. We worked together in a foundry when we were lads, in the early days of railway engineering. He went on to fame and fortune, unlike me. You've heard of him, I suppose. No? Well, he made his name adapting locomotives for the Great Western Railway. Under Brunel's patronage, that was. Then he got into the business of laying a telegraph cable across the Atlantic, did very well for himself on various boards, and got elected to parliament. Was made a baronet, too. Always clever and ambitious, but it takes more than that to be so successful. A case of being in the right place at the right time, as the saying goes. I've never managed that myself.'

'With a bit of luck,' said Runty, 'this colony will turn out after all to be a place where you can thrive. If you put your mind to it.'

'I'll do my best, be assured of that, Sergeant. And thank you for the encouragement. I see the rain has stopped, so I should let you get back to whatever it was you were going to do if I hadn't intercepted you. I hope my tendency to dominate the conversation hasn't been annoying.'

'No, no.' Runty rose to leave. 'I trust Mrs Browne is keeping well?'

The tone was casual but Thomas looked at him sharply. 'What have you heard?'

Runty seemed puzzled. 'Nothing at all. I just meant to express my good wishes. It must have been especially hard for her to lose a child under those circumstances.'

Thomas couldn't let it rest there. 'Yes, she's suffered,' he said, 'but she brought it on herself. And I'll tell you plainly, Sergeant, it's been a troubling time. Very tense between the two of us. I find it hard to forget what's happened, and she's become too fond of the bottle, neglects the new baby, the boy, young George…and there are other things, but I've said more than I should have.'

'I'll keep it to myself, don't worry about that, but I'm truly sorry to hear of your difficulties. Perhaps this new project will…who knows? Perhaps it will bring satisfactions you can both share.'

'Perhaps, but meanwhile there's a rift.'

*I talked too much, as usual,* Thomas thought as he watched as the detective waddle off along the wet street with his short-legged gait. Should have asked him about his work, and his family. Someone told me he's remarried; I didn't think to mention it. Must have been hard for him as a widower, I suppose.

Anyway, Rowe had seemed to listen patiently, and Thomas felt the need for a sympathetic ear more acutely than ever these days. Polly exasperated him, and he exasperated her.

## 32

# South Perth,
# April 1880 to November 1881

Standing near the stern and using the current expertly, the lighterman guided his barge with a long oar until he brought it to rest against the jetty. Thomas had watched its slow progress across the Swan from Perth as he waited impatiently for the supplies that would be transferred to his cart.

'I hope you've brought today's *Inquirer* with you,' he called out, hand cupping his mouth.

'Indeed I have, Mr Browne. I got your message about that.'

Paying no attention to the items being unloaded for him, Thomas seized the newspaper and turned its pages until he saw the large advertisement. He read it right through, slowly, and then read it all again with satisfaction at his carefully crafted phrasing.

The Alta Gardens Hotel
MILL POINT (Point Belches), SOUTH PERTH
THIS HOTEL, with its spacious gardens, recreation grounds, pic-nic park and premises now open, is intended to supply

the long felt want of an establishment combining the attractions of rural pleasure and out-door amusements with hotel entertainments and home comforts.

The Alta Tower, fifty feet high, has the ground floor fitted up as a refreshment bar. On the first floor is a spacious circular dining, supper and reading room, commanding extensive and beautiful views of Perth, the River, Mounts Bay Road, Mount Eliza, etc., and communicating with the newly erected grand balcony encircling the tower, upwards of two yards wide and one hundred and twenty feet in circumference. This balcony is also approached by outside stairs, so that ladies may ascend or descend without passing through the bar.

The second floor of the tower forms a capital smoking room and snuggery, communicating with a gallery on the top of the tower from which a view of unsurpassed beauty is obtained.

In combination with the ground floor of the tower is a spacious hall 31 x 18 feet, available for wedding, dinner, supper, dancing, music and other parties. The use of this hall, well lighted, can be secured for private pleasure parties from half a guinea per evening. In connection with the hall are retiring and dressing rooms for ladies.

In the hotel department spacious rooms are available for the use of visitors.

There is no tap room on the premises, neither is provision in any way made for the use of the building and premises for mere drinking purposes.

For the season the Alta offers special inducements as winter quarters for invalids, and for gentlemen fond of boating, fishing, etc., etc. Board and residence on moderate terms.

It is intended that the Gardens, now in part laid out and comprising nearly two acres of couch grass lawn, shall form a specially attractive feature of the establishment, provided with swings, merry-go-round, gymnasium, etc. etc., also grounds for croquet, archery, cricket, etc.

## ON SUNDAYS

the gardens and premises will be open to the public. No liquor will be sold to casual visitors; guests who use the hotel for board and residence during the day, and *bona fide* travellers by road or river, will alone form exception to this rule.

Inspection solicited and patronage invited.

Parties who may find a difficulty in proceeding from Perth to the Alta, will please give notice at the Alta Gardens Hotel Office, when boats will be placed at their disposal. The Alta boats will run at all times when inducement offers. With the incoming summer season a steam ferry will be established.

Licensee and manager

THOS. H. J. BROWNE

The Alta Gardens Hotel Office, Howick Street, Perth, opposite the Town Hall, is open daily for the transaction of all business relating to the establishment, engagement of rooms, boats, etc.

Perth, April 20, 1880.

This statement was sure to attract widespread interest. It would be seen, he believed, as an eloquent culmination to the series of advertisements appearing weekly for the last two months in *The Inquirer*, with more to follow throughout the year. Such an outlay was unavoidably very expensive, a significant addition to all the renovation work, furnishings and associated costs, but the expected flow of custom would soon recoup it all – and, more than that, would vindicate him triumphantly, demonstrating to friends and enemies alike that he was a person of substance, of uncommon talent. Someone to be reckoned with.

Meanwhile, many important details still required urgent attention. Some of the supplies now unloaded were for catering purposes, a few more items of furniture for the smoking room were due to arrive that afternoon, and it was necessary to finish cleaning and tidying the cottage rooms and the grounds. He anticipated a good turnout of visitors at the weekend; this was already Tuesday, so there was no time to lose. Once patrons began to arrive he'd be depending heavily on Polly to handle practical arrangements at the Alta while he worked at the office in the city. The mill cottage was to be home now for her and little George, but she'd also have to make it attractive to boarders, and the tower next to it was going to be a very public place, requiring her constant attention. She'd need to tend the garden, so that the kitchen would have fresh vegetables; she'd need to prepare food and provide drinks; she'd need to keep everything clean and tidy – rooms, bar, gallery, balcony, all of it; she'd need to welcome the guests, show them what the Alta had to offer, and generally ensure they had a pleasant experience there. He wished he could place more trust in her reliability.

Standing beside the loaded cart, Thomas shaded his eyes and looked towards the structure on which his hopes rested. He felt a throb of pride at the way he'd been able to transform the old derelict mill into the impressive Alta. It had required not only a considerable feat of imagination but also an uncommon set of professional skills. Nobody else in this colony could have conceived of such a project or brought it to fruition.

∞

'You said we could count on at least a hundred visitors every week. Definitely a hundred or more, you said. The numbers have been far less than that during winter and spring. And no wonder! It's damp and dreary here, Thomas, day after day. All very well for you, spending so much time over there in Perth – plenty of comfort and company – but for me and little George these last few months have been miserable. Just miserable.' Polly spat out the words with a hiss of resentment, and Thomas winced. 'I don't think you have any idea,' she went on fiercely, 'how much effort I've put into this place, trying to make your grandiose plan feasible. The whole thing is misconceived. It can't work. In the last fortnight barely half a dozen customers have arrived!'

'But the warmer weather will make a big difference,' he said. 'And with Regatta Day coming up I'll put a special notice in the newspaper, telling people the Alta is the only standpoint for a complete view of the races and sports. We can offer reserved seating. That should bring a large crowd here, and we'll do a brisk trade in ales and wines and refreshments. And then with the summer season, things will improve, I'm sure of it.'

'You're always so sure beforehand, cocksure, and so full of excuses afterwards.'

'That's unjust, Polly. I've planned this whole enterprise with great care, and put all my energy into it. We can't afford to fail. We must keep our nerve and redouble our exertions.'

But six weeks later, as Christmas approached, he had to admit to himself that patronage remained far below a profitable level. To the usual advertisement in *The Inquirer* he added this plea:

Having at considerable outlay brought these premises, together with the gardens and grounds, from ruin and wildness to a state and condition which I believe render the establishment worthy of patronage and support, I respectfully request a fair share of public favour, assuring my friends and customers that my best efforts shall always be directed to ensure their enjoyment and comfort. To wedding, select picnic and private social parties the Alta will be found to offer special advantages.

∞

During the long hours when nobody came to his city office to inquire about the Alta, Thomas immersed himself in reading. It took his mind off the financial problems for a while. He'd bought a copy of a novel that was becoming the talk of the town: written by John Boyle O'Reilly, the former Fenian agitator, *Moondyne* had been published the year before in Boston and recently reissued in Australia. Though much of it struck Thomas as rambling and sentimental, he found it irresistible because its main character was himself a convict transported to Western Australia, who escaped from custody, acquired the name Moondyne (Thomas knew where that sobriquet came from), and made his way back to Britain under yet another name, only to return to the colony as comptroller of convicts with a mandate to reform the penal system. There were further aspects of the story, too, that caught Thomas's attention – not least its recurrent theme that land ownership, if properly distributed, can redeem those who make good use of it.

The appearance of O'Reilly's novel brought back to mind the Irishman's bolt from a road gang in the Dardanup area. Even after more than ten years, Thomas could remember the whole episode clearly. The local whisper was that a genial young farmer, Big Jim Maguire, had organised the prisoner's escape with the help of his postmaster cousin, and that Father McCabe was behind the planning. One of the Maguire girls had attended Thomas's school, a large-boned child about twelve years old with hair as jet-black as his own, and he could still picture her in the playground surrounded by a huddle of her deferential peers as she smirked at the vicariously conspiratorial status they were conferring on her.

∞

Eighteen months after it had opened with such high hopes, he knew that the Alta was doomed. Although only a trickle of customers came to his office in Howick Street these days, others who wanted to have a word with Thomas knew to find him there. Visits from creditors and their messengers became increasingly frequent and acrimonious. Debts kept accumulating, and his requests for more time met with little sympathy. Payment was long overdue for building materials, for rented furniture, for the hire of boats that had ferried patrons across the river, for the purveying of food and drink, for the many advertisements placed in *The Inquirer* – there seemed no end to the demands. On top of it all, he found himself embroiled in arguments over land deals, his subsidiary line of work.

Swallowing his pride, he'd gone cap in hand to see Alfred Letch. Only a large loan would do, but surely this man – a paragon of self-made prosperity and a relative by marriage, who understood how hard it was for an emancipist to succeed – could provide that!

'I'm very sorry, Thomas,' said Alfred, clasping his hands in front of his rounded belly, 'but it's just not possible. I have no cash to spare, none at all. Indeed – this is strictly between ourselves, mind you – I'll soon need to negotiate a substantial overdraft with the bank, because I'm planning to move my business to a large building in Hay Street. When the railway station is finished, much of the city's commerce will drift away from St George's Terrace, and I must reposition my activities accordingly. Leasing and equipping new premises is financially risky, and these are difficult times, so I'm obliged now to conserve such resources as I have. I wish I could help you, but despite appearances my own prospect is less secure than it used to be...'

After that rebuff, Thomas could put off no longer the painful task of telling Polly how dire their financial situation had become. They'd kept apart for months now, seldom making any direct contact with one another. He slept in his city office; she and young George were staying in the mill cottage. It was a bitter estrangement. She'd blamed him for all their difficulties, voicing her anger in shrill tirades. He'd retorted with such cold censure – not just of her 'heavy drinking' but also of her reportedly 'wanton and vulgar' behaviour towards some of the Alta's male patrons – that any hope of reconciliation had evaporated. Confessing to her that his whole business was on the point of collapse would be mortifying but ought not to be further postponed.

To save the cost of a ferry ticket, he borrowed a dinghy and rowed across to Miller's Pool. It took longer than he'd expected. The November warmth sucked sweat from his pores and the unaccustomed exertion made his shoulders ache. At last he dragged the boat up on the sand and then, wiping his face continually with a damp handkerchief, walked slowly around to the cottage. Polly had evidently seen him coming. Impassive, she stood at the door without a word of greeting.

'I'd like to sit down,' he said wearily, 'there's something important I need to talk about.'

She moved aside and he went over to a chair by the open window. Eyes fixed on the floor, he tried to steady his breathing. He could hear faintly a high-pitched sound like the call of an osprey chick pleading for attention, but it seemed to be inside his head.

'I don't need to tell you we owe large amounts of money,' he began. 'You've known that. But things have gone from bad to worse. I'm being pressed mercilessly to settle most of those debts without delay, and now there's another thing – a real estate transaction that's gone wrong. I was paid a handsome sum in advance for property that turns out to have been bought previously by someone else. My client insists on immediate reimbursement, and I just can't produce the cash. I've offered a piece of land – land of our own – for equal value instead, but he refuses that proposal.'

He looked up at her, expecting a vituperative response, but she was pale with apprehension, and her voice quavered. 'So what happens next?'

'Court action, I'm afraid. He's taken criminal proceedings against me. As soon as the news of this gets around, the bank will stop my credit and people who owe me money for other land deals will withhold payment. Even if I'm successful in defending myself against the charge, I'll be penniless by then. It means ruin, Polly. I feel hollowed out, like a husk.'

## 33

# Fremantle, January 1882

'It ought never have come to this,' he told the chaplain as they sat together in the dark little cell. 'My solicitor should have been able to win me a reprieve. I'd offered restitution to my creditors, and with moneys owed to me I could have settled all the debts, given time. God knows I deserved leniency and respect! All these years in the colony my conduct has been upright. But where were the people I expected to stand up for me? My enemies must have prevailed on them not to speak in my defence. Even then, the situation could so easily have been retrieved if my relatives had been loyal. How could they abandon me at such a time? Unforgivably fickle!' He flung up his hands. 'George Letch, and especially Alfred – why didn't they provide guarantees to tide me over? Why didn't they appear in court and vouch for me personally? The sole person willing to testify today on my behalf was Rowe, the detective, who had no obligation to me but knew I deserved support.'

'Your indignation goes deep, Browne,' said the chaplain, rising to leave. 'That's plain enough. But I'm afraid it won't change anything. You've been found guilty, that's the long and short of it, and although sentencing is deferred until tomorrow I've no doubt you'll face incarceration. Old lags who break the law don't get gentle treatment. My duty's to help you accept your lot, with God's grace, and learn from it. Along with the writing materials you asked for, I'm going to leave this Bible with you now. I entreat you earnestly to spend as much time as possible reading what it has to say about justice and mercy. I'll visit you again in a day or two.' He moved towards the door and called for the warder. Large cockroaches scuttled into the corners.

Justice and mercy! Thomas tightened his jaw bitterly as the man left. The law had been used against him in a merciless way. Almost everybody who ought to have shown faith had failed him, yet he was the one who'd been publicly judged a failure. A burning rage gripped him – rage at those who should have stood up for him, rage at those who'd humiliated him. He'd been made to seem a fool if not downright dishonest, and it was this blackening of his character that distressed him most. 'To incur such debts,' the judge had intoned, 'with no hope of paying them proclaims incompetence and irresponsibility.'

The sheer injustice of it was overwhelming, and a surge of self-pity rose in his throat. He'd been brought low by others – some of them malicious, some cowardly, some perfidious, some just negligent. Agitated, he picked up the Bible and thumbed his way towards a prophetic passage that had struck him when he was young and lodged in a crevice of memory. *The Book of Isaiah, somewhere...Here.* 'He is despised and rejected of men; a man of sorrows, and acquainted with grief: and we hid as it were our faces from him; he was despised, and we esteemed him not.'

Even the women he'd married hadn't held him in the esteem he warranted. Eliza, his first wife, never really appreciated his professional accomplishments as he toiled to support their growing family. She'd become preoccupied with herself, and it was her insane profligacy that drove him despairingly into the fraudulent transactions that had wrecked his career. Then out here in the colony he'd done everything he could to rebuild his reputation, and marrying Polly had been part of that fresh start, but she, just like her predecessor, had shown no capacity to understand his exceptional qualities or provide the support that was his due. He'd seen at first hand her neglect of maternal and matrimonial duties, and what he'd heard about the increasingly dissolute way she'd behaved at the Alta Gardens must have a factual basis. Her drinking and flirting, her careless disregard for decorum – it had all contributed to the loss of public respect for him. And to the loss of vital income! If she'd been less of a sloven, the hotel would no doubt have attracted a larger number of well-to-do customers. In effect, she'd robbed him just as surely as if she'd taken money directly from his pocket, damn her! Polly liked to accuse him of being too ready to blame other people for his failings, yet she never took responsibility for her own. And when he'd gone to her parents and appealed for their help in making her see reason, George and Caroline had taken her side, snubbing him.

As he lay on his bed in the deepening darkness, hands to his forehead, his wild flurry of blaming began to turn gradually against his own lapses. Others had deserted him, yes, but wasn't it undeniable that he himself was a failure? Didn't the Alta Gardens disaster belong to a miserable pattern stretching back through his life? Hadn't he, after all, failed his children back in England, every one of them, despite his best intentions: a poor provider, poor protector, poor companion? Little wonder they'd ignored his letters asking them to join him in Fremantle; he'd brought shame upon them. He thought with remorse, too, of his sister in Bermondsey, Jane the fur-puller, her lungs filling with all that thick dust; instead of being able to rescue her from that situation, he'd let her down disgracefully. Hadn't he also failed those who, in the past, invested some faith in his potential: Stephenson, for one, and Fox, and Hardwick? They'd feel deeply disappointed in him if they knew about his downfall; in their eyes he'd be someone who didn't apply his talents with enough diligence and courage. And towering over them all, and over him, was the person to whose standards he had never lived up, could never live up: his implacable father.

∞

*The walls close in suddenly, and as the black passageway becomes narrower and lower he has to crouch like a hunchbacked dwarf and squeeze himself forward, unable to turn around. He tries to call for help but the sound of his voice is snatched away into silence the moment it leaves his lips. Just as he is starting to feel hopelessly trapped, the cavity opens out again and he emerges into a vast elongated space like a church's unlit nave but hewn from wet rock. There comes a fearful rushing noise, the roar of water as it pours into the chamber, a mighty swirling gush that sweeps up men and horses and flings them around in the darkness. He can feel himself being pulled down by the torrent, as if bound and cast into a bottomless pit. In an upper corner of the flooded cavern he glimpses a swollen shadow, the effigy of a judge in sable robes, ghostly, that looms like a final damning paternal rebuke.*

He gasped into wakefulness, his clothes soaked with sweat and piss. What time of the night it might now be he could not tell. There was turmoil in his heart, a whirlpool of conflicting emotions. One moment it appeared that nothing he'd aspired to or achieved had any firmer foundation than the powdery windblown dunes on which this godforsaken colony had tried to settle, or the shifting sucking waterlogged quicksand in the Kilsby Tunnel. Nothing mattered any more, nothing. All merely dust and ashes and mud.

And yet a moment later it was as if the very meaning of his life depended on a few precious things that must be cherished. His meticulous planning documents and drawings, which plainly showed the feasibility of the schemes he'd devised for vital public works – the railway eastwards from Perth across the Darling Scarp, and the other ambitious construction projects that could transform the colony – what would become of them while he mouldered in prison? The petitions in which he'd explained with such careful and cogent detail how people had wronged him – who would ensure that they were not dismissed and forgotten? Who could be trusted to safeguard his reputation and defend it against calumny? How would his infant son George learn that his father was no Satan, that he had a name to be proud of?

Vindication. To be not only absolved but also applauded. *Honour at last for Thomas Browne* – that's what he deserved. But there was no longer any hope of attaining it through his own efforts. Too late, too late. He was done for, damnably lost. Indeed, he himself, despised and rejected, had become an obstacle to the redeeming of his reputation, which would now have to be a task for someone else. Not that filching slattern, Polly, or her treacherous kin. The only trustworthy person to whom he could appeal was Rowe.

Daylight had begun to filter into his cell. He went over to the small table on which the chaplain had left paper, pen and ink.

Dear Mr Rowe,

Should any evil befall me, I ask you kindly to see to my funeral. The commission coming to me when your mortgage is executed will cover any expenses incurred in this way. One thing I enjoin upon you: do not let my wife, her father or any member of that family see my body or follow me to the grave. My wife has robbed me and wasted my substance. She is drunken and lewd, and has brought me to ruin. Her father aided and abetted her in these courses. In vain have I appealed to him to assist me to reclaim the woman. But for my wife I should not have been placed as I am today.

These are the true and last words of a lost and dying man who has lived industriously, frugally and honestly as you yourself can testify. I ask for this letter to be made public.

Thomas H. J. Browne 11.1.1882

He folded the sheet, wrote 'Detective Sergeant Rowe' on the verso, and waited for breakfast to arrive. Before long he heard a jangle of keys along the corridor and the warder came to his cell, bringing a pannikin of tea and a hunk of bread. After a few mouthfuls Thomas pushed the tray aside, stood up and rested his febrile cheek against the cold stone wall, eyes open but unseeing. Then the trance passed and he reached into a small fob inside his vest, drawing out a secreted packet of paper and opening it carefully. He tipped its contents into his mouth.

Feeling increasingly restless, he walked quickly to and fro. After ten minutes his neck began to twitch, and soon spasms were spreading to every part of the body. First one group of muscles would convulse, and then another, until his limbs thrashed. Nausea gripped him. He frothed at the mouth, vomiting again and again. Spasms in his belly made his back flex and arch violently. Breathing became more obstructed, more painful, as if a stake had been thrust into his mouth and right down his windpipe, and the last thing he felt was the sensation of slowly choking.

∞

'Thank you, Detective Sergeant, for responding so promptly to my message,' said the prison superintendent. 'Suicide in custody brings trouble for us here, especially when it's a poisoning. To have let strychnine into a prison! There'll be an inquest, and my warders are sure to be given a stern public reprimand, at the very least, for not searching Browne thoroughly. Anyway, he left a letter for you, and I wanted you to see it before we report what's happened.' He gave the folded sheet to Runty, who read it quickly and handed it back without a word, shaking his head.

'I know what it says,' the superintendent told him. 'You'll understand that I thought I should look at it before summoning you. It's unusual for a person who's going to kill himself to address his final written words to an officer of the law. I needed to rule out the possibility that the note might seem to incriminate you in some way. As you can see, it certainly doesn't do that. All the same I won't be surprised if questions arise at the inquest about your relationship with Browne, so give that matter some thought. Meanwhile, you should also consider what ought to be done with the letter. He wanted it made public. What do you think?'

Runty rubbed his forehead slowly, frowning. 'Difficult to go against the wishes of a dying man, isn't it? He's tried to entrust his reputation and vindication to me, and if I simply brush aside his wishes…well, in my book that would be a betrayal. On the other hand, it's clear he wasn't in his right mind towards the end. There are wild accusations here, and if made public they'd injure people unjustly. I haven't met his wife but I'm acquainted with her uncle, Alfred Letch, and from things he's mentioned I'm fairly sure Satan's picture of her and her family is distorted.'

'Yet presumably you think there's something to be said on his behalf. You did speak up for him in court when others wouldn't.'

'I did. He felt deserted, and I know there was a lot of good in him, a lot to admire. But there were bonds that held him tight. Years after receiving his pardon, he was somehow unable to think of himself as a free man. His mind was in hell. He'd been badly treated – though not, I believe, by his wife. He seems to have turned against her in a sort of mad anguish.'

'Even so, she's his next of kin, isn't she? Someone should tell her about his death before the journalists and tattlers get hold of it.'

'It won't be easy but I'll do it. Mrs Browne lives in a cottage at the Alta Gardens with her child. I'll go there immediately. As for Satan's letter, here's what I think: letting it be published would harm him along with those he traduces. For the sake of all concerned, it would be a kindness to file it away discreetly.'

# Runty

## 34

# Perth, June 1890

'*Inspector* Rowe, of all people! What brings you here after so long?'

'Good morning, Constable. Oh, I've just come down to Perth to attend to a few little personal matters – mainly seeing a lawyer about updating my will.'

'Feeling mortal, are you, sir?'

'No more than before. But with approaching retirement there are odds and ends to tidy up before old age slows me down. That's all, except I thought I'd poke my nose in here, too. Make sure you fellows aren't getting lazy now that I'm no longer keeping an eye on you. Anyway, it's good to look around the office and recall old times.'

'It must be – what is it? – over three years since you last set foot in our headquarters.'

'I left Perth a full four years ago.'

'And how's life been for you up Geraldton way?'

'Oh, fairly quiet for the most part. Which suits me well. I had my share of excitement over the years before getting the promotion and moving north. But Perth is bustling these days, isn't it? Plenty of development on all sides. Not surprising – the gold fever has brought so many men westwards, and of course a lot of their money must be filtering through this town. I can see it in the size of the buildings going up here now, the improved streets, new railway lines under construction.'

'The gold has made a difference, all right. Or the lure of it. Those rushes at Hall's Creek and Yilgarn were short-lived but they've certainly raised a thirst for further prospecting, and it isn't just the miners who dream of quick prosperity. All sorts of people around this town are coming up with ambitious business schemes – some hasty, some far-sighted.'

'Political changes, too – even sleepy Geraldton knows that the new constitution will make a big difference to us all.'

'Not long until we'll have our own elected parliament and Premier. Then the old colonial life is going to vanish in a puff.'

'But there'll still be criminals to keep detectives occupied.'

'We're busy enough at present, let me tell you, sir. Mostly routine things, easily solved, but occasionally there's a baffling case. I've got one on my hands right now. Remember Alfred Letch's new shop – the grand one he moved to in Hay Street just a few years before you left Perth?'

'Of course.'

'Well, a fire destroyed it just a few days ago. Gutted the place, and any contents that weren't burnt were badly damaged by water. Lost some of his family's personal possessions in the flames, too.'

'What an appalling misfortune!'

'We suspect arson, because we can't find any other cause of the blaze, but we're puzzled about motives. I've made no progress with my inquiries. Any chance you could spare the time to look into the case before you return north?'

Runty smiled wryly. 'I'm tempted. No hurry about getting back home, as it happens. But look – I've taught you all I know about detective work, Constable. If you can't get to the bottom of this puzzle then it's doubtful I could.'

'Too modest, sir! We all remember the superintendent's words about you – that there's nobody in any police force anywhere "more assiduous, efficient or truthful". An eloquent testimony, well deserved. So I'd be grateful if you could make time to help us inquire into the Letch fire.'

∞

It was a scene of complete devastation. Mounds of charred debris covered the ground floor and spilled out into the street: sooty bricks and masonry, fallen timbers, ruined remnants of furniture, iron melted and twisted out of shape. The roof had gone. Walls were cracked and discoloured.

Arson did seem likely, but Runty's investigation also confirmed that Alfred Letch had no known enemies, personal or commercial, being generally popular in Perth. His plight had attracted an outpouring of sympathy and support. He could have lit the fire himself, or had it lit by someone else on his behalf, but that looked improbable because he didn't hold any current insurance policy for the property.

Going to see Alfred at the Freemasons' Hotel where the Letches had lodged since the disaster, Runty hoped that casual conversation might elicit something informative, perhaps involuntarily. Long experience had shown him that an indirect approach often discovered more than interrogation would. Unexpected things, surprising connections. So they chatted casually for half an hour, their initial exchange of news leading into reminiscence about some of the ups and downs of their respective careers.

'Oh, I wouldn't say that gaining the rank of inspector has been a high point for me, not really. No, my peak came earlier, when I was seconded for a few months to New South Wales to review police arrangements for the big Sydney International Exhibition. As for my present role, well, the pay's good but the responsibilities hardly warrant a lofty title. Intended as compensation for transferring to Geraldton, I suppose. For me, though, a move up country was timely. There'd been a cloud over my head for a while. In the aftermath of Satan's suicide the colonial secretary's report on it to the Governor censured me for having "transactions" – land dealings – with a criminal. Remember?'

'Yes, I do. Absurd. Detectives can't do their job unless they mix with all types of men. But anyway, the work Thomas did for you as a real estate agent was clearly above board.'

'I was lucky the superintendent vouched for me stoutly in that matter. Lucky and grateful. He also had to defend my reputation against another slur at about the same time, when a lot of cloth for uniforms went missing and our branch was accused of covering up a theft. So it'd been a difficult period. Although the chief gave me loyal support, I was quite glad to leave Perth with a promotion when the end of his term approached. Things have worked out fine…But that's enough about me. This misfortune that's struck you, Mr Letch – it must be very hard to bear.'

'A double blow, really. To lose many of our private possessions along with the shop premises and most of the stock…it's heartbreaking. All those years of establishing and expanding the business, and nearly everything gone in an hour. The firemen did their best, and there were plenty of people trying to help us with waterbuckets. Everyone's efforts were futile. Foolish of me to have let the insurance lapse, but I thought I'd taken all necessary precautions against fire.' He bit his lip. 'Not that insurance would have enabled us to replace personal things, with sentimental value. My wife is quite distraught about losing them, as you can imagine.'

'What will you do now?'

'I think it's the end of my days as a merchant,' said Alfred, fingers nervously tousling his silver hair. 'Even if I had the energy at this age to get started again I'd need plenty of capital, and the bank would be chary of providing a big loan to anyone in my situation. But I still have quite a few horses and a bit of country property, so perhaps I can try my hand at breeding livestock.' He shrugged, before adding with a humourless and oddly tense laugh: 'It's ironic, but I'd played the piano at a Fire Brigade concert only two days before the fire.'

As Runty was leaving, he asked how Alfred's niece had fared in the years since Satan's death.

'Oh, Polly's had a hard time of it, as you can imagine,' Alfred told him, 'though the family has helped her. Recently an amiable sort of fellow, name of Merrilees, has been paying her a bit of attention. He has quite limited means but as Satan's widow she doesn't have many alternatives, and they seem well enough suited. By the way, the Alta Gardens has had a sad comedown. Been turned into a poultry farm.'

Back in the street, Runty mulled over their conversation and wondered whether Alfred Letch might have left something important untold. There had been, he thought, a brittle edge in the man's tone of voice – perhaps just registering the shock of his losses, or it could indicate a strained concealment, a holding back. So he went next to the Western Australian Bank, where the privilege of his inspector's rank allowed him to gain information promptly about Letch's business position – which, it transpired, had been dire: he was overextended financially. The bank had notified him a week before the fire that it planned to foreclose and sell his stock.

Runty walked to the courthouse gardens, sat on a bench and puffed on his pipe as he pondered Alfred Letch's character. Despite the youthful trespass that had caused his expulsion from England, Letch appeared to have led an impeccable life ever since, working hard here and earning public respect. But that didn't rule out the possibility of his having set fire to the shop. For someone like him, there could in fact be a motive – no less strong for being oblique – to destroy his own property in this way. Knowing he was about to be ruined after so many years building up his wealth and reputation, mightn't he consider that if his store went up in flames he'd be no worse off financially while his public standing would remain intact? Instead of the contumely and disgrace that would fall on him if his business failed, there'd be sympathy for his presumed misfortune. And perhaps he'd have speculated that the sympathy might even be translated into some material compensation: a number of his fellow citizens, regarding him compassionately as a hapless victim, could well take pity and donate money or goods to help him get back on his feet. He'd anticipate, anyway, that the bank would surely hold off after a seemingly accidental fire, giving him a chance to improve his situation.

A further talk with him might be useful. Strolling back to the Freemasons' Hotel, Runty asked at the desk for Mr Letch and waited in the foyer while the message was relayed. A few minutes later Mrs Letch appeared instead.

'My husband has just gone out, Inspector,' Amelia explained apologetically, after introducing herself. 'He told me not to expect him back before the evening. Is there anything I can help you with in his absence?'

'Thank you, Mrs Letch, but probably not. I wanted to continue my conversation with him about the dreadful conflagration. The circumstances of it. The possibility that it resulted from a deliberate criminal act.'

'Why would anyone want to do something like that to us?' She gestured to armchairs nearby, and they sat together.

'That's what I hope to find out. Arson does seem the likely cause, but as to why – that's a hard question to answer. Of course it could have been just a motiveless piece of stupidity by a drunken fool rather than anything spiteful.'

'In a sense it makes little difference to us, Inspector. Whatever the reason for it, the fire has robbed us savagely. Not just of our livelihood – in fact the material losses aren't the worst of it: Alfred thinks we can probably make a fresh start, because we still have our horses and some rural land. But many valuable personal items were destroyed, too. And more than that, the fire itself was a shocking, frightening thing to witness. Huge flames leaping from the roof. Rafters crashing down. The fierce heat. It brought back so much earlier grief. I've had such nightmares...'

'I'm very sorry, Mrs Letch.' It sounded feeble, but he couldn't think of anything to say that might comfort her. The earlier grief she'd mentioned must be the deaths of some of their children – he'd heard about that bereavement years ago – and he felt a sudden pang of compassion. For a fleeting moment it brought to his mind the scene when his own wife had lain dying – the agony in her eyes, so much blood, the flustered midwife's foolish reassurances, the cries of their frightened children, Sarah's final groans. He pushed the memory away.

Amelia wiped her damp cheeks. 'The fire could have been much worse – I have to remember that. Nobody was injured. And some irreplaceable things were rescued. This dear little keepsake, for one.' She reached into her reticule and pulled out a smoke-smeared locket. 'It's precious to me,' she said, holding it out for him to look at, 'because it belonged to my mother.'

Turning it over, he saw that it had something inscribed on the verso. Holding it on an angle to catch the light, he could make out a name: *Rebecca French*. His brow furrowed. It was as though the words stirred a sedimented memory in his mind, but if so he couldn't retrieve their significance.

'That name…' he said in half-muted tone, as if to himself. 'I feel I've seen or heard it somewhere before.'

But now Amelia had begun to weep.

'I didn't mean to upset you,' he said apologetically. 'I should leave. It's a distressing time for you. I'll call on Mr Letch tomorrow.'

'No, please don't go, Inspector. I need to tell someone about…about the anguish this fire has revived in me. There's something nobody knows, not even my husband, and to you I think I can speak of it. You're a stranger to me, but in your line of work I'm sure you're no stranger to guilty secrets. I must talk about this one now, and I feel able to confide in you. It would give me some relief to tell you what's come back now to haunt me.'

'You can count on my discretion if you think it may help you to —'

'I'm sure of that. The fact is, Inspector, I've been keeping a painful thing buried in the back of my mind for many years, hoping it would fade away, but this fire a few days ago has suddenly uncovered it again. So putting it into words may ease my conscience. I lost my parents when I was a child, you see, and I've never told anyone exactly what happened. The whole neighbourhood in our part of Tameside knew that our cottage burned down, and that my mother and father died in the flames while I escaped, but I'm the only one who knows how the fire started. You're the first person to hear this. Though it was a horrible accident, horrible, the blame was mine. I should have been fast asleep, but often after my parents had gone to bed I used to keep myself awake as long as possible because I was desperately keen to get as much learning as I could, so when the house was still and dark I'd light a tallow candle and sit quietly in my room, reading books I'd taken home stealthily from Sunday School. On this night I must have dozed off and let the candle drop, because the whole room was ablaze when I woke. I could hardly breathe. Somehow I managed to stumble through the smoke to the door and rush outside, calling for help. People came running, but not soon enough. By then flames were bursting through the windows and roof. Nobody could get in. My parents would already have suffocated.'

Runty could find no consoling words to reach into the redoubled grief of this woman he hardly knew. It was difficult for him to imagine her pain at seeing another home ablaze after trying for so long to efface the hideous memory of her burnt childhood. And how could any solace possibly arise for her from the ashes of such misfortune? Yet what Runty thought he did understand, because of its echo in his own experience, was how every loss rekindled earlier losses. For her, this fire had made the old anguished feelings flare up again, just as the sudden death of his own wife Sarah had taken him back to his previous bereavements.

Sitting with her quietly for a few minutes while he waited for her sobs to subside, he thought about her husband's likely culpability in the recent shop fire and decided there was no point pursuing that matter. A detective could sometimes choose to be a keeper of secrets. Even if Alfred had deliberately lit the fire, he hadn't exactly defrauded anyone. He'd simply inflicted damage on himself in a sad attempt to protect his name – and ironically, unwittingly, had ignited his wife's hidden guilt over the death of her parents.

Amelia made an effort to compose herself, dabbing at her eyes. Though the lids were now pink and puffy, he noticed that the irises had the same pale blue intensity as his own.

Runty was trying to frame a suitable form of words with which to take his leave when the name he'd seen on the locket came back plucking at his memory. 'It's a very strange thing, Mrs Letch,' he said, 'but when I looked at that locket of yours it was as if I heard a distant voice, which now sounds like my mother's, whispering to me down the years from fireside conversations we had during long dark evenings after my father died. This was in the Potteries, where I grew up. The town of Tunstall.' He paused for a few moments, silently dredging – until his memory pulled up fragments of those stories of hers about Tameside, where she'd once lived, and about how she met Hector Rowe, married him quickly and moved to Tunstall. And then with a jolt Runty recalled her telling him about her sister Rebecca, who had wed a local weaver, Will French! Runty could hear his mother saying, with what he now recognised as a bitter edge to her voice, 'A very plausible man. A charmer. But not a good man.'

'I'm sure,' he told Amelia, 'that Rebecca French was the name of my mother's sister.'

As it came gradually back to him and the implications began to take shape at the edge of thought, he told her about the last time he'd seen his mother, just before he went to the police job in London. She'd been having seizures. They knew that lead in the potbank glazes was poisoning her, that there was no remedy and that she was near her end.

'Holding my hand, she said she had a bad conscience and there was something I ought to know. But she'd become too ill to speak coherently. I kept leaning towards her, but I still couldn't decipher her murmurs. Then I heard distinct words: "Hector. Deceit," she said tearfully, and repeated it: "Deceit." I remember telling her not to upset herself, but I was protecting my own feelings, too. If my long-dead father had done something deceitful, I didn't want to know. Anything that might detract from his standing in my eyes was unwelcome. But she went on struggling to speak. "Harold knows," she said suddenly – that was her brother, I think, though I never met him. And then, "Fetch my sister. Want to talk to Rebecca." But it was too late. She just slipped out of consciousness and was dead within hours. Before long I was working in London, and I had no address for her brother and sister, so I never managed to make contact with them.'

Amelia stared at Runty in shock. 'I know some things...' Her voice faltered. 'Things that fit into the spaces in your story.' She sucked in a long breath. 'My Uncle Harold was usually a tolerant man, but a few years after the deaths of my parents he spoke harshly about my father's character and I insisted he explain his hostility. He told me that, just before marrying my mother, Will had made her sister Margery pregnant, and then spurned her, and soon afterwards she – Margery, the aunt I never met – went off hastily with a navvy from the Potteries, letting him believe it was *his* child she'd conceived. That must have been the deceit your mother spoke about – not revealing the situation to him. As for my mother, Rebecca, she had two sons, who both died as babes from the smallpox, and later I arrived. But you see what this means? About you and me?'

He nodded, dazed. 'We have the same…'

Amelia supplied in a whisper the word that had stalled on his tongue. He heard the sound of his own deep-drawn breathing as elation surged and half-thoughts tumbled. Not so alone after all, not utterly bereft. There were burdens to lighten, stories to share, perhaps affinities to cherish. For a family ruptured in England, the sudden prospect of healing in Australia.

She reached out a tremulous hand towards his forearm, and tentatively the sibling strangers touched, too astonished to be able yet to grasp all that their kinship might mean for them and others. For the moment, both caught only a glimpse of uncertain hopes: that some bonds could bring a kind of freedom, and that whatever corners of the world one's body might wander through it might still be possible to choose a place where the mind could come to rest.

# Afterword

Although I have invented most of what is in *The Mind's Own Place*, some aspects of this novel correspond partly to a framework of real people and events. To a large extent Thomas, Alfred, Amelia, Polly and Runty are imaginary characters, but each has a counterpart in recorded history. In telling a fictional story that incorporates particles of fact, I have drawn selectively on documentary sources and on the research of several historians. Here I acknowledge with thanks various background materials that were especially helpful in this process.

Some years ago I became interested in the tragic figure of Thomas 'Satan' Browne through a volume of biographical sketches of Western Australian convicts edited by Rica Erickson, *The Brand on His Coat* (UWAP, 1983). Browne's own extant paintings, drawings and letters whetted that interest, as did the residual structure of the old mill in South Perth, but the idea of writing a novel based in part on his remarkable life and demise sat in the back of my mind until I came across an account by Sandra Potter of the career of one of Browne's contemporaries. When I read her absorbing article on Alfred Letch in *Building a Colony: The Convict Legacy*, edited by Jacqui Sherriff and Anne Brake (UWAP, 2006), I saw how the two white-collar convicts could be integrated within one tale, not only because they were actually linked by marriage but also because of striking similarities and differences in their careers. For a few details concerning Polly – Alfred's niece, Thomas's wife – I went to the Battye Library's rich trove of historical documents, where I read a diary written by her father George during the family's voyage to Western Australia in 1872. Another component in the interlocking set of narratives emerged from Erickson's passing reference to Detective Sergeant Rowe as someone who befriended Satan Browne. I discovered more about Rowe, the colony's first detective, from Mollie Bentley's *Grandfather Was a Policeman: The Western Australia Police Force 1829–1889* (Hesperian Press, 1993) and Peter Conole's *Protect and Serve: A History of Policing in Western Australia* (WA Police Service, 2002). Knowing that Rowe travelled to Fremantle with Irish political prisoners on the *Hougoumont*, the last convict ship to sail to Australia, I studied Battye Library copies of diaries and memoirs of the voyage written by some of those Fenians – John Casey, Denis Cashman and Thomas Fennell – along with related material. I found no sources of information about the woman Alfred married, Amelia French, but from Jan Gothard's book *Blue China: Single Female Migration to Colonial Australia* (Melbourne University Press, 2001) I was able to gain an impression of people whose background would have been similar to Amelia's. More general historical scholarship shed light on various aspects of life in the Swan River Colony, especially Alexandra Hasluck's admirable early study *Unwilling Emigrants* (Oxford University Press, 1959) and Michal Bosworth's *Convict Fremantle: A Place of Promise and Punishment* (UWAP, 2004). Some specialised studies were also illuminating, for instance articles in the journal *Early Days* by J. H. M. Honniball (1980) on Prince Alfred's visit to the colony and by Dorothy Erickson (1990) on convict jewellers. I delved into records of transportation through the 'Convicts to Australia' website (members.iinet.net.au/~perthdps/convicts/con-wa42.html) and read accounts of Alfred Letch's trial with the help of online documents available through the Western Australian Genealogical Society at membership.wags.org.au/images/stories/documents/sigs/convict/news/con_hashemy.pdf. I also found the historical sections of the Fremantle Prison website very helpful (www.fremantleprison.com.au). And I gratefully used, too, the excellent digitised repository of newspaper archives assembled by the National Library of Australia at trove.nla.gov.au.

But though valuable as a stimulus to storytelling, historical sources cannot dictate the content or shaping of a novel. A writer of fiction about times past can take the liberty of deciding not to pursue verifiable details beyond a certain point, relying instead on the imagination to supplement or modify them for the purposes of a thematically coherent plot with credible characters and motivation. In devising those parts of *The Mind's Own Place* that relate things experienced by my five main characters during their pre-emigration years in England, I largely chose to ignore whatever may really have happened to their historical counterparts, and where those actual people lived. Arbitrarily I decided to situate young Thomas in Newton and London, young Runty in Tunstall, young Amelia in Ashton. Nearly everything in the novel relating to their youthful pathways is fictitious. For Polly and Alfred I followed to some extent the general contours of the lives they are known to have led in Essex, but again most of it is purely imagined.

Unlike a historian, a novelist must sometimes allow the demands of the story to take precedence over validated evidence. For instance, in the case of Thomas Rowe (who becomes Runty in my novel), I took advantage of a convenient discrepancy in the historical records. The real-life figure on whom I've based my character is said by some to have travelled on the *Hougoumont* as a warder with his wife and children, but the ship's manifest does not bear that out; it does, however, list 'Thomas Rowe' as one of the convicts on that voyage – and so I decided to make this an undercover identity for him, regardless of whether that was really true.

In the process of creating small worlds for my characters to inhabit convincingly in different parts of nineteenth-century England before they came one by one to Western Australia, I found rich information in various books, articles and online resources. The internet has been a great boon; for instance, the chapters that recount Thomas's experiences in Newton make use of materials on the history of that place assembled by Steven Dowd on his excellent website (newton-le-willows.com) and of Sir Daniel Gooch's diaries (1892) accessed in digital form at archive.org/details/diariessirdanie00goocgoog.

To gain an understanding of the growth of railways I consulted Henry Booth's *An Account of the Liverpool and Manchester Railway* (1830; reprinted by Frank Cass, 1969); John C. Bourne's *Drawings of the London and Birmingham Railway* (Ackermann, 1839); Frank McKenna's *The Railway Workers, 1840–1970* (Faber, 1980); David Brooke's *The Railway Navvy: 'That Despicable Race of Men'* (David & Charles, 1983); Terry Coleman's *The Railway Navvies: A History of the Men Who Made the Railways* (Hutchinson, 1965); and R. S. Joby's *The Railway Builders: Lives and Works of the Victorian Railway Contractors* (David & Charles, 1983). Particularly helpful in evoking the Potteries were Simeon Shaw's *History of the Staffordshire Potteries* (G. Jackson, 1829); Charles Shaw's *When I was a Child* (Methuen, 1903); and Arnold Bennett's *Clayhanger* (Methuen, 1910). For the experience of Tameside millworkers I relied partly on *Songs of the People: Lancashire Dialect Poetry of the Industrial Revolution*, edited by Brian Hollingworth (Manchester University Press, 1977).

Insights into Victorian English life generally, urban and rural, came from many writings, including contemporary periodicals and books – for example, the multi-volume *Penny Cyclopaedia of the Society for the Diffusion of Useful Knowledge* (Charles Knight, 1833–43) – and more recent sources such as Pamela Horn's *The Real Lark Rise to Candleford: Life in the Victorian Countryside* (2nd edn, Amberley, 2012); *The Victorian Novelist: Social Problems and Social Change*, edited by Kate Flint (Croom Helm, 1987); Priscilla Metcalf's *Victorian London* (Cassell, 1972); Donald J. Olsen's *The Growth of Victorian London* (Batsford, 1976); and *Early Victorian England, 1830–1865*, edited by G. M. Young (Oxford University Press, 1934).

I give warm thanks to a cordial group of critics who gallantly read a large part of this novel in draft form and gave me their discerning opinions: Brian Edwards, Alison Jaquet, Gale MacLachlan and Wenche Ommundsen. I'm also grateful to other friends whose responses to my previous novels have been especially encouraging: they include Erica Becker, Noelene and John Bloomfield, Geoff Bolton, Ross Chambers, Brenton Doecke, Trish Dowsett, Robyn Gardner, Paul Genoni, Nick Hasluck, Lorraine Jacobs, Yvonne Laing, Rosemary and Charles Lancaster, Duncan Mackay, Vera Mackie, Lesley Maloney, Linda Martin, Edith Moore, Dawn Oliver, Paul and Kathy Rossiter, Brian Shepherd, Michael Stanford, Andrew Taylor, Brenda Walker, Jennifer Weir and Helen Wildy.

I'm glad to acknowledge, too, the appreciative letters and messages from numerous people I've never met, and the stimulus of interesting questions and comments from members of book clubs and reading groups, and from audiences at talks I've given in libraries, bookshops, educational institutions, writers' centres, literary festival sessions and elsewhere. For timely practical assistance I'm indebted to staff of the Battye Library in the State Library of Western Australia, Marlene Anderson of the Royal Western Australian Historical Society, Courtney Fowler in the School of Humanities at the University of Western Australia, and Jenna Lynch at the City of Perth History Centre.

Those whose professional expertise has turned my manuscript into a handsome book deserve a special salute, particularly my editor Nicola Young for all her scrupulous work, and the director of UWA Publishing, Terri-ann White, for her steadfast support.

CPSIA information can be obtained
at www.ICGtesting.com
Printed in the USA
FSOW04n2351250615
8252FS